PRETTY BAD THINGS

From the Chicken House

I loved the start of *Catcher in the Rye,* and I think Holden Caulfield would get PRETTY BAD THINGS. Today, he might even sound like Paisley. They're both cool, angry, and reckless.

Paisley and her brother, Beau, are the sort of teenagers we would all like to be, but would never dare! They're wild and dangerous, but they really love the people who matter most.

Get ready for the ride of your life!

Barry Cunningham
Publisher

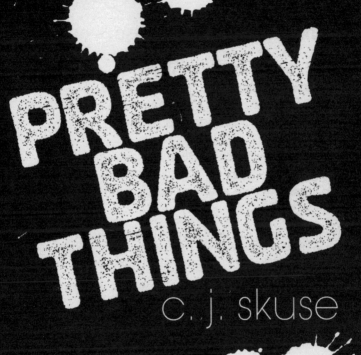

PRETTY BAD THINGS

c. j. skuse

Chicken House

2 Palmer Street, Frome, Somerset BA11 1DS

Text © C. J. Skuse 2010
First published in Great Britain in 2010
The Chicken House
2 Palmer Street
Frome, Somerset BA11 1DS
United Kingdom
www.doublecluck.com

Cover design by Steve Wells
Interior design by Steve Wells
Typeset by Dorchester Typesetting Group Ltd
Printed and bound in Great Britain by CPI Bookmarque, Croydon
The paper used in this Chicken House book is made from wood grown in
sustainable forests.

3 5 7 9 10 8 6 4 2

British Library Cataloguing in Publication data available.

ISBN 978-1-906427-25-2

For my dad

CHAPTER ONE

Paisley

School counselor's office, Immaculate Conception
Academy, Lodi, New Jersey

Simpson fumbled getting the tape into the VCR. She was all, Which button is it?

And I was like, How old are you and you can't even work a friggin' VCR?

'I'd like you to watch this and tell me how you feel about it,' she said, finally getting her fat ass out the way so I could see the screen. The music started up over CNN's flashy intro. The words came up: CNN BREAKING NEWS: SIX-YEAR-OLD NEW JERSEY TWINS MISSING. MOTHER FOUND DEAD. CNN's Kim Slaughter appeared—devil-red lipstick, concrete bouffant, gray suit, serious face—shuffling her papers.

Good morning, I'm Kim Slaughter and this is the news you're waking up to on Monday, March twentieth. It's seven a.m. We can go live now to our NBC affiliate in New Jersey, where Jake Williamson is outside the house where this tragic story is unfolding. Jake, what's going on down there?

Yeah, do tell, Jake, I thought. What *is* going on down there?

Thanks, Kim. And tragic is definitely the operative word in this story. I'm here standing outside the Argent family's house on Forest Way, Clifton, a quite unassuming residence where an extraordinary story began to unfold earlier today.

Cue montage of worried faces, woman in a red coat biting her lip, tracker dogs in bushes. Then back to Jake.

This is what we know: at three fifty this afternoon, Mae Wong, who lives next door to the Argents, dropped the twins Beau and Paisley home after school, as she normally does every day, and went home with her own kids. And then, approximately five minutes later, a 911 operator received this call. Take a listen …

Cue the blue screen and scratchy tape recording.

OPERATOR:	*911 Emergency. What's the problem?*
GIRL:	*Hi, um … I think my mom needs an ambulance.*
OPERATOR:	*Is your mom sick?*
GIRL:	*Uh-huh. She's on the couch.*
OPERATOR:	*Is she awake or asleep?*
GIRL:	*Asleep. (Background crying.) I said, 'Mom, wake up,' and she didn't say anything.*

OPERATOR:	*Okay, are there any grown-ups around?*
GIRL:	*No.*
OPERATOR:	*What's your name, honey?*
GIRL:	*Paisley Jane Argent.*
OPERATOR:	*That's a pretty name. Can you tell me where you live?*
GIRL:	*1175 Forest Way, Clifton, New Jersey.*
OPERATOR:	*(Background crying.) Is someone else there with you, Paisley?*
GIRL:	*Beau's here.*
OPERATOR:	*Who's Beau?*
GIRL:	*He's my twin brother.*
OPERATOR:	*How old are you, Paisley?*
GIRL:	*We're six and four days old.*
OPERATOR:	*You're very smart to call 911. Did you learn that at school?*
GIRL:	*Mmm-hmm.*
OPERATOR:	*Okay, there'll be someone to help you real soon. You just keep talking with me and we'll wait for them. They're coming.*

Jake appeared again. I was kinda glad. I started lip-synching along with him.

Now we know the little girl on the tape there, Paisley Argent, didn't stay on the line. An ambulance showed up at the house around seven minutes later and the body of her mother, Sylvia Argent, was found in the living room. But Paisley and twin brother Beau were nowhere to be found …

Maggie Simpson stopped the tape. The picture went to

black. She set the remote down on the table and put her hands on her lap. Maggie Simpson wasn't her real name. That was just what I called her 'cos she had spiky blonde hair and would sit there in our sessions, pouting and puckering her lips as she listened to me, like a baby sucking a pacifier.

'You okay?' she said, eyebrows peaked in fake sympathy.

I looked at her. 'What did you expect?'

'I thought maybe that might have brought back some bad memories for you, hearing yourself as a little girl.'

All these counselors had one mission: to get me to cry. And there was no way, even if they pricked my eyeballs with pins or splashed lemon juice into every cut, no way was I gonna cry.

'You rather I started bawling?'

'No. I just want to know how it made you feel, seeing that news item again.'

I shrugged. 'Hunky-fucking-dory.'

Simpson smiled, and there was a definite roll of eyes. 'Can you relate to that little six-year-old girl anymore?'

I sat back in my leather chair and played with my hair. I was running out of boredom indicators. She didn't have a clue how to deal with me. None of them did. It wasn't my choice to have counseling. I was forced to have it. I was one of the school's 'special cases.' Like the piano genius in my Music class who only ate orange food. Or the autistic girl in Science who liked banging her head against the fire door.

'Tell me about what happened. You and your brother came home from school, found your mom … and you went to find your dad to tell him she was sick.'

'She wasn't sick. She was dead. I do know the difference.'

'Okay, so you both headed out to go tell your dad. But you got lost, didn't you? In the woods. Were you scared?'

'No, we had the time of our lives. No parents, no peer pressure …'

'Why did you go to the woods?'

'We didn't mean to go to the woods. The woods were at the back of the golf club.'

'Your father worked there?'

'I thought you knew my history? No, he sometimes went there for dinner after work,' I sighed, in the same sing-songy way little kids read out poetry.

'Was your brother scared when you were in the woods? Did you look after him?'

I didn't answer.

'Your brother's called Beau, isn't he? Are you close?'

Still nothing. We were having a staring competition now.

'You're twins, aren't you?'

I was rock solid. Not even blinking.

'Is he the younger one or the older one?'

I wasn't going to talk about Beau. Beau was off limits. I didn't want him going through this torture too.

'The sooner you express yourself the sooner you can leave.'

'Yeah, we're twins.'

'Some twins don't get on. Do you?'

'Yes.'

'Do you ever experience that strange telepathy with Beau that some twins get? You know, do you feel pain at the same time as him? Have the same dreams? The same feelings?'

'I sometimes get the urge to touch my dick.'

'I am trying to help, you know.'

'No shit.'

'Would you at least try to open up? Just go with it. No one else can hear.'

She had a pockmark on her face that kept catching the light. We're talking crater-sized. The last counselor was better than her. I called her The Jawbreaker 'cos she had this really large lower face and big donkey teeth that could crush rocks. Then there was Pretty Shitty Blah Blah at Sacred Heart. I called her Pretty for short. Except she wasn't. She was the kind of person who looks pretty to start with but gets uglier the more you learn about them. I could call most people Pretty.

This one, Simpson, was so nervous I only had to sneeze and her coffee cup would rocket up to the ceiling. Such was my reputation, I guess.

'Your father's imprisonment …' she began, then stopped for me to fill in the blank. I wasn't going to. But then I did 'cos she was looking at me and going all puckery again like she was gonna explode.

'He didn't kill her, if that's what you're thinking. Our mom.'

I could see her balk, checking her notes again. *Father robbed hotel staff at gunpoint. Been in prison for the last eight years. Mother overdosed. No wonder. No fucking wonder.*

'What do you think about your recent behavior? Do you know why you felt compelled to do that to the piano?'

I shrugged. 'I was bored. I'm a fuck-up. That's what fuck-ups do.'

I had to meet up with the school counselor—whoever it happened to be that term—in their office every Tuesday and

Thursday after school to talk through my 'issues,' while sitting on a bean bag with my shoes off. I'd done this as long as I could remember. In every school it was the same—different days and different color bean bags, but the same kinda set up. The rooms always stank of coffee and on the walls were posters of kids with their heads in their hands, saying things like, 'We get the blues too' and 'Amy didn't like being laughed at.' I'd feed them all the usual crap of finding life so tough 'cos I was away from my brother and Mommy never showed me any affection, and they'd look at me sympathetically and give me meditation exercises and all that kinda fuckery. It was bullshit.

'Do you ever think about your mom? How do you feel about her?'

'She hated me. It's no biggie.'

What was I supposed to say? My mom did hate me. She hated Beau too. She hated us so much she used to drink to forget we were there. She'd hit us. She'd lock us in the basement for hours on end. She hated us so much she took her own life. I don't know what that is if it isn't hate.

Simpson looked at me, eyes all smoky with compassion. Luckily my bullshit shield kept out oncoming attacks of kindness. What's that stuff they froze Han Solo in at the end of *The Empire Strikes Back*? Anyway, it was like I had that all around me. No one could get through my shield of 'that.'

Immaculate Conception Academy (ICA) was the best boarding school in New Jersey—highly academic—turning out America's finest girls since 1908. It was also the most expensive. I knew that 'cos I'd been kicked out of all the crappy ones. Our Lady of the Oranges, Rambuteau, Satan's School for Girls

(Bayonne High) and Sacred Heart Academy – been there, done that, broken the windows. My grandmother realized that to keep me out of her way permanently she had to spend some real dough. I had this 'volatility' problem. My dad got the blame.

Simpson checked her notes. 'Your father's in prison, isn't he?' She was getting confident. 'How do you feel about that? Do you miss him?'

I picked my nails. I wasn't gonna answer that. I didn't want to tell her anything about my dad. I only ever talked about him to Beau.

'Your grandmother tells me that when you went home for the summer you didn't fight as much.'

'That's probably because we're not talking as much.'

'Oh, you've had a fight?'

'We always fight. So we don't talk to each other.'

'Why don't you get along?'

'Uh, because she hates me?'

'She must think a lot of you.'

'How do you work that out?'

'Well, she's spending a lot of money to give you a good education.'

'No, she's spending a lot of money to keep me as far away as possible.'

I remembered the day she'd dropped me off at Our Lady of the Oranges when I was seven. There was little me, drowning in my huge uniform, standing on the huge mosaic steps with the principal's hands on my shoulders. My grandmother, Virginia, stood there, with Beau beside her. Nowadays I call her the Skankmother. She's too Botoxed to be called Granny. As we stood there, she kept straightening my tie. I hated that.

'You'll make lots of friends. We'll see you at spring break.'

I looked up at her. 'I'll be good, I promise. I won't say any more bad swears and I'll help tidy my room and I won't be mean to Beau …' I'd have said anything to go back to Los Angeles and go to school with my brother.

'We have to catch our plane. You take Mrs Lloyd's hand.'

Beau held out his toy owl, Two Wit, to kiss my owl, Two Woo. 'Bye Pais.'

'Where's Beau going?' I kept asking her, but she didn't seem to hear it. 'Where's Beau going?!'

She finally looked down at me. 'Stop whining and go with Mrs Lloyd, please.'

'We'll keep you informed, Mrs Creed,' said the principal. 'And we'll take good care of Jane.'

Five schools later and they still always called me by my middle name. I hated that.

'Do you want to talk about those marks yet?' said Simpson, scoping my legs.

I sighed. When were they gonna learn? I decided to throw her a bone. 'No. It … it's too painful,' I lied, pulling down my skirt hem to hide my cuts. Counselors were born to be lied to. I liked to watch them lean forward and get all excited 'cos they thought they were on the brink of something.

'You know, some young people do it because it's the only outlet they allow themselves. Opening their skin becomes a way of leaking out what's troubling them. Do you have any friends that you talk to about it?'

I shook my head. 'No. I'm saving up for some of those Harajuku girls. You know, those Japanese chicks you can pay to be your friends and they don't say anything, they just carry your bags and stuff. Gwen Stefani used to take hers everywhere. You can tell *them* to get out of your face and they'll fucking listen.'

She did the lean-forward thing. 'You can talk to me. You can always talk to me. You can think of me as a friend, if you want.'

That was a big fat hairy lie. The older I got the bigger and fatter and hairier the lies got. She was no friend. Just like the counselor at the hospital when we were six. *It's okay, you're gonna be alright. Your dad'll be here soon,* she'd said. Yeah, in about ten years maybe. Eight with good behavior.

I reached into my pocket for my chocolate peanuts.

Simpson took a deep breath, then blew it right out. 'You remember in our last session together we spoke about the possibility of you moving to another facility, one that might be able to help you …'

'Yeah, a nuthouse,' I said. I popped a blue M&M in my mouth and began flicking it around on my tongue. I liked to suck them until just the peanut was left.

'A behavior-modification facility—quite a different thing. I think they'll be able to help you. There's one in California as it happens, so you'd be nearer your grandmother …'

I scoffed.

'Well, nearer your brother then.'

The M&M almost shot right out of my mouth. Nearer

Beau? Yeah, sure, where do I sign, I thought. But of course there would be a catch and I knew what it was.

'That'd be right. Get me all cozy in this nice little nuthouse, regular visits from my brother, trips to the zoo, all nicey nicey, and then zap the fuck out of my brains. I can see it now. I'm just staring into the abyss with stuff coming down my chin. Shuffling around in my slippers. *Buh buh buh buh buh buh buh buh.* I've heard electric shock treatment is a real winner.'

'It wouldn't be like that.'

'Knock it off, I know how this works. You just want me outta Jersey. If you can't turn me into a High School Musical wannabe you ship me off to La La Land where they'll put those little wires on my temples and turn me into a vegetable.'

'I can assure you that's not what happens. But it's true that your problems may be a little beyond my expertise … Have you tried reading that book I lent you?' She looked down at my legs again.

I looked down at my legs again. 'No,' I said, bowing my head. *Chicken Soup for the Teenage Soul.* I was using it to balance my nightstand. Simpson sighed. Her breath reeked of stale coffee.

I wasn't self-harming. I only liked them to think that. I was just really bad at shaving. I have no patience, no interest in doing it right at all. I scrape and scratch away and I'm done in like five minutes. I don't see the point.

My M&M was ready, just the peanut left. I took it out of my mouth and split it in two. The little bunny was there. The bunny that was always there whenever I opened a peanut. It had been something I'd noticed when I was about eight. I don't think I first discovered it, though. That was probably Columbus or somebody. It's the middle bit where the two halves join.

'So, I'm a crackpot. S'that what I put in my next letter home to the folks?'

Simpson sighed. 'No, I wouldn't put it like that. But you do seem to be incredibly … tense. You have a lot of frustration and I can completely understand that after what you have been through. And if we could identify what's causing …'

I crunched down on the nut and switched off. I was so frickin' fed up of hearing the same old, same old. Yeah, I was tense. Yeah, I needed help. Yeah I was all outta love. I'd read somewhere that the best tension-reliever was sex and that would have been great if I could get it. Only problem was, Immaculate Conception Academy for Girls was pretty dry of tension-relievers. No men, just three hundred and sixty-five mechanically-engineered lesbians who'd do it with a broom handle if it looked at them the right way.

But a week after this crunch meeting with Maggie Simpson and the threat of being sent to the cabbage patch, a miracle happened. A blinding light shot down from the August sky and this angel appeared before me in paint-splattered jeans. His name was Jason and he was helping the school gardener. He was seventeen, had a perfect V-shaped torso and spiky brown hair. I was convinced we were soul mates. I even took more interest in Classics because of Jason and the Argonauts. I imagined that was him, sailing forth to retrieve the Golden Fleece and doing all this heroic shit, when really he was downstairs filling wheelbarrows with weeds. I don't like dropping the L-bomb ordinarily, but I guess, I suppose, it was sorta love. In a way.

I was smoking a sneaky one before class when he said his first words to me.

'Who are you?'

'Paisley. Who are you?'

'Jason.' He grabbed both handles of his wheelbarrow and checked out my skirt, or rather my belt. 'You always dress like that or is it just for me?'

'What's the matter, too long?' I said, hitching it up a little higher.

Pretty soon we were sharing cigarettes behind the storage shed, talking about movies. And then it got physical. I've always seen couples stroking each other and going all cupcakey and sending text messages every five seconds and stuff, but me and Jason weren't like that. We were more your frantic smash-and-grab sessions. Kissing but missing, like magnets. Grappling like wrestlers. Not Elizabeth and Darcy, but romantic all the same. And then I kinda understood the point of shaving.

I remember everything about our nights inside the storage shed. The spicy smell of the wood and the stinking rubber of new tennis balls. The candlelight flickering, making our shadows bigger on the wall. His hot breath in my ear. His skin on mine, his hands on my back. Feeling down my glossy, smooth legs. All that kinda crap. We'd talk too, all night long, about nothing in particular and he'd listen to me. Just like Beau does. Not interrupting. Not going off on some boring tangent. Just listening. Laughing. Passing cigarettes and laughing. It was like having Beau there in a weird way. Although with me and Beau it had been candy not cigarettes.

It felt like it was the start of something. The start of me feeling something other than anger.

'Tell me you love me,' I'd say to him.

'Of course I do. I love you so much,' he'd say. And I'd believe him.

'I love you too,' I'd whisper into his shoulder and hold him real tight.

How sweet. How heartbreakingly sweet.

We talked. We kissed. He tasted of green apples. He smelled of grass cuttings and wood smoke. He held my head and stroked my earlobes. And for a short time at school, I was happy. I lived for our nights in the shed. A softer, kinder Paisley was born. Desk lids were scored with *P.A. Loves J.T.* instead of *When I Die Bury Me Upside Down So The Whole World Can Kiss My Ass.* My grades rose. I noticed birds and clouds. Tension drained through me like a sieve.

So you can kinda guess what's coming next.

CHAPTER TWO

Beau

9976 Bizcocho Drive, Cahuenga Blvd East,
Hollywood, California

I shouldn't have been there, *ergo* I should never have known about it. What happened was, I had to come home from school early to change my clothes. O'Donnell and his merry men had found a new way to humiliate me—they'd dunked me head first into the trash cans by the cafeteria. Despite the walk back in the California sunshine, my Eels T-shirt clung to my skin like food wrap.

I walked in through the back and Concepción our maid (Connie to us) was in the kitchen reading a letter.

'Hey,' I said, making her jump about a mile in the air, and

she fumbled the letter back into its envelope.

'Ooh, what's that, Connie?' I asked, thinking it might be from her son, Nando, who'd been sent back to Mexico a few months earlier. I knew she was desperate to hear from him.

'It's nothing. No, don't worry,' she said, flapping her arms like she had ants down both sleeves. She noticed my soggy T-shirt. 'Oh, you are wet. I will wash—'

'No, I just had an accident at school,' I said, trying to sound nonchalant.

She went to put the letter in her apron and I saw the front. 'That's addressed to me and Paisley.' That's when my heart started to thump real hard. I asked her who it was from but she wouldn't tell me, just kept going on about taking my clothes off so she could wash them. She practically had my shirt up over my head before I wriggled away.

'Connie, if that letter's for me I wanna see it, okay?' I tried my best to be polite, really I did, but I still felt bad for raising my voice to her.

She sighed, took the letter out of her pocket and placed it quietly on the counter. Then she walked from the room and I heard her go upstairs.

I looked at the envelope. *Mr Beau and Miss Paisley Argent.* It was postmarked Spurina, Nevada. I picked it up and slowly pulled out what was inside. Words in scrawled blue pen covered one side of a small piece of white paper. And this is what it said:

To my Wonder Twins,
Well, here I am in Spurina like I said. It's not Las Vegas but it's

close so maybe when you come visit we can go see the lights. Eddie's putting me up for now in his duplex. It's kinda on the small side, but it has four walls and a shower so it's good enough for me. As I've explained in all my other letters, it's just a stopgap. I'll get a good job in time and my own place and maybe then you guys could come see me. You're both probably doing so well, you don't need your old man back in your lives, sticking his two cents in. But whatever you think, I'll be here waiting,

Dad XX.

There was a rush through my whole body and this water-clear release in my head. Dad. He wanted us. He'd always wanted us. He'd gone to jail when we were six, charged with armed robbery. Now he was out of jail. A free man. A free Dad! We hadn't seen him, hadn't even heard from him the whole time he'd been inside. I held in my hands the first shred of contact we'd had with him in ten years.

But 'other letters'—what did that mean? When did he say he'd be staying in Spurina? Who was Eddie? How did he know we were doing 'so well?' I didn't think we were doing so well. Who'd told him that?

'Connie?'

I couldn't hear her upstairs and found the lack of floorboard creaks troubling. I heard a distant clatter coming from the far end, near my room. I two-stepped it up the stairs, finding her in the spare bedroom, sitting on the floor in front of the bureau, a shoebox of letters on her lap. She was crying into the hem of her apron.

'This is all,' she said to me. 'Miss Virginia made me throw

away the presents. This is all yours now. I want no more of this. It is too sad.'

I looked down at the letters. There must have been fifty of them. 'How long's he been writing to us?'

She smiled, her wide eyes melting into moons. 'You and Paisley were seven. Your seventh birthday a card came. He loves you so much, Beau. So much …'

I started bawling, as is my wont. My sister Paisley says I cry way too easily. She never cries if she can help it. Once when we were kids we were freewheeling on our bikes down the street and Paisley fell off and slid along the concrete until she'd scraped off all the skin down the side of her leg. When I'd got to her, she was pretending like she hadn't been crying, wiping her eyes and saying she was fine. She could barely walk. 'I'm gonna have a cool scar,' she said and got straight back on the bike like nothing had happened, the blood still trickling down. She's always been like that. I think it's because she knows if she starts crying, it'll be hard to stop. She says tears are a sign of weakness. At least, that's what our grandmother always told her.

'You kept them from us?' I said.

Connie got up and handed the box to me, closing the bureau door behind her. I hated to see her cry. She'd always snuggle us if we cried as children. It had always been her job to feed us, tuck us in, take us shopping and give us cuddles.

I still stank of the rotten kitchen waste I'd been dunked in at school but offered her a hug anyway. I tentatively put my arms around her, feeling her tense up, and then go limp and cuddle me back.

'You kept them all this time?' I said, feeling her nod against my head.

'I might lose my job.'

'It's alright.'

We released each other and she tapped the top of the box. 'These are yours now. Please, I don't want them. You read them.' She pinched my T-shirt on my shoulder. 'Please change your clothes. I will wash them before I go.'

And then she left the room and me and the box and disappeared down the stairs. Moments later I heard the vacuum cleaner humming in the den.

I stripped off my rancid T-shirt and I sat there, all afternoon, reading through every single letter Dad had sent us from prison. Letter after letter that my sister and I had never seen. I held each one like it was some ancient document that would spoil beneath my finger grease. Each one took me back ten years in time, back to New Jersey. Back to Paisley and me as children. Back to Dad and how it used to be when he took us out. To the park, to the golf club, to eat pancakes on low-lying tables where he had to bend over to eat. To hotel lobbies where he'd show us coin tricks and we'd play Baby Blackjack for candy.

Then I knew who Eddie was. I wandered back in my mind to the times when Dad used to take us with him on his trips into the city (he was a sales rep for New Jersey Gardenia who sold toiletries to hotel chains). He'd give us Junior Mints and Mike & Ikes if we behaved. We got to go inside these plush hotels and play on the grand winding staircases, go in and out the elevators, slide around on the pristine marble floors in the bathrooms while he did his work. Just like in that children's book, *Eloise at the Plaza*. Sometimes if the hotel was real busy, Dad'd get someone to watch us—usually a real old weener who'd keep reminding us how lucky we were and tell us about the crap Christmas presents he used to get as a kid, like oranges and bones. But sometimes we'd get a concierge like Eddie.

Eddie at The Roosevelt was awesome. Like Will Smith only shorter. He always wore this pristine black uniform with a burgundy collar and he'd show us coin tricks like Dad's and make us laugh with stories about the guests, telling us who was super rich and which ones were just super weird. 'Suits' he called them. Suits with golden wives. Certain companies would hold conferences in the hotel and there'd be a horde of suits with matching designer luggage. The men would always do the checking-in and the wives would stand around, sighing and clicking their heels against the marble. Me and Paisley would take our candy up to the mezzanine and find ourselves a quiet nook where we could look down on the marble lobby, staring at the twinkling chandelier, watching the tourists check in and out, and waiting for Dad to emerge.

I remember the last time he took us into the city. It was our birthday the following day and as a pre-birthday treat he took us to this diner in Grand Central Station where we had burgers and cheese fries. Dad had a BLT. I was dying to ask him about the fight he and Mom had had the night before. Our neighbor, Mr Wong, had even called over to complain because it was thumping through his walls. Mom going all high and screechy. Dad being all deep and defensive. And then him all high and defensive and her all deep and judgmental. Paisley and I shared a room above the kitchen, which was where most of their arguments took place. That night Mom had called us 'little shits' and complained that Dad was never home to help, and always gave us candy to curry favor. That part is sort of true. Dad did buy us a lot of candy. You want me or my sister to do anything, you give us candy. It's kind of a key to get in with us.

In the diner, Paisley had ketchup all around her mouth. She asked Dad about the wives at The Roosevelt.

'Are they made of gold, Dad?'

'No, honey. Why d'you say that?'

''Cos they look gold.'

'No, they're not gold. They sure got a lot of it, though. I wouldn't mind a piece of it myself.'

'Do they have jobs?'

'No, I don't think so.'

'What do they do all day?'

'I don't know, honey.'

I couldn't wait any longer. 'Are you and Mom going to get a divorce?' I said.

I remember him chewing real hard on his sandwich and frowning. 'Why d'you ask, son?'

''Cos we heard you shouting again last night.'

He took another bite of his sandwich and scrunched up his napkin to wipe his chin. Then he said, 'I'm sorry, guys. We thought you were asleep.'

'We were,' said Paisley. 'It woke us up.'

Dad shook his head. 'We just had a little argument, like you guys do sometimes. We're not gettin' divorced.'

'Where does it hurt you, Dad?' Paisley asked him.

'What do you mean, baby?'

'You told Mom you were broke. Where are you broke?'

Dad bowed his head and wiped his chin again with his napkin. When he came back up he was smiling. He grabbed the menu from the stand. 'Who wants cheesecake? Let's see what they got … ooh, strawberry I think. Or Chocolate Swirl. Y'all want Chocolate Swirl?'

We nodded and dunked our fries in our joint pot of ketchup.

I remembered it so clearly. On the way home, Dad throwing Peppermint Patties over his shoulder for us in the backseat, them raining down on us like stars. Me and Paisley snuggling down into the blanket.

'Try and get some sleep, okay guys? Traffic's gonna be pretty bad gettin' back into Jersey. We got a long drive.'

About a week later, Dad went to work like usual but didn't come home. We just assumed she'd kicked him out. We didn't know about him going to prison until later. Mom spoke to us less and less and started talking to bottle necks more and more. And then pretty soon, she wasn't saying anything at all. Paisley and I were the ones who found her.

Paisley misses Dad like crazy, even now. She's always talking about him. His on-the-spot bedtime stories in which we had starring roles. His BLT subs—the best in Jersey, he always said. The way he always called us his Wonder Twins. I kinda resigned myself years ago to the fact that he didn't want us anymore. Finding the letters threw me all out of whack. I didn't know how I felt now. I didn't know what to do.

All afternoon spent worrying about it and reading and

re-reading the letters brought me to one conclusion: I needed to tell Paisley. That was the next step I had to take. But I didn't know how to do it. She was banned from all the computers at her school so I couldn't email her. I tried calling but I kept hanging up the second I heard the voice on the other end. I couldn't work out what I would say. I knew I'd get all tongue-tied and say the wrong things and she'd go on the rampage and get all Paisley about it. For the sake of her school, I needed time to work out the best way of telling her. I decided to write a letter. I spent all evening at it. My numerous attempts lay beneath me on the carpet in slowly uncurling balls.

Pais, I have to speak to you urgently …

Sis, You are seriously not going to believe …

Dearest Paisley, This is such a hard letter to write, I don't know how you're going to take it …

Pais, I don't know how to tell you this …

Paisley, This is really difficult to say, so I'll just come right out and say it …

PJ, Well, look what just turned up on our doorstep …

Dear Sis, You will not believe what happened today. I came home from school and Connie was in the kitchen …

Paisley, I have some really big news so call me …

P, It's about Dad …

Pais, Remember our dad, well he hasn't just abandoned us from his prison cell, he's actually been writing to us for ten years and our grandmother didn't think it right to tell us …

However I ended up phrasing it, I knew one thing for sure: she was gonna go ballistic.

CHAPTER THREE

Paisley

Immaculate Conception Academy for Girls, Lodi,
New Jersey

I caught Jason screwing a prefect. Not a significant prefect,
not Emily-Jane Bulow or Jessica Walsh, the two most popular
bitches in school, but Mandy Fugazi—Paris Hilton in a
smashed mirror. Diseased little alley cat too. She'd once done
five St Anthony's boys behind the tennis courts, using an empty
potato chips packet for protection. Alright I'll admit, I'm no
Jonas Brother when it comes to chastity, but Mandy had those
kinda eyes. A slut's eyes.

Seeing those two skanks together became another one of my
mind replays. Like the time we found Mom's body. In those

moments between being awake and asleep, my brain has a habit of puking up bad memories. Like finding Mom dead. Being lost in the woods. The time Dad was pushing me on the swing and it swung back and caught his head and made him bleed. And from that day on, this scenario: getting to the storage shed twenty minutes early. Taking three tokes of my cigarette. Hearing the floorboards; a giggle. Rubbing a space on the dusty window. My cigarette dropping to the earth. Seeing them naked. Her lying beneath him like a doll. Him looking up at the window and smiling. Him carrying on. Harder.

I ran back to the dorms. Ran and ran and ran, like some stupid hamster on its wheel, running off its night energy. When I got below our window I stopped, knowing that my heavy breathing and wheezing would wake up the others. I couldn't go in. But I couldn't go back. And because I'd stopped running, I started to feel it. The punch to my stomach. The big black boot stamp to my ribcage. I needed to keep running so it wouldn't get me. So I ran deep into the woods behind the school and spent the night there, nestled in the nook of a large tree trunk. I think I was born to live in a fucking tree trunk.

And when my breathing got less and the pain came back, I started thinking about my brother, Beau. The last time I went girl-scout under the stars, he was with me. But now I was on my own. No frightened twin brother to hold my hand. No more angel of salvation in paint-splattered jeans. Just me. Fucked-up, fucked-off me. I let it take me over. This was why I didn't cry. Because it hurt so damn much.

I made out like I'd forgotten about it when I saw Jason

wheeling his barrow up the sports field a few days later. I had this stinging sensation behind my eyes like I wanted to cry but there was no way I was gonna. There was no way I was gonna punch him either. Why would I waste my calories on that son of a bitch? No, I would not be conquered, not by a guy. I took my big black boot sole and stamped down hard on any feelings I might have had for him. I wrote myself some angry poetry and this little story about a woman who cut the dicks off her former lovers to make necklaces and then bought a jewelry store and made a fortune. It helped. I concluded Jason was merely a 'get-me-through.' Like when you're forced to watch a really boring movie and it's numbing your brain, so you develop a little crush on one of the stars, just to get you through it. A get-me-through. That's all Jason had ever been. That's all any guy would ever be.

Apart from Beau. And Dad.

But even though I'm a vegetarian, I still have meat-eater's incisors so naturally I wanted revenge. And it was while I was thinking up how to wreak my revenge on this little douche bag that I got a letter from Beau. And this letter, this little one-line letter put the whole stupid Jason incident into proper perspective.

Beau usually emailed me, but since I'd been banned from all computers for making fake IDs, he had to go old school and write. When I first saw the letter, I immediately thought it was bad news. A long ramble about a beating he'd gotten from the O'Donnell gang at his school, written by his nurse. A wordy speech about how he was finally at the end of his infinite tether with the Skankmother and was planning to run away for sure.

But it wasn't. It said just six words.

Paisley, Dad's been in touch, Beau x

I read it again and again. And it came screaming forward at me like one of those magic eye posters that your brain has to unscramble before the hidden picture comes into focus. I stopped reading and held it to my chest. Dad. What? Dad's been in touch. Our dad? My dad? I had to say it a couple times before I wrapped my brain around it.

Over the years Dad had become this god to me. I constantly thought about him, wore old rock T-shirts that reminded me of the ones he used to wear, watched his favorite movies until they became my favorite movies. *Dog Day Afternoon, Serpico, Bonnie and Clyde, Cuckoo's Nest, Assault on Precinct 13, Psycho*. I never stopped wondering why he didn't contact us. Wondering if his brown eyes still twinkled like Beau's did when he smiled. If it would still feel the same to hug him. If he was still as big. At school I'd fantasize about him in class. Him breaking out of jail and stalking across the desert to look for us. Putting a bullet through the head of the first guy who stood between him and his kids. Bursting through the door of the Latin room, sunlight flooding in from behind, and saying in his gravely Dad voice, 'Come on, Paisley, I'm gettin' you outta this dump.' The fantasies were always killed when the bell went. I hadn't been stupid enough to think any of them could come true. Until now.

I went from lying in a pit of stinking, slashed-heart despair to being thrust up into the sunlight like a beach ball, held under the water and then bursting up into the sky. I paced up and down our dorm like some crazy-assed bear in the zoo. I had an open-ended air ticket back to LA so I could easily get a cab to Newark Airport and be on my way back there within twenty-four hours. But the principal, or Super Turbo Bitch as I knew her, would never let me go without the Skankmother's permission. And there was no way Skank was gonna give permission. It meant all the stops would have to come out.

I needed to get myself expelled. A.S.A.F.P.

And a week after the traumatic event with Jason, four days after receiving Beau's letter, an occasion presented itself to me.

The whole school lined up for lunch in the long corridor outside the refectory. Jutting off at various intervals were our classrooms and the fiction and reference libraries. Right at the end was the school chapel. This was where we'd meet every morning, give praise for stuff, get scared to death by the tall plastic Jesus figure on the altar and kneel on uncomfortable cushions 'til the woven imprints of crosses were tattooed on our knees. On the occasion in question, Mandy Fugazi, aka Sluttina Fug Face, had the misfortune of standing right outside the chapel, and therefore at the end of the lunch line, just as I joined it. The corridor reeked of meat and onions.

'Hey Mandy,' I said. She just looked at me, like I was clowning.

'Oh, hi,' said Fug Face, turning away. I knew exactly what I would say. I'd played it over and over in my mind to get it right. I took a few breaths before delivering it; I didn't want to stumble or mispronounce anything. I wanted it to be just right.

'Mandy,' I said, 'I've got this great book if you ever wanna borrow it. I know you're into that kinda stuff.'

She looked blank, as she well might. Fug Face didn't read. A halogen light flickered above our heads among the wooden eaves and cobwebs. She had so many zits under her make-up I could have joined them up and made a shape.

'Kama Sutra, it's called. Yeah, it shows you all these different sexual positions you can get into with your boyfriend.' I leaned in closer. I could smell him. Grass cuttings and wood smoke. 'You looked kinda stiff on the floor of the storage shed the other day.'

Fug's face went scarlet. The low mumbles of conversation stopped as the others listened in. I could see some of them giggling behind their hands. But I wasn't finished. Yet.

'It's okay if that's what the guy likes. But one day you might want to be a bit more adventurous. You know, try opening your legs a little?'

She looked daggers at me. No, not daggers. Swords. Swords with flaming blades and poisoned tips. She lunged at me, pushed me back against the pin boards, grabbing my hair, pulling it any way she could.

'You bitch!' she screamed at the top of her lungs. 'You were spying. You perv, you complete psycho perv!' Her voice echoed, ricocheting off every wall as we grappled. That's all she could do: grapple and pull hair. She was such a girl. That's how girls fight, they go for the hair. I had never fought like that. That was foreplay to me. I pushed her and swung right back, clocking her across the left side of her face.

Thwack!

Whoomph, down she went. I can still see her eyes close as my fist caught her cheek, the slow-motion jet of blood shooting from her mouth like a little red fish.

My arms were pinned back.

Cries of, 'Oh my God'—'Is she dead?'—'What happened?'—'How awful,' echoed in my ears as I floated along the corridor, propped up by two teachers, Miss Randle and Mr Patrick. Every pair of eyes was on me, from the prefects right the way down to the tiny ones in their claret-and-gold lunch overalls, gawking at me as I passed them. Some had their hands on their mouths, others tried to pretend they were suddenly very interested in their shoes. Soon there were no more giggles, no more murmurs of disapproval. Just big eyes. And me, desperately trying to kick and wriggle out of my restraints, screaming at the top of my lungs: 'Go on then, do it. Do it, you assholes. Put me out of my fucking misery!'

And then *bam*, I was in the principal's office, standing tight-lipped before the massive wooden desk with its row of paperweights and picture frames. Super Turbo Bitch, that day in gray trouser suit and sad new bob haircut, glared at me all the way through her lecture.

'I'm not tolerating it anymore, Jane Argent,' she said finally in her English Royal accent, her nose all pointy and high in the air.

'For the past few terms, your behavior has become progressively worse. Our school motto encourages us to give everyone a fair chance to fit in. But you are an example of everything that is wrong with this school and everything I want to be rid of. I think you'll agree I've given you quite enough chances, spent enough of our funds on providing you with counseling and you have done nothing, absolutely NOTHING to improve.'

Here we go again, I thought. Come on, then, do it. You know you want to. Rub this dirty little stain out of your clean little school.

She stood up and faced me, leaning over the desk. 'Punching a student?' The 'P' of 'punching' was packed with enough spit to spray my entire face. I motioned to wipe it from my eye.

She huffed. 'How am I going to explain to Mandy's parents that she has been punched? That she may have a broken jaw? Hmm?'

I started laughing. I couldn't help it. 'What can I say? I made the bitch famous. They'll be talking about it for years to come.' My heart was thumping in my ears. This was my chance. Four schools down, one to go. She was giving me all the right buttons and I was pressing them all like a little kid on a keyboard.

STB snarled. 'Disobedient, arrogant, rude, insolent … I could go on.'

I sucked the tips of my near-frozen fingers in an attempt to give them the warm kiss of life. Every word was a shout. A criticism. An order. As though saying it at the right volume and spitting it at me like a cobra was gonna make me bow down to her. It wasn't. Nobody could make me do anything.

'… ruthless, obstinate, rude …'

'You already said rude.' I picked at my teeth with the tip of my long purple nail. I'd had enough by this point. I couldn't look at the woman anymore so I concentrated on the William Morris wallpaper and tall dark-wood bookcases all around me. I don't know if it was my near-hypothermic state in that freezing office or the putrid waft of stale coffee I was getting off her breath but it all seemed to be closing in on me. Like the garbage crusher in *Star Wars*. Or was it *Empire Strikes Back*? The one where they rescued the princess, anyway. It used to be Beau's favorite movie, up until he saw that French one with the chick on the bike. Now he likes that one better. Thinks it makes him look more intelligent.

'Look, I get the point,' I said finally. 'I'm crap. Can I go now?'

'That's what you want, isn't it?' she roared, sitting down on her swivel chair and folding her arms, her too-tight jacket taking the strain at the shoulders. 'And that's what you got from all your other schools. They couldn't handle you so they just let you go. I know you too well.'

'You don't know me at all,' I shouted. 'Most of the time, you people ignore me. And when you're not ignoring me, you're whining on about me not joining in or not being good enough for this or that … and it's "waaah, waaah, waaah" in this ear, "waaah, waaah, waaah" in that ear. Is it any wonder I'm so goddamn ANGRY?'

I'd used this same speech when they'd kicked me out of Rambuteau. There were two of them then. I managed to bring one to tears and pull the other one's toupée off. STB wasn't a crier. She didn't wear a rug either.

'With a family history like yours I'd say your behavior was written in the stars.'

Mee-ow. Okay, I thought. Let's try this …

'You can't honestly tell me I'm single-handedly … bastardizing the entire private school system. I'm a drop in the ocean compared to some of the things that go on here that you don't know about.'

'Such as?' she said, hands searching for things to do on the desk—papers to shuffle, pens to put back in the pen-holder, a stapler to realign so it was perpendicular with the edge of the desk. Everything had to be perfect.

I counted them off on my fingers. 'Your highly-decorated head girl has her own strip show on YouTube, half the eighth graders are bulimic, I'm pretty sure our drama teacher smokes crack, and your apprentice gardener has been screwing most of my year.'

She looked like she was waiting for a golf ball to drop into her mouth.

Her whole body rose and fell with her breath. She picked up the phone.

'I suppose the piano incident wasn't your fault either?' she said, dialing.

I thought about it for a second. 'No, that was me.'

She spoke into the phone. 'Morrie, could you send Jason to my office, please … I don't care, it's urgent.' She put the phone down.

I leaned in for the kill.

'And while I'm spilling all these unfortunate beans, I don't suppose you've sat in on any of your husband's German classes recently, have you?'

'Don't you …'

'… he can suggest things with a long ruler that would make your eyes bleed.'

'… DARE. You HORROR of a girl,' she bellowed, squinting the words out as though the force was hurting her eyes. 'I could sue you for slander.' Drawn up to her full height she rounded the desk and marched over to the office door. She opened it, turning to deliver her parting shot.

'Get out of my school.'

Mission: Accomplished.

'You are a bad seed, Jane Argent. Your future looks *very* bleak to me.'

I stepped into the corridor and turned to deliver *my* final blow. 'My name is Paisley. And at least I *have* a future. I wouldn't give a bucket of piss for *yours*.'

I'd heard that line in a movie once and I'd been dying to use it. Luckily my great brain managed to bring it to my attention at the perfect moment. The door slammed in my face, the bang echoing around the stony hallway.

'Yeah, thought that'd do it,' I said.

I stood there for a moment, blinking myself firmly into reality. That was it. I was outta there. My heart still thumped in my ears. I couldn't think about it anymore. I couldn't dwell on it. Five schools. Five schools and not one of them could deal with me. I didn't even know if *I* could deal with me. All I knew was I had to get to Beau and we had to get to Dad. Life would be better then. *I* would be better then, I was sure of it.

There was a school brochure on the hall table. All the pictures inside were of happy, fresh-faced girls: a shiny blonde in an immaculate tunic lighting a candle in the chapel; a girl sprayed in achievement badges playing the flute in the music room; a circle of cross-legged Girl Scouts sitting around a toadstool, listening intently to a fat woman reading a book. I was never the girl in the brochure. I was always the back-of-head in the science lab or the out-of-focus-blob on the baseball field. I took the brochure in my hands and tore it right down the middle.

As I started walking up the staircase to the dorms, the front door opened and Jason lumbered in, taking his boots off on the doormat. For the splittest of split seconds, I felt that disgusting pang in my chest again, like I still loved him. It was a relief when the anger came back and I remembered what he had done to me. What I had seen.

He looked up and saw me.

'What have you told them?' he glared.

'Everything, darling.' I carried on walking.

He came over to the banister and grabbed my hand.

'If you've told them about us sleeping together …'

'Sleeping together, screwing together. Eating Chunky Chips Ahoy together …'

'I'll tell 'em it's all bullshit. You're a kid. And you're a kid with a bad rep. They'll never believe you.'

At that moment, Super Turbo Bitch appeared in the doorway to her office, behind Jason. She must have heard us. He hadn't seen her.

'But it did happen, Jason,' I said, raising my voice so STB could hear every word, and fake crying, lip quiver and all. 'You said you loved me.'

His hand felt rough and sweaty on mine. 'Give it up, Paisley. It won't work. I got a good rep here. You're not gonna blow this for me.'

'That's not what you said before!'

'Stop it, alright?!' he whispered, leaning in to the banister. 'I'm just gonna tell them you're lying, then you'll be out of here and that will be that.'

I stopped fake crying and looked at him. 'But that *isn't* that, is it? I got proof. I kept our first condom. A souvenir to remind me how much I meant to you.'

'Shut up, you know we never used a condom …' He couldn't help shouting at me and it wasn't until he turned that he saw Super Turbo Bitch, glaring at him with nostrils like caves.

He turned back to me, as gray as a cliff face.

I smiled and whispered. 'Don't that just stick it in and break it off?'

In the dorm, I packed up my stuff and found my plane ticket and passport. I threw off my school shirt and tie, replacing it with my AC/DC *For Those About To Rock* T-shirt, an exact copy of the one Dad wore when we were little. I kept my school skirt on and hitched it up another inch. It actually went really well with my chunky socks and boots. I kept my stripy tie too; it made a cool wrist wrap. Everything else, the coat, the yellow sweats, the sewing kit, the white shirt, could go burn for all I cared.

I could hear them all in the refectory as I walked to the school entrance. The echo of, 'For what we are about to receive, may the Lord make us TRULY thankful, Amen.' The eager scraping of chair legs and clank of metal kitchen utensils.

I strode on. 'Assholes,' I said. 'All of them, assholes.'

CHAPTER FOUR

Beau

9976 Bizcocho Drive, Cahuenga Blvd East,
Hollywood, California

I was sitting at my desk, awaiting Paisley's call to pick her up from the airport. I couldn't wait to see her. I didn't want to wait to see her. I had been waiting too long. I opened the lid of my hibernating laptop and clicked on the 'TV Archivia' link in my favorites, then logged into my account. All my most wanted videos came up as thumbnails. I clicked on Oprah's face.

'They're doing marvelously, yes,' said my grandmother in an odd Madonna-esque English accent. Ever the actress, she was rehearsing for a play in London at the time. 'Beau's very good at baseball and he's taken quite a keen interest in art.' She was sat beside us on this vast squashy lemon couch. Paisley had her hands on her lap and her feet crossed over; I was wearing some kind of lederhosen. Our grandmother retrieved a piece of paper from a nook in the couch and showed the cameras. It was a painting I had done of myself and Paisley playing in the gardens. I remember doing it at school.

The audience 'aaahed' in chorus and Oprah asked, 'And what about Paisley? How you doing, little Miss?'

The camera zoomed in on my sister, dressed in her little white smock and tights, hair in silky blonde pigtails. She smiled at Oprah and nodded.

'I'm really good, thank you.'

And the whole audience just melted. Then she started squinting. She developed it not long after we moved to California. Ten years on, I still have my own nervous tic where I can't look anyone in the eye for longer than two seconds when they're talking to me, but Paisley's only lasted a couple months. It was pretty bad though, and the camera wasn't on her for long.

'She's just wonderful,' said Virginia, smiling widely. 'Yes, she's a very happy little girl. They're both very much loved. I just feel so … so blessed that we've been able to make the most of what was a terribly tragic situation.'

I then looked up at Connie and said 'What's tragic?' Oprah clapped and laughed and there was another round of applause from the studio audience and a pastel-colored cutaway to commercials and whinnying saxophone. After the break, Oprah had wheeled us in our new bikes, but that wasn't available for download. Virginia didn't let us keep those anyway. We'd already won bikes on *All Star Kids Fun House*.

Virginia made sure she got to tell everyone our story. We had interviews on ABC, CNN, *60 Minutes*. Appearances on *Ricki*, *Montel*, *Regis and Kathie Lee*, *Rosie O'Donnell*. We did endorsements for Chunky Chips Ahoy, Lucky Charms and Wonder Gummies. She even got us invites to the Nickelodeon Kids' Choice Awards as guests of N'Sync.

Wonder Gummies was this healthy kids' candy, which was supposed to contain all these vitamins. When we were lost in the woods, all we ate for three days was a packet of them that Paisley had in her pocket. So everyone went all hoop-la about this miracle candy and the company wanted us to front a new campaign.

I clicked on the Wonder Gummies thumbnail.

I remember being taken down to the studios with Paisley, both of us dressed in nasty white overalls with these pink and blue bubbles on the pockets. The ad was pretty corny, even then. We had to pretend we were walking through this plastic forest, rubbing our tummies like we were real hungry. And then we'd come upon this house made of candy and start gnawing on it, like Hansel and Gretel and the gingerbread house.

Then Paisley had to say, 'Gee Beau, this Wonder Gummy house is delicious.'

And then I had to lick a wall and say, 'Sure is, Paisley. And did you know Wonder Gummies are fat free *and* give us essential vitamins and minerals too?'

Except I couldn't say 'essential.' I kept saying 'senshal' and Virginia would give me daggers off-set every time I messed up. It took about twenty takes, and even then the director wasn't happy and changed it to 'vital.'

'Enunciate, Beau, there's a good boy,' Virginia would say. 'Big smiles, Paisley Jane. Come on, you can do better than that.' And she'd do this quick clap after every order, like we were performing seals or something.

And then this voice would come over saying, 'Wonder Gummies are helping keep America fit and healthy. Did you know that a child's daily portion of Wonder Gummies contains as much calcium as a glass of milk? It also provides vital daily nutrients including Vitamins D and E, folic acid and zinc.'

And then Paisley would be licking a Gummy window and she'd say, 'Hey, try the window, Beau. It's made of Wonder's New Honey Gummy. It tastes good.'

Virginia would be screaming at her from the sidelines, 'Rich in potassium!'

By this time I'd be sitting on the roof of the house chewing on the chimney and saying, 'I'm not done up here yet. Mmm, raspberry flavor. You gotta try this.'

And then the voice would come on again and say, 'Give the kids what they love and what they need—*(cue kids shouting)* Wonder Gummies!'

I laughed. I remembered Virginia storming onto the set, pulling my sister's overalls down and smacking her across her bare legs. I stopped laughing.

'You WILL get it right. You will stay here ALL NIGHT if you have to.'

It had been good to think of us as kids again, me and Paisley, remember the good times. But the remembrance of every good time was tainted with bad.

I've always been afraid of Virginia, more fool I. But she didn't scare Paisley at all, even when she hit her. Paisley would always just stare up at her. Whenever she sent Paisley to her room without food I'd go up afterward and sneak her some Apple Jacks or something, and we'd sit in a little blanket cave on her bed and eat them straight out of the box. I knew when she'd been crying. I always knew when Virginia had got to her. And there'd sometimes be a new hole she'd kicked in her closet door or a tear in the wallpaper behind her headboard. But only I would ever notice these kinds of things. Nowadays she and Virginia don't speak to each other at all if they can help it. She's allowed home for the holidays if she's lucky but that's it.

Paisley always used to say our grandmother was a vampire 'cos she hated garlic, *always* wore dark shades in sunlight and didn't believe in God. Virginia did have a reflection in our mirrored hallway, though, which I picked her up on, but Paisley told me it was because our grandmother was the queen vampire so she could have a reflection. Once, a bird or something crashed into our bedroom window at night and when we looked it had gone. Paisley convinced me it had been Virginia, flying up to check on us and I didn't sleep properly for days after. I hated all that kinda stuff: vampires, werewolves. Paisley's not afraid of things like that. Ghosts and gargoyles. 'It's the living you wanna be scared of, Beau, not the dead,' she says. And I know she's right. But that's just the way I am. I think when we were babies she won the lottery of the good genes; she's cute, quirky, blonde and badass. I'm short, dark, scared and superfluous.

I clicked on the *Regis and Kathy at Home with* Special and scrolled through it. I'd watched it a bunch of times but I wanted to see the last shot again, of us jumping in the pool. The rest of the clip was just our grandmother standing in our mirrored hallway with a backdrop of her glass statuettes for Best Daytime Soap Actress, 1984 and 1986.

'*We're looking forward to Christmas and as you can see, the twins are doing great,*' she said. And then she looked deep into the camera and said, '*And can I just take this opportunity to thank every single person who has sent cards and money to the twins. We still receive gifts from all over the country and it is heartening to know that America thinks so highly of them. We are investing in their future and have set up a trust fund for them, which will pay for their education and care. We try and respond to every single letter we receive, but are sometimes a little overwhelmed. We thank you all from the bottom of our hearts.*'

I laughed. *We're looking forward to Christmas.* Which Christmas was that? The Christmas she left us with Connie's family to go skiing with the raisin millionaire? Or the Christmas she left us with Connie's family so she could get wasted on Scotch at home because she'd been dumped by the raisin millionaire? I could see through her like she was one of those glass statuettes. *We're investing in their future.* New pool. State-of-the-art fire pit and sauna. New furniture. Bathroom fixtures. Carpets. Nice future.

On one particularly brave Saturday afternoon a couple years ago, I searched Virginia's bureau and found the details. Me and Paisley had over ten million dollars coming to us when we were eighteen.

Ten million dollars!

I couldn't believe it. People had been so kind, sending us money when we'd been found, knowing full well that we had nothing else to look forward to. No Mom, no Dad. No home. I checked the bureau often when I knew Virginia would be out. The latest correspondence from the bank said they were 'looking into the misuse of finances issue' and putting a lockdown on all withdrawals from now on. Since we'd lived with her, she'd creamed off three million dollars of what was sent for us.

The total then stood at just under seven million.

The day we were sent to live with Virginia was scary for us. You have to remember that we were only six and we were fresh out of a group children's home where we'd been placed after leaving hospital. We thought it was gonna be like *Annie*, when the little curly orphan goes and stays with this gazillionaire. We thought we'd walk into the mansion and there'd be footmen twirling around on mops, maids folding silk sheets and a happy dog padding around all covered in soap suds. What *we* got was a ramshackle duplex in West Hollywood, a part-time Mexican housekeeper, a gardener called Popeye who had two fingers missing from his right hand, and a grandmother whose sole preoccupation was to get us in the papers. It was better than the children's home and Connie was always good to us, but she had her own family. It never felt like home.

And while the cameras were there we could never be ourselves. We had to be the children our grandmother wanted us to be. Clean, cute angels with rictus grins and well-rehearsed waves, always happy or studying. Not the kids we were. Me, who sucked on wet washcloths until they were gray and stank like wet dogs. And Paisley, who answered back and stole food for us when Virginia wasn't looking so we could have midnight feasts in our blanket cave on my bed.

When the cameras had gone, we were just messy kids; naughty kids; disgusting kids. We'd chew cookies then spread the chewed mix out on top of other cookies and eat them. We'd spit up on the back of our grandmother's padded velvet coat when walking behind her in a store and draw patterns in the trails. Once we drew all over ourselves in black marker and pretended we'd gotten tattoos. We broke the lock on the booze cabinet and took sips from all the bottles. We cut each other's hair with gardening shears. We'd wash stray cats in talcum powder. We'd pee in the pool. We'd pee in the fire pit too. Our knees were always bloody and scraped and we always had the best time when we were doing something we shouldn't.

In the end Virginia realized that smacking our butts or locking us in our rooms was no deterrent. She found the hole in the wall between our rooms, the hole Paisley had bored with one of Virginia's own stiletto heels so we could talk to each other. That was when she lost it and decided to send Paisley away.

It was always new and fun and exciting being a kid. I liked being disobedient. I can't bring myself to do the fun, naughty stuff anymore. I'm too afraid. I hate being a teenager.

I'm supposed to be stealing purses and notching up my STD count. Hanging out in the Little League field after dark, chugging brewskis and doing eight balls. Getting bong flu or getting shit-faced in sweatboxes on Hollywood Boulevard or at frat parties in the Valley. I'm supposed to pack a knife and rob old ladies or be planning a shooting on my blog. But that's not me.

I like simple things. Reading. Observing. Watching the green parakeets up on the pylon wires outside the house. I like the cool breeze on my face through my bedroom window when I'm writing at my desk. I like French movies, pop music, pomegranates. I'm reading Sartre and Simone de Beauvoir and trying to teach myself French using a four-CD kit I got from a thrift store. I want to live in Paris some day.

That's why I get called 'nerd' or 'pussy' and dunked in trash cans. I try not to look them in the eye anymore. I hide behind my hair. But I can't change. I won't change.

I closed my laptop and stared out the window. I had a bag of peanut M&Ms on the desk and I reached over and plucked one out, a blue one. I carefully crunched away the blue shell and licked away the chocolate until just the peanut remained. Then I split open the two halves.

And there inside was the little bunny that lives inside every whole peanut. Paisley taught me that.

And then the phone rang.

CHAPTER FIVE

Paisley

```
Terminal 4, Los Angeles International Airport,
                California
```

'Hey,' he said with a thin smile and a lift of his eyebrows.

'Hey,' I said, dropping my bag. He picked it up and we made for the exit. I hate airports. 'There's too many fucking people in this world.'

'It's good to see you, Pais,' he said, giving it puppy dogs.

'You too.' We hugged. I'd seen him like a month before during summer vacation so it wasn't one of our usual squeezes, full of unsaid *God I missed you*s. He was definitely fatter since the summer. The Skankmother had been feeding him up. But I didn't mention it. It was too soon to go into that old brother–sister routine and I knew he'd get all worried and start going on and on about diets he should try, so instead I cut straight to the chase.

'D'you bring the letters?'

'No, they're at home. I hid them under my bed.'

'Good job.'

We walked through the automatic doors and I took my first breath of Californian air. It felt good. Then we played cab dodge to cross the road to the parking lot where Beau had left the Skank's white Pontiac Fiero.

'D'you wanna grab something to eat? I didn't have breakfast yet so …'

'No. First things last. I wanna get back and see the letters. How many are there?'

'I don't know.' Beau started the car.

'She hasn't treated you to your own wheels yet, then?'

He shrugged. 'I don't mind. The Fiero's a sweet ride.'

'It's not yours, though, is it? I thought you were looking at Subarus.'

'She said they were too expensive.'

'Can't bear the thought of you having a little bit of freedom, can she?'

'It's not like that.'

'It so is.'

He clearly wanted to change the subject. 'So, good flight?'

'Not really,' I said, looking out the window at the palm trees. 'Didn't sleep.'

'You're officially expelled then?'

'Yeah. So what else did Dad say? Where is he?'

'Spurina.'

'Where the hell's Spurina?'

'It's this little place just outside Las Vegas.'

'Why there?'

Beau shrugged. 'He's staying with a prison buddy. Remember Eddie from the Roosevelt Hotel? Him. He's got a place there.'

'Oh. So why not come see us first?'

'Maybe he wants to get his soaps business up and running again. He talks a little about heading for the Las Vegas Strip. You know, for the hotels ...'

'But why can't he do all that in LA? We have hotels here. God, we're so close to him, Beau.'

'I know,' he said. 'So what was it this time, why'd they expel you? Demolished another Steinway? God knows you tried everything else to get outta there.'

'I punched a girl. And I liked it.'

Beau laughed. 'Why? What did she do to you?'

I shrugged. 'Stuff.' That was our code for 'Don't ask me about this under any circumstances.'

'Something pretty bad, then,' he said. 'So I guess *Chicken Soup for the Teenage Soul* fell on deaf ears?'

'Just get me back home.'

'As you wish.'

Beau eased the Fiero into Bizcocho Drive and up the slope until we came to the paved driveway of the house. She'd had the outside repainted again, white this time, and there were more palm trees out front. It was something different every time I came back; it never looked like the same place. New pool, new downstairs, new dining furniture. Same old Skankmother, though, if you didn't count the injections.

She wasn't home, thank God. Out at the salon having her landing strip de-fuzzed, apparently. Connie wasn't there either. She had finished for the day. The place was spotless and I could smell chocolate as soon as I walked in. She'd baked one of her special chocolate pizzas for us and left it on the kitchen counter. It said *Welcome Home Paisley* in marshmallows. We both tore off a piece and went upstairs to Beau's room. He slid out the shoebox from under his bed and emptied it onto the carpet.

'I can't believe they're from him,' I said, yanking one of the letters from its envelope. 'But why'd Skank hang on to them? If she never wanted us to have contact …'

'Virginia didn't keep them. Connie did,' said Beau, munching on his pizza, watching me rifle through the envelopes like a monkey ripping open bananas. 'Hey, be careful.' He had read through all the letters before, at least twice. I picked up an early one, dated December 1997.

'This the first?' I asked. Beau nodded. The postmark was 'EJSP.' East Jersey State Prison. Where he was sent after the robbery. I knew the history of the place from the Internet. Beau gulped down the last of his pizza and took the letter from me. He read it aloud.

I never stop thinking about your mom. She was beautiful. I have this necklace of hers that I carry with me all the time. It was almost taken away from me in jail but I still got it. I know she put you through some stuff, but she was sick. I should have gotten her treatment. But I kept following this big dream I had of getting some money together so we could all get out of Jersey. Make a better life somewhere else. Do you know she taught you both how to swim? I'll tell you all that and more when we're together again. I'll make that my job. To tell you both about your mom.

I listened with my mouth open, like some retard kid at group story time. I didn't remember Mom being 'beautiful.' She was older than Dad and she had short bleached hair always scraped back. Her blue eyeliner looked like it had been dug into her face, and whatever she was doing she'd have a cigarette between her fingers. But Dad said she was beautiful. I wished to hell I could remember the beautiful part. And the swimming lessons. All I remembered was the screaming and the smell.

Beau read out five more letters. The word 'love' came up a lot. I was glad.

'Did he put kisses on the bottom?' I asked. Beau showed me the page in his hands. Two kisses. I touched them with the tip of my finger.

'Are you finished with that?' he asked, noting my untouched pizza slice balanced on my knee. I nodded. He took it and started picking off the marshmallows.

I lay back on the carpet, trying to take it all in. I wanted to cry, I wanted to shout and I wanted to grab hold of that bitch's scrawny neck and force her head down the nearest toilet. 'He didn't forget one single birthday, Beau. I knew he didn't abandon us, I fucking knew it!' I yelled.

'Sssh,' said Beau. 'He DID abandon us, Paisley. He gave up the right to freedom when he robbed that hotel ...'

I sat up. I couldn't believe what Beau was saying. 'We were poor. Dad didn't know what else to do ...'

'You're just quotin' lines from the trial. He held a gun to a woman's face. Him and his friends deserved what they got. Whichever way you look at it.'

I pouted. I'd watched that video over and over on TV Archivia before I'd gotten banned from the computers. Dad in his suit and handcuffs. His face creasing up when he talked about us. The judge looking at him beneath his half-moon glasses. Him being led away on the echo of 'fifteen years.' He didn't serve fifteen years; they let him out after eight. But we hadn't seen him since we were six. And now we were sixteen. That made ten years. I always was good at take-aways.

'He's still our family,' I told Beau, pulling tufts out of the carpet.

A car door slammed outside and Beau sprang to his feet and meerkatted over to the window, looking for signs of the Skank. 'I think she's back from the salon.'

'Still terrified of her, then?'

'You know what she's like. If she sees the letters, she'll fire Connie ...'

'She won't do a damn thing with me here. I ain't 'fraid of no ghost.' I looked at him. 'What's your curfew like?'

'What curfew?' He licked his greasy fingers. 'School then home. That's it.'

Beau had the same haunted look on his face he had as a kid back in Jersey. Whenever our parents were arguing. Whenever we hid in our tree house until Mom had passed out from shouting.

He was still at the window. 'Oh, it's not her. It's Matt.'

'Who's Matt?' I asked, carefully placing the letters back in the shoebox.

'The new gardener.'

'The new boyfriend you mean.' I got up and joined him at the window. 'So he's the latest tomb raider, is he? Younger than the last one. She spent any more of our trust fund lately?'

'No,' he said. 'Except the lake house. In Utah. I saw a picture of it in her desk drawer. Lake Peligno. She bought it a while back. It's pretty remote.'

'Why the hell'd she buy in Utah?'

'For holidays, I guess. A retreat.'

'Yeah, somewhere she can retreat for her week-long benders.'

I went back to the shoebox and tucked it under my arm. My eyes started stinging. 'Why didn't he come get us, Beau?'

'Dad? Because Virginia wouldn't let him. He tried. Completed his parole, got a car and drove all the way from Jersey. Says so in one of the letters.'

I looked at him. 'He came here? He didn't even know I was in boarding school in Jersey?'

Beau shook his head. 'He and Virginia had a fight. She got a restraining order, said he threatened her, tried to hit her, all kinds of stuff. It's all in the letters.'

'She got a restraining order? What was he, some kind of wastoid?'

'No, he says he'd got his act together and come to get us. She was the one who called the cops, said he'd been drinking and wanted to hurt us. He hadn't. But she told him that if he set foot inside the state, she'd have him back in jail.'

'Bitch,' I yelled, pacing across the floor.

'Ssh …' Beau stuffed his hands in his pockets and bowed his head, his clean dark brown hair falling down over one cheek. 'Look, she's had a lot of problems lately.'

'Oh what, California run out of Botox or something?'

'She checked herself into rehab a couple weeks ago. Said it was the hardest thing ever …'

'I'll bet it was. Probably realized they didn't have a free bar.'

'It's not just booze. She's got all these pills in her cabinet. Just like Mom.'

'Mmm. Well the apple never falls far, does it?'

Beau stuffed his hands in his pockets. 'We have to do something, don't we?'

'Uh, yeah,' I said. 'We've gotta find Dad. A.S.A.F.P.'

Beau didn't want to do anything about it but he knew I wouldn't let it go. 'But I got school and stuff …'

'Which you hate,' I reminded him.

'Yeah, but—'

'But what?'

He sighed hard. 'Well, alright, but we'll just bail, okay? Just run away and that's it. No need for revenge. You won't … do anything, will you?'

I looked at him. 'Do anything?'

'You know. No Paisley-esque parting shots, like in Beverly Hills.'

'That security guard had it coming, Beau. He'd been stalking us for weeks, up and down that mall. Just 'cos I got skulls on my backpack.'

'Yeah, but you made a laughing stock of the guy. Please, just this once, for me, can you not do anything to Virginia? She's not the type to forget it. She's not like the security guard. Our last gardener, Marvin, you know she sued him for sexual harassment?'

I sighed. 'Yeah, you told me about that …'

'But it was her harassing *him*. She's got a mind all of her own, trust me.'

I laughed. 'Yeah, a mind of her own but a vagina that belongs to the world.'

'Paisley …'

'Alright, alright. We'll just disappear quietly, if that's what you want.'

'Yeah,' said Beau, suddenly enthusiastic. 'We can go find him and she'll never know where we are.'

I put my finger to my chin and tilted my head like I was really thinking hard. 'Yeah. Running away's good; I'm on board with that.'

'Cool.'

Then I went up to him. 'But as for the no-revenge thing?' I squeezed one of his eager, pitted little cheeks. 'I don't think so.'

He deflated like a Bubble Yum balloon and went back to look out the window.

I was only thinking of one thing as I walked along the corridor to my bedroom. *We get out of here, we find our dad.* That was all there was to it. My bag was already packed from school but I unzipped the side and threw out the textbooks, replacing them with two clean push-up bras, my favorite holey fishnets, some ripped blue jeans and some rock T-shirts. Springsteen, Metallica, Bowie. I knew it'd impress the hell outta Dad if I was wearing one when we met up. Like father, like daughter. Apples and trees again.

There are a lot of shitty dads in the world, and as an armed robber mine would probably rank among them. But he never hit or hurt us, never locked us up. And when he held up those people in that hotel, he wasn't stealing their money to gamble it away on booze or drugs. He was stealing it for his family. He couldn't see another way out. He wasn't the perfect dad. Just *my* perfect dad.

I realized I'd used up the last dregs of my allowance on a veggie burger at Newark Airport. I had next to no cash.

I paced back into Beau's room. He had three neat piles of clothes laid out on his bed – one for socks, one for underwear, one for pants. His toothbrush and toothpaste were wrapped neatly beside them in a white face cloth. He could totally rock the whole 'white and nerdy' thing sometimes.

'How much money you got?' I asked him.

'Uh, 'bout seventy bucks. Why?'

'I got about fifteen bucks in the world, that's why.' I turned to leave.

'You seen my new razor?'

I turned back. 'Uh, why?'

'I wanna shave before we go.'

I just looked at him. 'As if. Your balls even dropped yet?'

He squinted at me. I walked back into my room and slumped down on my bed. We wouldn't get far on eighty-five bucks. The lawn mower started up outside. I got up and looked out the window. Matt the gardener was walking up the edge of the small lawn, watching his own arm muscles tense as he pushed his throbbing engine along. He was good looking in a comic-strip kinda way. But in the good tradition of our grandmother's gardeners, he was probably screwing her, so that made him a total ass clown.

Still no sign of her. A little light bulb came on in my head as to how we could fund our yellow-brick quest for Dad. I went back into the corridor and tried her door handle. I'd never been inside her bedroom in the whole ten years we'd lived there. The sound of a car pulling away came from outside. The front door banged. Then came the throaty cough, a memento from twenty years of smoking and another twenty trying to give up.

That was her.

CHAPTER SIX

Beau

9976 Bizcocho Drive, Cahuenga Blvd East,
Hollywood, California

I poked my head out from the other end of the corridor. Footsteps at the bottom of the spiral staircase.

'I won't be long. Help yourself to a beer from the fridge,' came Virginia's voice. I darted back inside my room as Paisley darted back inside hers.

Seconds later I poked my head out again to see Virginia going into her room. I saw the shadow move around, heard the sound of drawers opening, her closet opening. Two bangs as her high heels were thrown to the back. The *flip flop* of her pool mules as she crossed to her en-suite bathroom. Water running, pounding the bathtub. Low light. The cloying scent of burning roses came wafting my way. This was her ritual after a long morning doing nothing in Beverly Hills—she'd light all the candles around the tub and run the hot tap until the water was scorching. Then she'd go downstairs for a while to allow the water to cool and the oil burner to do its thing.

She came out and shut the door. I pulled back.

'Beau? Are you home?'

It was all I could do not to answer. I bit down hard on my quivering tongue. She carried on down the stairs. I stayed behind the door until I heard the distant sweep of the patio doors to the garden. I went over to the far window and saw her go outside, dressed in her long red silk gown and mules, barely hiding her white bikini underneath. She was talking to Matt and twizzling a length of her long black hair. When she had settled on her sun lounger to sunbathe, I heard a little rattle at the end of the corridor and poked my head out again. The bedroom door was wide open, and Paisley was inside.

I was drawn to follow. 'What are you doing?' I asked her in a forced whisper.

She was already rooting through drawers. 'What do you think I'm doing? I'm funding our trip. Shut the door behind you.'

'Are you crazy? She's run her bath—she'll be up here any second.'

'I'm not scared of her.' She was hunched over Virginia's dressing table, rummaging through crystal dishes full of trinkets and sundry bottles of anti-wrinkle cream, bypassing them all in favor of the large red leather jewelry box.

'And if I know our grandmother the way I think I do, she'll be busy screwing the gardener in the sauna, which gives me just enough time to do what I gotta do and get out before she even notices. Ooh, that's pretty.'

She bent down to search through the bottom drawers of the bureau, her blonde hair running down her back in waves like octopus tentacles.

'God, Paisley, please don't,' I said, my ribcage contracting like a trampoline which she was happily jumping on. I edged back out the door, leaning my face against the frame. 'We're so dead.'

'Stop being such a wuss. Why don't you grow a pair and come help me?'

I tried to be strong and take a stand. *Do the right thing. Walk away. Just walk away.* But she was leaving, with or without me. And I didn't want her going off on her own. And I didn't want to stay here any longer if it meant she wasn't coming back. Counting down the days until my sister flew in for the school holidays was how I got myself through it. So I did what I always do. I did what Paisley told me to.

Cautiously I moved further into the room, to stand by one of the four posts of Virginia's unmade bed. Paisley stood on the chaise longue beneath the window, which looked out on the back of the house and the valley below it, and began tugging at the Japanese silk drapes from Fukuoka. They wouldn't come off their pole. So she started taking things off the high shelves. Ornaments, candlesticks dripping in years' worth of hard wax, a clock, a diamond-encrusted snow globe with a little girl ice-skating inside. The chaise was draped in a black silk robe and several items of white lacy lingerie. Virginia's patent pink leather belt with its huge gold buckle shaped like a lion's mouth was curled up in the nook of the chaise. Paisley stepped all over them leaving dusty marks.

'I've got some bubble wrap in my room. D'you want some?' I said.

She turned and looked at me in disbelief. 'You would have bubble wrap for occasions like this, wouldn't you? Grab me a bag from the closet.' She reached up further, to a small wooden box at the very back of the top shelf.

'Bet you there's a stash in here. Maybe it's her emergency liposuction fund.'

I made for the closet next to the bathroom, the flickering light from the candles around the tub catching my eye. Steam rose in little drifts above the motionless water. Everything gleamed. The gold taps, the deep white tub, the gold claw feet.

I remembered when it had arrived from Italy. Paisley and I had sat at the top of the stairs, swinging our legs through the banisters, watching the men hoist it up the stairs. It was just after we'd done an update on our story with Oprah.

I took out the black beach bag with the little white flowers sewn into it and threw it up to my sister, who was still standing on the chaise. She caught it and began filling it up until it bulged and the handles wouldn't meet. She stopped filling momentarily to admire the snow globe, giving it a little shake and watching the glitter float down on the little skating girl.

'Pais, I'm not kidding. She catches us, we're dead. We're beyond dead. We're history. Come on, Paisley, please, let's go. Put that down.'

'I'll hear her coming,' she said.

'No you won't. You never hear her coming. And then all of a sudden she's there, like … like a crack in the window letting in a chill.'

'Poetic, Beau.'

I went to take the snow globe from her but she moved away.

'No,' she said. 'All this stuff was bought from the proceeds of OUR story. She got famous and rich because of US. This snow globe is ours. All these little knick-knacks and trinkets are ours. That jewelry is ours. We're taking it back.'

'Alright, alright,' I said, backing off and returning to the door frame.

'I'm gonna need a bigger bag,' she said, throwing the snow globe down onto the silk bedclothes and marching out of the room with her swag.

The doors swept open downstairs.

'Shit, that's her,' I said, edging further back into the corridor and closing the door very gently behind me. Paisley came out of her room with her backpack and the swag bag and tried to get past me.

I blocked the way. 'Paisley, we've got enough now. Let's just go.'

'I'm not finished,' she said, trying to get past me again.

'Look, I'll grab my stuff and we'll go out my window, okay? We can be gone before she even knows what we've done. Shh. I think I can hear her.'

'I'm getting the snow globe and then I'll follow you down. Go start the Fiero,' she said, handing me both bags.

'What? You can't take her car. She loves that thing.'

'Just do it.'

And she disappeared back into Virginia's bedroom leaving me standing there, dallying as usual. I checked for signs of anyone coming up the stairs, then ran along to my bedroom with the bags. I slid open my balcony window, my palms sweating on the door handle, and stepped out onto the little balcony. Seeing no one around, I dropped my own backpack down onto the patio, followed by Paisley's, and yanked one of my bed sheets free, tying it around the handles of the swag bag and easing it down too. Reluctantly I climbed over the balcony and let myself over and down until I hung by my hands on the railings. I dropped down onto the lawn and stumbled backward, falling flat onto the grass. Getting up, I checked around to make sure I was still alone and grabbed hold of the bags, running along to the front of the house to dump them beside Virginia's Fiero. My hand was shaking. I pulled the key bunch out of my pocket and pointed the ignition key at the car, pressing it down and down again until it flashed and opened for me.

I threw our packs in the trunk, and ran around to the driver's side to start the engine, bending over and putting the swag in the passenger's foot well.

As I came back up, I was face to face with Matt. He was crouched down, leaning on my door.

'Hey Beau,' he said. 'I could have sworn I just saw you ripping off your grandmother. That didn't really happen, did it?'

I just looked at him. The engine was still humming. He stood up so his head disappeared above the car. 'Out.'

I got out but left the engine on.

'I think you got some explaining to do, don't you?' he said, wrapping his thick muscly arm around my neck. 'Come on inside.'

And he marched me back into the house.

CHAPTER SEVEN

Paisley

9976 Bizcocho Drive, Cahuenga Blvd East,
Hollywood, California

'Just do it,' I shouted.

I felt bad for ordering Beau around the whole time, but I knew it was the only way he was ever going to do anything. He'd always been the same. If it were up to him we'd still be in the womb.

I went back into the Skank's room. The snow globe glinted on the other side of the bed. I made my way around to grab it and saw the drawer of the nightstand was slightly open. Once, when me and Beau were little, we'd been snooping around in there and found this book with color photographs of people doing each other over car hoods.

But the book wasn't in there anymore. Just a clean pile of lace panties. And on top of them, a shiny silver gun.

The handle was black, the barrel was silver, and I couldn't resist taking it out, molding my fingers around it. *Eclipse Target*, the barrel read. I'd seen one in a movie but it didn't look as beautiful as this one. This one shone. I touched it, held it against my cheek.

I'd heard her, the Skankmother, talking about getting a gun once when her circle of poolside bitches had come around for afternoon gin and sympathy. How the crime wave was getting worse, how she didn't feel safe walking in LA. How it was her right as an American to 'bear arms and defend herself.'

I didn't think twice. I tucked it in my skirt at the back and pulled my T-shirt down over it. Done. It was there. The cold metal against my skin made me shiver, momentarily, but then it was warm and it stayed put against me as though it had always been there.

I closed the drawer and took the snow globe from the bed, holding it up to the window. The diamonds twinkled around the base.

I felt a presence behind me. Like a crack in the window letting in a chill.

'I see you're home, then,' came the greeting. I turned. There she was, a cougar on two legs, almond-eyed. Expressionless. She'd had a boob job since I last saw her, and yet more Botox shoved in her face. The outer corners of her eyes made her look like someone was working her with strings from behind. Her silk robe was open to reveal part of her white bikini underneath.

'My my, Grandmother. What big tits you've got,' I smirked.

She gave me the thinnest, coldest smile and closed the door behind her. 'I got the phone call from your principal. What was it this time? Drugs, sex or violence?'

'What can I say? I learned from the best.'

I held the snow globe tight and made for the door. She barred the way.

'Move!' I hollered. She just looked at me, clearly trying to frown but the Botox wouldn't let her. She looked at the snow globe, then back at me. Then at her empty window.

'Oh, that's the game, is it? You were stealing *my* car and *my* things and then running away, were you? Is that how I raised you, Jane?'

'Wrong on three counts,' I told her, brandishing the snow globe in my fist like I was about to smash her over the head with it. 'Count one, that's *our* car. You bought it just after *we* got you on *Montel*, remember? Count two, these are *our* things. And three, *you* never raised me or Beau. You just paid somebody ELSE to.'

She sighed. 'Is it any wonder? Your own mother couldn't bear to look at you. Your father went to jail to get away from you.' I moved in close to her and grabbed the door handle. The door opened, but she slammed it again. 'You disgust everybody.'

She always played the 'absent parent' card in shit-uations like these. I'd never exactly gotten used to it but we argued so often I'd come to expect it.

'*I'm* disgusting?' I laughed. 'At least I'm not some chronic slut who fucks her handymen.' Come to think of it, actually I

- 66 -

was. But I wasn't telling her that.

'Vile. My ears are not garbage cans, Jane.'

'No, but your ass is. Get outta my way.'

'No, you will damn well stay here and face up to what you've done.'

'You think I'm gonna stay here for all eternity? You can't lock me up like a fuckin' prisoner. I'm not Beau.'

She smiled, hands on her hips. 'Where will you go, hmm? You don't have any other family, do you? You're sixteen. Face it. I'm all you've got.'

'No you're not. We're going to Dad's. We found his letters. Connie kept—'

'Dad's?' she repeated. She stared at me, wide-eyed like some weird bird. 'Dad's what? Dad's boarding house? Dad's homeless shelter? They don't send ex-offenders straight to luxury mansions, you know, honey.'

'Whatever. It'll be a palace compared to this shit hole. Get outta my way.'

'He hasn't even called you,' she giggled. 'What's wrong with this picture, Jane? Yeah, he wrote, but that was in jail. He had nothing else to do.'

I gripped the snow globe so tight the diamonds pressed into my palm; I thought my fingers were gonna crush right through the glass. For Chrissakes don't cry, I thought. Fuckin' pussy. Think of Dad.

Her words were like knives but I just swallowed them down. 'He came to see us when he'd done his parole. You drove him away.'

'And he never came back. The End. When he knew he

couldn't get his little fingers on your money he skedaddled out of here faster than you can say *gold digger.*'

'Liar,' I said, making for the door handle again. Her face tensed and she slammed herself back against the door. We were so close I could feel her hot breath on my face. It stank like kerosene.

'You're in for a big disappointment if you think he's going to scoop you up in his arms like he used to. You're not his cutesy-wootsy babe in the wood anymore.'

'Move your ass—'

'Think about it,' she grinned, her eyes wide and black. 'He didn't care about you enough to stay outta prison. And that's when you were children. Why would he give a damn about you now? Some monstrous little teenage … maniac?'

'Because he loves us. Remember love? It's in the dictionary, next to *lush.*'

She pressed herself harder against the door, like a dough cutter.

'Alright, you can go. I'll *allow* you to go. But you're not taking your brother with you. You can go, Jane, but he stays. And that is mine,' she said, clasping the top of the snow globe.

I snatched it back. 'My fucking name is PAISLEY.' I turned to the window and pitched the snow globe toward it, sending it smashing through the glass. There was a pause and a tinkling of glass as it hit the air, then it *boomfed* on the driveway below.

I turned to her. She drew a full breath and glared, the way vampires always look at their victims right before they suck the shit out of their necks. She grabbed hold of my shoulders and shoved me backward against her closet. I grabbed her chin and forced it upwards, then pushed her back onto the bed and bolted for the door, but she caught my foot with her freezing hands and held on.

'Get off me. Get the fuck off me!' I yelled, kicking, hoping to catch her face with my boot. She let go, only to tackle me to the floor and grab my head at the sides, slamming it down into the carpet. I wrenched away from her and stumbled to my feet. She got up, helped by the bed, her hair even more of a mess and the sleeve of her silk robe torn. I laughed, catching my breath before she lunged at me one final time and with one supreme push, shoved me backward into her bathroom. She grabbed the door handle and pulled it shut.

I could hear her outside the door, propping the chair under the handle, panting.

'I've had it with you,' she shouted, all breathless and squeaky. 'I don't know what to do with you. Now you stay in there until you damn well cool off!'

I lay half-slumped and all crazy-breath against the tiled wall under the towel rail. I remember Mom saying the exact same thing the time she locked me and Beau in the basement. *Now you stay there until you damn well cool off!* She couldn't handle us either. The only light in the room came from the candles lit around the full bathtub. My mouth stung and throbbed like it had a little heartbeat. I touched my bottom lip. Blood. I yanked down some toilet paper from the roll to hold against it as I stood up and looked in the mirror. A cut. My right cheek was cut too. She had caught me with one of her diamond rings.

'It's nothing, it's nothing, it's nothing,' I whispered, stamping my foot on the tiled floor, my whole face throbbing.

'Stop-it-stop-it-stop-it-stop-it.' I dampened the tissue under the faucet. My hand was shaking. I turned off the water and dropped the soggy wad in the basin. I sucked my lip and checked the mirrored cabinet above the sink. I was gonna have a cool bruise. I could always guarantee a good scrap with old Skank. Most grandmothers taught their granddaughters to bake or sew buttons. Mine taught me how to fist-fight. The girls at school were so weak. They always went for the hair or clothes. I never got hit like I did with her.

The cabinet was ajar. I opened it. I saw all the little pill bottles lined up on the shelf. Oxycodone. Vicodin. Lorazepam. Hydrocodone. Tylenol. Ativan.

Ativan. I remembered one of the doctors overdosing on it in *ER*. Anxiety problems. I pocketed it.

I tried the door handle. Jammed solid. I sniffed, wiping my nose with my bare arm, expecting a trail of snot but seeing red. I wiped it on one of her pristine white bath towels and began kicking at the door, lightly at first, and then fuck-it-fast. Faster and faster and harder and harder, until it started to weaken, buckling and chipping at the latch. Then it swung right out before me onto the empty room. She was gone.

I took two of the lit candles from around the tub and held them up to the Japanese silk drapes from Fukuoka.

'Fuk-u-Grandmother,' I laughed. Damn right I'm a maniac.

Conducting my own little orchestra of fire up both drapes, I swung the candles back and forth, watching the orange flame flick higher up the fabric, smelling the burning silk, the heat fanning my sweaty face. Ecstasy prickled through my body, making my hairs stand on end.

'Oh, you need locking up, Paisley Argent,' I said, throwing the candles onto the bed and striding across the room, slamming the door behind me.

There was no sign of the Skank upstairs. Outside the Fiero was running. All our stuff was in the open trunk but Beau was nowhere near it.

'Fuck,' I said, reaching through the driver's window to turn the engine off. As I looked to the house I saw Beau coming out, Matt the gardener just behind him, his huge ham forearm clamped around my brother's neck.

'You must be Paisley,' the brute said.

'And you must be Matt,' I replied.

I looked up. I don't know what made me look up. A flickering. The fire had gotten as far as my bedroom.

'Can't let you do it. Can't let you take off with your grandmother's things.'

The Skankmother appeared behind them in the doorway. She walked straight out, right up to me and threw down a bundle of money at my feet.

'One thousand. That enough to get you gone?'

'That and my brother,' I said, picking it up. Beau was barely standing as Matt had hold of his neck. He was trying to prise his arm away but Matt's arm was big, wrestler big. He looked like Thor, only with girlier hair. The tendons flexed under his skin. My brother looked at me with his desperate brown eyes.

'I get it. You need Beau so you can still claim the money.' It was all screaming back to me now. She needed one of us, and who was easier to control? 'If I'm not coming back, he won't stick around.'

'Oh he'll stay,' she glared back at me. 'If I have to keep him under lock and key he'll stay. Beau's a good boy.' Matt tightened his grip. Beau closed his eyes.

'How much she paying you to do this, Matt? Or did she promise you a slice of our trust fund?'

Skank's face lit up. 'Beau stays. You go,' she said.

'You know there probably isn't that much left now, Matt,' I warned him. 'She's creamed off most of it paying to send me away and then there's the new furniture, the new tits ...'

'You better scram, girly,' said Matt, tightening his grip on Beau's neck. Beau's face was getting redder and redder.

'Reckon she's spent three million already.' I waited, looking from Skank to Matt and back again.

'Go,' Matt told me. The Skank folded her arms.

'Beau, get in the car,' I said.

'Mmugh?' he garbled, his throat constricted, feet barely touching the ground.

'I don't think you heard me, Jane. Beau is staying here. But you can go. Be free.' She ushered me away with a flap of her hands, like I was some little fly that wouldn't get the hint. 'You don't have to wait until you're eighteen. I'm giving you your freedom right now. Take it. Go on. It's what you've always wanted, isn't it?'

'No. What I wanted was my dad back, you evil bitch.'

She smiled at me, one of her huge stretched smiles with her big red trannylicious lips that looked like she'd been injected with Joker venom.

'Okay.' I turned on my heel. I walked to the car. 'Good luck putting the fire out,' I called back, getting in the driver's seat and slamming the door.

I started the engine and stepped on the pedal. *Skreeee!* I looked in the rear-view mirror. The Skankmother was scurrying inside on her own screams and Matt had loosened his grip enough on my brother so he could wriggle free and run to the car.

I was rolling out of the driveway when the passenger door flew open and in scrambled Beau, breathless and gasping theatrically.

'My God, Paisley,' he panted, reaching out to shut the swinging door and turning to look through the rear window. I shifted into gear and stepped on the pedal.

'She should have known not to leave me in a room full of lit candles.'

In the mirror, I could see the flames licking out of my bedroom window, lapping up at the milky afternoon sky like tongues. Splashes and sparks and debris flew out. It looked kinda pretty.

'Shit, Pais. You set it on fire?' Beau wheezed. 'Oh shit, this isn't happening. This just isn't happening …'

'Then let's pinch each other and wake up,' I said, looking over at him. His hands were at his temples, like he was trying to massage away the last few hours.

'That's her home. She's gonna be pissed, she's gonna be so pissed!' he kept saying.

I kinda wanted to stick around and watch the old woman melt under the weight of her plastic skin, but we couldn't. I put my foot down and kept my head forward, leaving the whole sorry mess in the rear-view.

CHAPTER EIGHT

Beau

Somewhere in the Mojave Desert, Interstate 15

'Why d'you call us the Wonder Twins, Dad?' I once asked him. I must have been around five, I guess. I was helping him mend the backyard fence.

'Because that's what you are. You and Paisley are my Wonder Twins. You took a long time to, well, come along.'

'What do you mean?'

'Never mind. Point is, when we finally got you, we were real happy.'

'Was Mom happy?'

'Yeah, Beau, she was. You know, there are these superheroes called the Wonder Twins, too. They're a brother and sister. To get their powers, they have to touch hands and say, "Wonder Twin Powers: Activate!" When you and Paisley were babies, your cribs used to be next to one another and when one of you would wake up, you'd stretch your arm through the bars to reach for the other one. Like if you touched hands, you'd activate your powers too. It was the cutest thing.'

'Do me and Paisley have super powers?'

'You're both pretty super to me.'

'Who cried most, me or Paisley?'

'You,' said Dad, without even thinking. 'But all we had to do was put you in the crib with your sister and you'd shut right up, every time. Like magic.'

So that was us as babies. The Wonder Twins. Better together. When we went missing in the woods, the news anchor who broke our story to the nation called us the same thing. Wondrous. Wonderful. Wonder Kids. They said we had kept each other alive. I didn't get what was so amazing about us until I read all the news reports years later. There was a spate of child murders around the time we got lost. Kids would vanish for a couple nights and then their bodies would show up somewhere. Near the swings in a park in Elizabeth. Floating on a pond in South Orange. On the roadside near our elementary school. But we were found, alive. Everybody just went nuts. And what with it being March and us being out in the open for three nights alone. And us being six. We were little wonders. America loved us.

Now we were thieves. Arsonists. America wouldn't think us quite so wonderful now, that was for sure.

The Fiero thundered along the endless desert road, two and a half hours into our journey. It seemed to take forever to get to Spurina, just like tomorrow seems like next year when you're a little kid. I'd been biting my nails the whole way from Virginia's house, or rather Virginia's ruin. Because that's what it was now. Like Thornfield in *Jane Eyre*. Just charred remains. I still couldn't believe what had happened. We were on the run now, whether we found Dad or not. Virginia would have the cops onto us for this, make no mistake. My bitten fingertips were red raw, and throbbing like each one had its own little heartbeat.

'Such a boring road,' said Paisley, switching radio channels. She had all the windows down and the warm gritty wind was whipping my hair up around my face. The whole ride out of LA, her white-knuckled fists had gripped the wheel and her jaw was tight and twitchy. When we got out on the open highway, she started to relax. Her hands slipped down and she sang along to the mullet rock blaring out of the radio.

'It's a beautiful road,' I told her. Alright, it was still a running buffet of desert, but the sky was brightly blue in every direction as far as the eye could see, broken only by mini explosions of cloud. I looked at Paisley. The corner of her mouth glistened. It was cut and swollen. I reached out and placed a fingertip on it. She jolted away.

'What?' she frowned.

'It's bleeding again.'

'Leave it. It'll scab over.'

Pretty soon I felt a nudge on my arm. She handed me half a pack of peanut M&Ms. I don't know where she got them from. I took them and popped a green one in my mouth.

'Wonder what those mountains are?'

'Who cares?' she said, scraping her hair away from her face.

I glanced toward the speedo.

'I'm within the speed limit, Gramps,' she informed me.

'What will we do when our money runs out? We've only got like one thousand eighty-five dollars.'

'Sell the antiques. Dad'll know some prison dudes who can fence the stuff for us. He's sure to. And he'll have gotten work at Caesars Palace and, I don't know, maybe we can get jobs there too as pool hands or something. I heard they got like five pools.'

'Prison dudes? Like that Eddie guy he's living with?'

'Yeah.'

'I don't think Eddie's gonna be too happy about putting us up as well as Dad.'

'We can rent somewhere. Between the three of us, it'll be fine.' She shivered and grinned. 'God, I'm so excited. We're gonna see Dad, Beau! Long fucking last.'

She was watching the road, so I didn't need to smile. I couldn't share her enthusiasm at all. I didn't like not knowing where we were going. Not knowing where we were gonna sleep tonight. Everything was so messed up. I rubbed my throat. It still hurt from being half-strangled by Matt. The M&M was ready. I took it out.

'Bunny?' she said.

'Yeah. A good one too.' I held it out to show her. She smiled. 'How long will it take to get to Spurina?'

She squinted and pulled the sun visor down to shield her

eyes. 'I don't know, few hours? Jesus Christ, it's hot.' She put the windows up and turned on the air conditioning. Within seconds the car was a refrigerator on wheels.

I stared through the windshield and watched the white lines disappear beneath us. I wondered if this would be the road that would lead to him. What his first words to me would be. What he looked like. If he'd started to go gray. If he would hug me. If he would cry.

My throat felt taut, as though Matt was still wrapped around it. I coughed to try and clear the pressing pain.

'I seriously think that ape damaged my larynx.'

Paisley rolled her eyes. 'You're fine.'

A song came on the radio and she squealed and reached for the dial.

'Oh, this is a classic. This can be our road-trip song. Dad used to love this.'

'Who is it?'

'The Boss, of course. Springsteen. "Born to Run." She turned the volume up until it became distorted and screamed her lungs out. 'De-niw-niw-niw!'

It was my turn to roll my eyes. I leaned my head against my window. I wondered if the fire at our grandmother's house had hit the news. If we didn't find Dad, I didn't know what Paisley would do. Dad had always been kinda like her version of Kryptonite. But a good Kryptonite. I only had to mention his name and her face would release its pulled tension, her eyes soften. When we were little kids she would tantrum all the time, especially if Dad wasn't home. She'd kick out at walls and doors and Dad was the only person who could calm her down. All he had to do was hold her hands and ask what was wrong and she'd stop. One minute she was peanut brittle, the next she was marshmallow. It was like flicking a switch. I didn't like to think about what she'd do if we didn't find him. She'd already burned our house down.

Paisley turned down Springsteen. 'You can put that French crap on, if you want,' she said. 'Those two losers in turtlenecks. Foley and Douche.'

'*Folie à deux* …' I corrected, feeling my head become heavier. 'I didn't bring it.' The air was cool and soft from the vents and I drifted into nothingness, lulled by the gunning engine. The sun bounced off the hood of the car in little shimmers. I was with my sister and we were okay. It was all going to be okay …

HONNNK HONNNK.

I woke with a jolt, opening my eyes and sucking in the drool that had run down my chin. A gigantic juggernaut was passing us by.

'M—where?' I said, licking my salty lips.

'Back with us, sleepyhead? We're about twenty miles out of Spurina.'

I opened my eyes wider to focus. 'How long've I been asleep?'

'A good hour. You missed all the fun. The traffic getting into Barstow was a real hoot. You got the last letter? I think it's Green Mango Road. Find the house number.'

I fumbled around in my backpack to find the envelope. 'Uh, yeah, 659 Green Mango Road, Spurina.'

She clutched my arm. 'Oh my God, Beau. We're actually

going to see Dad again. Can you believe it?'

'Now?' I asked, sitting up in my seat. 'We're going there now?'

'What did you think we were going to do first, take in a show? Dad's the whole reason we're here.'

'But it's like nearly dark, and we're tired, and we need to think about getting a room or something. We can go find Dad tomorrow.'

But Paisley wasn't gonna quit so easy. 'No way. Dad is here and I'm seeing him today. And God help anyone who tries to stop me.'

We rolled through all these quiet little townships, which looked much the same as any other. The early evening light made everything look clean and happy. Kids were out on bikes, people in strappy vest tops and sandals were drifting around at their own pace. There were signs for golf courses, art galleries, craft shows, a farmer's market, a petting zoo, new apartment complexes. Everything looked so ordered and sanitary, like the town in *Edward Scissorhands*. Something just didn't fit here. Dad, at least the Dad we knew, definitely didn't fit here.

We started coming across street names that sounded like fruit. Orange Tree Court. Pineapple Road. Plum Way. And then, around the corner from Plum Way, was Green Mango Road.

'Green Mango Road, there it is, there it is, Beau,' said Paisley, turning the corner and ogling out the window for signs of house numbers. Every house was colored differently, pastel blue, pastel pink, pastel orange. 'Six-five-six, six-five-eight. Where the hell is six-five-nine, Beau?'

'It's there,' I said, pointing to a duplex on the street corner. 'Six-five-nine.'

Paisley pulled up on the spotless yellow stone driveway next to an immaculate Ford and turned off the engine. She got out, slamming the door, and immediately went up to knock. I took my time. I still hadn't fully woken up. I still wasn't sure if I was just dreaming all this. And I still didn't know what I would say when I saw him. I'd kinda figured I'd think of something during the drive. But then I'd fallen asleep. And here we were. I couldn't think straight.

The heat outside our icebox hit me like a sheet of hot plastic. Even at this hour the sun still showered down in pulsing black waves. I followed Paisley to the door, hanging back a little, already wiping the sweat from my eyes. I didn't know what would be best, a hug or a handshake. A 'How are you?' or a 'Long time no see.' I cleared my throat.

A black guy answered the door in a lemon shirt and navy shorts, like he'd just been called away from a barbecue. It was Eddie. Will Smith, but shorter.

I glanced at Paisley, who seemed unfazed.

'Hey, is Buddy home?'

The man glanced back inside the house and stepped out, closing the door quietly behind him. 'I'm sorry, Buddy?'

'Yeah, Buddy Argent? He wrote us and gave this address.'

'We're his kids,' I cut in. 'He said you were an old pal of his and that you'd put him up after he'd finished his parole.'

'Oh.' He stepped back inside. 'Yeah. Are you … Paisley and Beau?'

'Yeah, so is he here?' said Paisley.

'Uh … no.'

'No?'

'I said he could stay here a couple weeks.' He looked behind him again into the house. 'That turned into a couple months and I had to …'

'Let me guess, your wife was giving you static and you kicked his sorry ass onto the street.'

'Look, I'd just gotten married and moved out here and we were trying to make a go of things. And then Buddy shows up, asking to stay, and I let him. And he was here for a long time. But … I gotta get on with my life.' The man looked at me. 'We wanted to start a family and …'

'What, did he keep walking in on you or something?' said Paisley, stomping away from the door and back to the car.

'It's okay. You don't have to explain,' I said to the guy. 'We just thought he'd be here, that's all. It's just kinda disappointing. Sorry if we disturbed you.'

The guy smiled and then laughed. 'Damn, Paisley and Beau. You two sure grew up since I last saw you. Do y'all remember me? At the hotel?'

Eddie had been the inside man on the job, the Concierge. He knew when people were checking in, going out for the evening, what they put in the safe. He laughed and clapped his hands together.

'God, your dad never stopped talking about you two.'

'Really?' I said.

'Yeah. All the time. You'd be, what, fifteen …?'

'Sixteen.'

'Sixteen now? Yeah, Paisley was this little blonde hothead

who always got her own way. And you were this quiet little dude, always smiling.'

I raised my eyebrows and pushed away a sweat bead.

Eddie's smile disappeared. 'I think Bud was under the impression you two didn't wanna see him.'

'It's a long story ...' I said, not wanting to elaborate further on the whole letters debacle. I stepped away. 'Nice to see you again.'

'Sorry I couldn't be more helpful,' he called out. 'Your dad talked about gettin' work on the Strip. Pal of ours works at a bar in Caesars Palace. You could try there.'

'Okay, thanks.'

Paisley was slumped in the driver's seat when I got in. It took me a while to build up the courage to say anything.

'He said to try the Strip. Caesars—'

'I heard.'

'We'll find him, Pais. It's just gonna take more time.'

She started the engine and reversed out of the drive.

'It's not gonna be like the woods,' I told her, checking her reaction. I tried to sound optimistic. 'We'll get to him. Whatever it takes. Okay?'

She just nodded.

CHAPTER NINE

Paisley

Las Vegas Boulevard, aka 'the Strip,' Las
Vegas, Nevada

Car horns blasted. Engines revved. Lights flashed. Music
pumped from roadsters, cabs and ginormous electronic screens
called Jumbotrons. It was full-on night-time and we had hit a
stream of traffic. This was it—the Las Vegas Strip.

On both sides of the street were these large looming hotels
which looked like they'd been designed by children. We were
stopping and starting the whole way down the street 'cos of the
traffic, like a car in a board game when you keep throwing
ones. But for the first time since we managed to escape from
LA I was glad. I wanted to take in all the sights, make mental

notes of where we should go look for Dad, and maybe have a little fun too.

Beau was goggling it all like his eyes were kaleidoscopes. This big shiny bronze-colored building with the word *Wynn* scrawled across the top of it was definitely the biggest, but then this sprawling Italian-style one came into view and that looked bigger.

'Keep a look out for Caesars,' I said to him, flipping the bird at a cab driver who was giving me the eye through my window. 'Piss off, pervert.'

Along the other side of the Strip there was a ton of building work going on, and presumably they were busy building even bigger and better and more wacky hotels to fill in the gaps between the others. Hundreds of tourists lined the sidewalks. We halted at the lights and got a good look at them all, swarming like bees in a golden hive. Hawkers peddled portable ice-boxes filled with bottled water. Guys and gals strolled hand in hand, some catching buses, others posing for photographs, laughing, stopping to admire and point things out. Everything was busy, everything was loud, everything was big, everything shone like cheap jewelry.

Beau brought his head back inside the car. 'Pais, I just had a thought. We're not gonna be allowed in any of these places. They're casinos and we're totally underage.'

'It's cool, I got a fake ID.'

'Oh. Great.'

The computer equipment at my last school, ICA, was pretty tech-tarded, but I had the basic stuff to cope with this small task. 'It was surprisingly simple. Me and these two other girls did it on Photoshop. Color printer, couple butterfly pouches and a laminator. It got me banned from the computer lab, but it was totally worth it.'

'It can't be very good. They'll suss it a mile off, you'll be slung out.'

'I made you one too.'

'You did?' he said, almost touched but still all paranoid android.

The Paris, Las Vegas hotel loomed over us, looking like some insanely ornate office block with its own Eiffel Tower and big blue hot-air balloon statue out front. That just blew Beau away. Next to Paris was a giant Planet Hollywood hotel, and then we saw the MGM Grand with this gigantic gold lion stood out front.

'They got real lions in there too,' I told him. 'I saw this documentary about Las Vegas on the plane on the way over from Jersey. They got cubs sometimes.'

He looked through the rear window. 'If we can get a room at Paris that'd be way sweet,' said Beau.

'Not if you're gonna go all quoting Sartre and spouting how pathetically pleasing the joint is the whole time. I don't think I can handle that, bro.'

'Not pathetically pleasing, *esthetically* pleasing.'

I looked at him. 'I know, Beau.' I loved it when he corrected me. It made him feel all intelligent and high and mighty, and then all embarrassed when he realized I didn't need correcting.

'I wonder if they speak French in there,' he said, then answered his own question. 'Maybe not. They might have some French people working there, though. This is Vegas, after all.

Anything's possible.'

Another hotel was shaped exactly like the New York skyline with an Empire State Building, Chrysler Building, Statue of Liberty, Brooklyn Bridge, and there was even a roller coaster looping around the outside of it. I could hear the screams of the passengers as it twisted and zoomed across the front. We had to stop again for some tourists on the crosswalk but we could watch these fountains in front of the Bellagio Hotel dancing to 'Hey Big Spender' and on the trumpet parts the water shot up into the air.

'Oh my God, this place is awesome!' said Beau. I didn't think Vegas was going to be Beau's cappuccino, guessing he'd think it bawdy and seedy, but for some reason he was really soaking it up. I leaned across him to get a better look out his window.

The car rolled on until the Strip became quieter, darker. The hotels became motels and the strolling tourists turned into vagrants sleeping on the sidewalks. I scoped a little pink motel right at the far end, illuminated by a tiny neon sign and a large green shamrock. *The Lucky Inn.*

We pulled into the parking lot. After everything we'd seen on the way, it was pretty disappointing. Beau just stared at me. He obviously had his heart set on a suite somewhere with valet parking and gold taps but we just couldn't afford it. The buzzing neon sign and the trash can with the cluster of derelicts rifling through it welcomed us to reality. I turned off the engine and went to get the bags from the trunk.

'You can't be serious,' said Beau, shutting his door.

'The big hotels'll ask too many questions,' I said. 'We'll stay here so we can be more incognito.' I handed him the swag bag and his backpack. 'It's just until we find Dad. Then we can give him the antiques and he can sell 'em off and we'll be able to afford something better.' I waited until Beau had turned his back, before I reached through my window and stuck the keys back in the ignition.

There was no one in the tiny brown reception room when we walked in. It was all cheesy wood paneling, damp on the ceilings and pink chintzy drapes. A plastic Elvis figurine was wiggling his hips on the counter beside a miniature flashing sign saying *Welcome to Las Vegas*. Beau copped a glance through the window at the massive pyramid of the Luxor hotel then looked back at me and rolled his eyes.

A blonde woman appeared from a back room and came to the desk, glitterbag flashy and chewing gum like her mouth was mechanical.

'Hey there.'

'Hey, do you have a room?'

'Got twelve of 'em. Twelve rooms, twelve vacancies. Double, yeah?'

'Uh, two queens please?' I said, offended, sifting through my wad of bills courtesy of the Skank.

She just looked at me. 'You know, you're lucky to get a room. There's a big rock concert over at the Mandalay this weekend and Britney's in town tomorrow.'

'How come you got twelve empty rooms, then?' I asked.

'Won't be empty tomorrow,' she said.

'Whatever, how much for the week?'

'Five ninety.'

'Five ninety?' I cried.

'Like I said, Britney's in town. We're the cheapest on the Strip.'

'I'll say,' I muttered, picking the money from the roll of bills. I slammed it down on the counter. She was lucky I was too tired to argue.

The woman teetered over to the back wall for our key and placed it down on the counter. 'You got no blow-dryer and don't flush the toilet with the shower on 'cos it gets, like, extra hot. Okay, you're all set.'

'Thanks bunches,' I said, smiling my fakest.

Our room was basic to say the least. Two queen beds, draped in what looked like leftover gingham sacking. It stank of dog blankets, and the leather-effect headboards were spewing yellow foam at the corners. We each had a nightstand, and there was a small desk and chair with a telephone directory and Lucky Inn stationery set. A sliding wooden partition opened to reveal a very small avocado bathroom suite with a cracked shower door. There was a big warning sticker on the side of the tub. **Prolonged exposure to water may cause osteoporosis, heart disease and birth defects.** Fu-larious.

'Well, there's a bed, so I'm happy,' I said, throwing my backpack down on the floor and flopping onto the bed nearest the bathroom. It looked kinda gray and hard but it was so soft it felt like I was lying inside a loaf of fresh bread. Bedgasmic.

Beau stood by the window. 'How much money we got left?'

'I don't know. Have a look.'

I threw over my jacket and he rummaged around in the pocket.

'There's, like ... there's not even five hundred left!'

'Yeah, well. You heard what she said. Can I just get a little shut-eye, please?' I hadn't slept in, like, two days.

'Do we get breakfast at least?'

'I had to pay by the bath towel, Beau, what do you think?'

He dropped my jacket on the chair and went to the window. 'Oh my God, Paisley ...'

'What?'

'The car is gone.'

'Huh?' I levered myself up. Beau had his hands on the glass and his mouth wide open.

'Our car, the F ... Fiero, the goddamn car, it's gone! Oh my God. We gotta call the cops—'

'They work fast round here, I'll give them that,' I said, leaning back down.

'Who?'

'Those hobos we saw hanging around the trash can. Musta taken it.'

'You knew they were gonna take it?'

'We had to lose it, Beau. It's hot. Cops are gonna be after us. Skank may even come after us. We don't wanna draw attention to ourselves.'

'How the hell are we gonna get anywhere? Now we're stuck here!'

'We'll have found Dad by the end of the week. He'll look after us.'

'Paisley ...'

I turned over and tried losing myself. I could hear him sighing and padding around the floor. Zippers. Unpacking things. I heard his bed springs. Then a sigh. And pretty soon, a snore. I opened my eyes a little and turned onto my back, reaching down beside me into my backpack. I pulled out the letter.

So how's my little girl? I don't suppose you're so little anymore. I always think when I see you, I'll be able to scoop you up in my arms like I used to when I came home from work. You'd come running downstairs to see me and jump from the bottom stair. I remember the last time we saw each other, I tucked you in for the night. You reached up and hugged me so tight. If I'd have known that was gonna be the last time, I'd have made that hug last longer. I love you, Paisley. Dad x

CHAPTER TEN

Beau

The Strip

The next morning we hit the Strip. It was hot in Vegas. 'Day-am hot!' Paisley kept saying. Much hotter than LA. I was half starved from the day before and wanted to eat something before my stomach started munching on my other organs, but she insisted we went straight to Caesars Palace to look for Dad. We split the difference. We went to Caesars Palace to eat.

The hotel itself took some navigating around. The place is enormous. It's obscene opulence times twenty, with extensions to the rear and fountains to the front. It's perfectly trimmed hedges and A-list limousines. It's marble pillars and gilt statues and people who smile at the right wallet.

I'd only ever heard about Caesars when there was a big concert on HBO or something, but to actually see it was unbelievable. The Forum Shops' entrance to Caesars was a mall in itself and we weaved our way through its maze of designer stores and boutiques. The place was echoey and smelled of cinnamon and caves. There were a few tourists around, looking through windows and throwing coins into the huge ornate fountains that spanned the base of the escalators. We found this little café called the Stage Deli. I got the works: coffee, orange juice, three huge buttermilk pancakes with whipped butter, maple syrup, sausage links, bacon, eggs and toast. And I ate every single crumb of it, aside from a triangle of toast which I insisted Paisley ate. She just ordered a fruit platter. Then we got into an argument over the tip. Paisley doesn't tip. She doesn't believe in it.

We walked through the main casino, where Paisley saw the sign for the Concierge's desk. It was at the very front of the hotel in the massive pillared reception area that looked more like the check-in for an airport. A snaking line of tourists with large suitcases was already waiting and it was only, like, nine thirty in the morning. Out front, white limousines and cabs were pulling up one after the other and men in burgundy uniforms were falling over themselves to load luggage onto gold carts.

The Concierge wasn't at his desk. I rang the bell.

He appeared. A tall, thin, mustachioed guy with strangely tiny hands.

'Good morning, welcome to Caesars Palace, my name's Leon, how can I help you this morning?'

He'd taken so long introducing himself I'd almost forgotten what we were doing there. Then I remembered.

'We were wondering if you could help us. We're looking for somebody.'

'Are you lost?'

'No, we're just looking for somebody. An employee. We were told he might be working here.'

'I'm sorry but I'm not at liberty to give out information about employees. That's confidential.'

Paisley broke in. 'We just wanna know if he works here or not.'

'No, it's quite out of the question, I'm afraid. If it's a matter of employment references, you would need to speak to our—'

'Look, jerk-off,' she said, leaning into the desk.

I butted in. 'His name's Buddy Argent. We're … friends of his. We just need to know if he's here or not.'

'I'm sorry, son, but I am not at liberty to discuss employee information with members of the public.'

'Don't "son" him, you patronizing bastard,' Paisley shouted, marching off straight into the casino. She turned as she walked. 'Fuck you, you know that? Fuck you!'

I turned to the Concierge, my cheeks aflame. 'I'm sorry. It's just really important that we find him. Thanks anyway.'

He threw me an alarmed look and nodded, gesturing to the old ladies behind me to come forward. You had to know how to handle my sister and if you didn't, you got your ass handed to you. I felt a little sorry for him. He thought he had power before he met Paisley.

I saw her amid a sea of tourists and flashing lights and the whir and woo of a zillion machines. Old women in baseball caps jamming slots with quarters and fishing out tickets. Guys with sunburn in Hawaiian shirts pummeling buttons and swigging beer. The whole place smelled strongly of sweat and decade-old cigar smoke. A blonde waitress sauntered over, draped in a toga.

'Sir, can I get you anything?' she asked me, hand on hip.

I shook my head, amazed she didn't even ask my age. I attempted a smile but I felt myself blushing and my head automatically dipped. She was real cute. I needed to get to Paisley.

I headed through the casino and back out into the mall where Paisley had been heading. More tourists were milling around and I could just see Paisley's head right at the end of one of the streets that made up one arm of the huge shopping complex in that part of Caesars. She was sitting cross-legged beside one of the marble fountains, staring up at the ceiling which was painted to look like bright blue sky and clouds. This big god-like statue was in the middle of the monument, sat on a throne and smiling with hollow eyes. Moldy green coins lay at his feet. I could smell the stale water and chlorine as I got closer.

I sat down next to her on the balustrade. 'Pais?'

'I know I overreacted. I don't wanna talk about it.'

'Okay. Let's keep asking around then. Yeah?'

'Yeah.'

I wanted her to look at me. She did. She jumped down and I followed her.

That day we walked the length and breadth of the entire hotel. There were six towers to the complex: Augustus Tower (where there was a spa and a couple wedding chapels and some very snooty-looking restaurant where this waiter gave both of us the evil eye), Centurion Tower, Roman Tower, Palace Tower, Octavius Tower and Forum Tower, where we had eaten breakfast. Eddie Green Mango hadn't mentioned any one in particular so we had to try all of them. Forum Tower seemed to be the hive of all activity, so we asked at all the bars and restaurants in there. No sign of Dad, nor anyone who knew him. Planet Hollywood let us sample chicken strips in their new barbecue sauce, so we stayed there and had dinner.

And then we kinda settled into the spirit of things. People were nice to us, so it was okay. Paisley was okay. Frustrated, but okay. And I was doing my best to help her forget about Dad for a while and just have fun. I didn't say as much, but I was having fun too. We sat with some random kids, watching the fish in the Caesars aquarium while their parents were in a store. A boy and girl, about seven or eight. We gave all the fish names and little personalities and me and Paisley made up a story about them going about their daily business under the water. I could have talked to those little guys all day.

But instead we did as much of the Strip as we could, evading certain death on crosswalks and bypassing the many street sellers we came into contact with: guys touting water or show tickets; women wearing too much mascara offering discount vouchers for the monorail or the Fashion Show mall; a giant M&M with legs handing out leaflets and posing for photos.

The following day, we headed to New York New York, where we walked through this casino that was like an indoor

Central Park but with slot machines. It even had street signs and fake stone pathways, and I kinda felt at home. Dad used to take us to Central Park sometimes to see the boats on the lake or go to the zoo. There was a mock-up indoor Coney Island too, upstairs from the casino, with all these arcades and games. We found a dance machine and ate Twizzlers while stomping out a rhythm together, side by side. The song was called 'Everlong' but I'd never heard it before. Paisley said she liked it. I kinda did too. We even had a little audience watching us.

And I wonder,
When I sing along with you,
If everything could ever be this real forever,
If anything could ever be this good again ...

We did that same song three times. Our audience stayed for all three times. We were perfectly in sync. It was a good song. It sounded like us. Those lyrics were going around my head all day long.

If everything could ever be this real forever,
If anything could ever be this good again ...

Our audience even clapped when we'd finished.

We played the arcades for about two hours, throwing balls into baskets and into rings and Hoops over Las. I got thirty tickets for Skee Ball and won some jellybeans and a monkey pencil topper. Paisley was real good on the basketball and won like fifty tickets, and she picked for her prizes two packs of heart-shaped stickers, a bag of Jelly Bellys, and a light-up popsicle ring that glowed through her cheeks when she sucked it. She managed to get seven of those stickers on my back and neck before I sussed her and had her peel them off me.

After a slice of pizza and a blue Gatorade from a vending machine in the lobby, the only slot we could actually play, Paisley did the Manhattan Express roller coaster that goes round and through the hotel (I wimped out and waited for her in the gift shop) and then she suggested we go to the other end of the Strip to get some good views of the place.

By the time we reached Stratosphere, this endless knitting needle pointing right up into the warm Las Vegas sky, I had just come around to the idea of going up to the observation deck. But I was adamant I wasn't going on the rides. I sat watching the casino from afar from the Under-21 'safety area' while Paisley got the tickets.

'There you go,' she said upon her return, handing me my ticket.

I looked at it. 'Pais, my ticket says Observation Deck and Big Shot. What does yours say?'

She showed me.

'Huh? Yours says Observation Deck and three rides. Big Shot's a ride.'

'Yeah, I asked if you could just go up but they have this law and if you're going up the tower you have to do at least one ride. Otherwise you can't go up.'

'I can't.'

'Yeah, you can,' she said, taking my arm and guiding me up the stairs to the security check. 'I'll be there. We'll hold hands if you want. Big Shot's just this big donut going up and down on a stick and you're strapped in.'

'Yeah, but it's right at the top. It's like the tallest thing in the world!'

We joined the end of the security line.

'I did say to you I didn't want to do any rides, Paisley …' I kept saying.

'I know, but you have to. Come on. You might even, just maybe, enjoy it. Have a little fungasm maybe. Don't be afraid of it, Beau.'

I fretted the whole time in the line. She kept trying to reassure me, patting my hand and stuff, but I was really starting to sweat, especially when we were frisked and asked to take our belts off by security.

In the elevator, I really started to panic. 'Paisley, I can't. I just can't. What if …' I leaned in to her, 'what if I need to go pee?'

'*Do* you need to pee?' she asked, prompting looks from others in the elevator.

'No, but it happens to people when they're scared. They pee.'

I only stopped whining when we got out and saw the view. It was absolutely incredible. We were standing behind the glass and looking down on tiny little Vegas, laid out beneath us like a child's model built from matchboxes stuck with sequins.

'It's so beautiful,' I gasped, sticking a quarter in the observation telescope.

'Yeah,' she said. 'Can you see our motel?'

I swept the telescope around as wide as it would go. 'No, I can see Paris. We still haven't seen Paris. We gotta do that.

Maybe tonight, yeah?'

'Yeah, yeah,' she said. 'I'm gonna get a Slushie and then I'm gonna go do my rides. You want?'

'No thanks.' I didn't take my eyes off the telescope.

'Aren't you gonna come watch me risk my life?'

'Yeah, I'll be there in a minute.'

I watched Paisley do her rides from behind the glass on the other side of the Observation Deck. If I thought my sister was crazy before, I *knew* she was crazy now. There she was, spinning around on this big umbrella contraption, nearly a thousand feet in the air, dangling off the edge of a building. Who in their right mind puts three thrill rides a thousand feet up in the sky? And she wasn't even holding on! She was laughing. Waving! If it had been me, my knuckles would have burst straight through my skin from the sheer pressure of holding on so tight.

I met up with her when she came off, retrieving her Slushie from a temporary locker beside the ride. '*You're* Insanity, let alone the ride,' I told her. 'How could you do that?'

'Just gotta be done, Beau,' she said, taking a big old slurp of her Slushie. 'When in Vegas …'

Next she did X-Scream, which was this little eight-seater roller coaster, stuck out on a limb from the building, that kept going up and down on its little track, as though about to fall off the edge. I didn't open my eyes to watch her for most of it. Any second I thought she was gonna come flying out and fall to her death. But again she laughed and waved, and again I felt like the cowardly turd waiting for it all to stop.

I handed her Slushie to her again when we met up. 'Weren't you scared?'

'Nah,' she said panting, taking in multiple sips and getting cold headache. She pinched her nose. 'Piece of cake.' She showed me her tongue. 'Blue yet?'

I shook my head.

'Come on,' she said, linking my arm and tossing her cup into a garbage can. 'Now we're both doing Big Shot.'

'Paisley …'

'I'm not scared, Beau. So you shouldn't be either.'

'Yeah, but I'm not you. I'm really not.'

Paisley didn't hear any of my pleading, my fretting, my declarations of illness.

'Sorry, I'm a little deaf at the moment, Beau. Must be all the FUN I'm having!' she shouted in my ear.

We took the lift up to the highest level of the tower and joined the line for Big Shot. A dude at the top was taking our tickets. I stood in front of my sister. I put my hand behind me and she grabbed it. I thought of the Wonder Twins, the real Wonder Twins. The superheroes, touching hands to activate their powers. I wondered if it would work for us, if just a touch of my hand could give me Paisley's courage. Then I realized how stupid that was.

'It's alright,' she whispered in my ear. 'You're gonna be fine.'

'Okay,' I kept whispering to myself. My palm was as slippery as a starfish.

We took our seats and buckled ourselves in.

'Do these bars come down? Why hasn't he come around to put the bars down? What if he's forgotten about this side of the donut, Paisley?'

'He's coming, look.' And the guy came around to our side

and checked our belts and pulled down the large red bars to hold us in place.

'Y'all ready for this? Sit tight,' he said to me.

'Hell, yeah,' said Paisley. 'You wanna hold my hand, Beau?'

I shook my head, gripping the bars at my shoulders, tugging on them a little to check they were secure. I was belted, strapped down, locked in. I couldn't fall out.

I heard the song from the arcades in my head again.

If anything could ever be this good again.
The only thing I'll ever ask of you,
Gotta promise not to stop when I say when …

We sat there, poised. I shut my eyes and breathed in. Once, twice, three times, waiting for the off, for the jolt, the zoom, the screams.

'Paisley …' I said.

'Yeah?'

'Are you scared yet?'

'No. So neither should you be. This is gonna be great.'

She looked at me. I briefly opened my eyes and nodded. And on my next intake of breath, the donut was released and shot *up and up and up and up* into the sky, way faster than anything ever, and right up to the top of the spire on the tallest tower in the whole wide world.

'WHOOOO HOOO,' Paisley yelled. 'Look, Beau, look at Vegas. Look, you can see everything! Look at the desert!'

'I can't open my eyes!' I screamed. 'Oh my gaaaaahhhhhhh-hhd!'

And down we went and then *whoosh* up we went again in a puke-inducing upsurge, lingering for a second at the top where I briefly opened one eye, and then *schoom* down again, guts to the floor, eyes to the skies, and then *whoooooosh* up again, four times over. On the fifth time, I opened both eyes at the top and it was like the camera shutter came down. I only looked for a moment, an instant, but the view was enough to last my lifetime. Everything was so much smaller and more beautiful. I couldn't see the dirt or the depression or the gambling addicts. I couldn't see the pimps or the 'hos or the hobos. I couldn't even feel the heat. I just saw Vegas. And it was beautiful.

We gently came down and stopped, exactly where we had started.

I still had my eyes shut.

'You did it, Beau,' said my sister. 'You did your first ever thrill ride. Look at you, Stuntman Mike!'

I opened my eyes. 'Is it gonna move again?'

'Nope, we're done.' Then the dude appeared and let us out and I clambered off and promptly stumbled over to the railing and gripped on like the drama queen I am.

Paisley came over to me and put a hand on my back.

'I was really scared, Pais,' I told her.

'I told you, you don't need to be. I'm strong enough for both of us.' Then she asked, 'Shall we go check Paris now? You can try out your French on some of the mesdemoiselles.'

Still clinging to the safety rail, I shook my head. Sweat droplets flew from my face and hair ends. 'I need to cool off.'

We knew from our extensive investigations at Caesars that it had like five pools, so we headed back there and followed the signs. It did cross my mind that we'd be kicked out for not being guests or not having the right attire to be poolside, but there was no one there when we walked through to the pool areas so Paisley snagged us a couple fluffy white bath towels from behind the desk.

And we chillaxed on sun loungers by the pool for the rest of the afternoon, eating jellybeans. Paisley got us a couple ice-cold strawberry-and-banana smoothies from the poolside shack. I thought about when we were kids. We'd sometimes spend whole afternoons lying before the fireplace in the den with our sketch pads, a box of jellybeans and super pack of pens, drawing and planning each room and each brick in our grandmother's house as though it were our own. Being there with Paisley was like being a kid again. And it felt great.

'Try lemon and cotton candy,' she said, cross-legged on her lounger, squinting in the sunlight. She had stripped down to her underwear. I was still in my T-shirt and jeans. I'd taken my sneakers off, though, and I was lying down. I had loosened up a little.

I pushed my shades back up my nose and felt two beans land on my chest. 'Mm, yeah. Pink lemonade. That's good.'

'I've got marmalade. Two tangerine, one lemon and a lime.' She tossed me over two blueberries and a buttered popcorn. 'Blueberry muffin combo. Flavorgasm, trust me.'

I chewed the life out of them. 'Yeah, that's the best.' All possible combos were tested until only a couple root beers and a strawberry daiquiri rattled in the bag and both our stomachs groaned with greed.

I looked over at her and she smiled. Her nose wrinkled up,

just like it did when she was little. She held up a blue bean to show me.

'Think any of these are magic beans?' she asked me.

'Probably not. God, I'm so sleepy.' The warm breeze on my face was bringing me to whole new levels of happiness. I could hear subdued chattering from the other sun loungers and swimmers around me, but nothing too intrusive. Little kids giggling and splashing in another pool a few yards away behind a pink-flowering hedge. More toga-draped waitresses saunter-ing around with trays of empty glasses. One came and took my empty smoothie cup. I pretended I was asleep behind my shades.

Then Paisley went and ruined it.

'We're kinda out of money.'

'What?' I croaked, leaning up.

'Almost out.' She sifted several receipts out of her wallet and went through them. Breakfast $35.75. Two Stratosphere tickets at $65.90. Chicken wings, steak fries and two iced lemonades $39.04. Candy $46.71. Feminine care and shaving gel $18.78. Smoothies $18.00. Deuce tickets $10. More candy $48.63.

We worked out we'd spent around $180 on arcades and snacks too. Even so I wasn't prepared for the total she gave me.

'We got … thirty-two nineteen.'

'Shit. We kinda went a little crazy, didn't we?'

Paisley started laughing. 'Yep. So back to my original point, we're kinda out of money.'

I leaned back. I thought I would be more worried than I was. I was so lethargic I could have fallen asleep mid sentence. 'It's not funny. We'll have to get jobs.'

'Yeah. That'll be easy. Two sixteen-year-olds with no quali-
fications, no references and no home. Vegas'll be cryin' out for
us.'

'We haven't found Dad yet and we got no money. What else
can we do?'

'Are you getting in the pool?'

That was the last thing I heard her say. I must have drifted
off. When I woke up, she was gone.

CHAPTER ELEVEN

Paisley

Apollo Pool, Caesars Palace, the Strip

Beau had eaten so many jellybeans he'd crashed on his lounger by the pool. Candy always had that effect on him, even when he was a kid. It didn't affect me at all but it always put Beau into a sugar coma. I watched him snooze for a little while, his forehead creases disappearing, his dark brown hair falling across his face, his long eyelashes fluttering on his cheeks. The best part about Beau is that, though he is actually really beautiful for a boy, he has absolutely no fucking idea.

I went into the ladies' changing rooms, intent on just cleaning myself up, making myself look less underage, before I headed into the casino in search of bulging back pockets or short-sighted grannies with buckets full of quarters. I took off my faded Queen T-shirt, replacing it with a lonely white fitted blouse I'd found hanging on a gold hook by the wash basins. There were other clothes around I could have chosen: a gold camisole, a pukey pink sarong, a psychedelic red-and-yellow shirt with big black buttons.

'No. Go simple, Pais,' I said to myself.

I bagged my boots and looked for another pair of shoes; there were silk mules, f-expensive-looking strappy sandals, red kitten heels. I went for stilettos, black with a silver heel. They were ever-so-slightly too big so I stuffed the toes with toilet paper until they fitted. Women staying at Caesars were either too stupid or too trusting with their stuff, and I didn't care which. Bags were lying around for the taking, but on inspection I found they were just pool bags, not purses, so no money. There were make-up bags lying around, too. I put on some blazing red lipstick and fired up my eyelashes a little. I've never really seen the point of perfume but one of the bags had a little bottle in so I sprayed some of that on as well. It smelled like the Skank – lust and dead flowers. The shirt was a little tight and the heels a little high but I ain't as fussy as Goldilocks. I checked my look in the mirror, pushed what little boobs I had up in my bra and undid two buttons. I looked good. I shook out my hair. I looked older.

I strutted back through those wide marbled passageways like I was the new owner of the place. If I looked or acted sixteen years old in any way or form, they'd kick my ass outta there for sure. To my way of thinking, the dudes scoping for under twenty-ones would be so knocked out by my T&A they wouldn't think of carding me. Think mature, think mature, I kept saying to myself. Be cool. Back across the lobby, the wind from outside blowing my hair as the doors opened and closed, tourists goggling my fabulous bare-leg-high-shoe combo. I had sunshine in a bag and I knew it.

Without making too much of it, I ventured onto the casino floor. I bypassed the blackjack, craps, roulette and mini baccarat tables, glided past the Keno area and hung around the slot machines waiting for someone on Jeopardy, Wheel of Fortune, Megabucks or Blazing Sevens to leave their purse or wallet vulnerable. I was trying to walk as steadily as I could. My feet were killing me and my bag was tugging on my shoulder from the weight of my boots. I checked coin trays, sizing up some redneck tourists who'd had a few too many, waiting on an opportunity to fleece them. A group of guys watched me from one of the tables. One of them in a leather jacket smiled. I was gonna be all, 'Yeah, as if. Keep dreaming there, Leather Boy,' but I didn't. I smiled back. Might get a free drink out of it, I thought. What was the harm?

A fat guy was leaning on the side of an Elvis machine as his girlfriend played. He was talking to a young couple. They were chatting about moving in together and the fat guy was all like, 'Been there, done that, divorced the bitch,' and he sounded like the kind of guy you meet on holiday and can't shake off. He'd had hair implants too by the look of it. Bad ones. Total midlife going on. I made a bet with myself that he had a Ferrari. I pretended to play a neighboring slot and listened in for a good ten minutes. The Midlife had no awareness of me, even though I did look badass delectable. He was too busy talking about himself. He didn't even notice that his wallet was teetering suicidally out his ass pocket. Running out wasn't going to be easy in my heels, but I could do it. I knew I could do it without him seeing.

But his girlfriend ran out of quarters, so he had to dip into the wallet to get some bucks for her to change up, then tucked it back down deep into his pocket. Chance wasted.

I looked over at the guys at the table. They had moved. Another ship sailed.

I got bored real quick of fishing for loose change after that. I headed for the bar that overlooked the casino. I slipped as gracefully as I could onto a bar stool and ordered the most mature drink on the menu, an iced tea.

'Can I see some ID please, Ma'am?' said the bartender.

'For an iced tea?'

'I'm sorry.'

It had to happen. I huffed and puffed around in my bag and found my wallet. I pulled out my Photoshopped ID and handed it to him. He looked at me. He looked suspiciously at it. He handed it back.

'Thank you.'

Then he went off to make my iced tea. I scoped the bar. It was nearly six thirty and there were a few guys hanging around, sitting at tables. Mr Suspicious returned with my tea and took my money and went to the cash register to get my change. It was loaded with cash. It was a good job I'd left the Eclipse back in the motel room that day or I might have just cut out the middleman, or at least the barman, right then and there.

The iced tea was pretty terrible.

By a quarter to eight, the bar was a little busier and more guys had gathered to watch some football game on a screen in the corner. I fixed my eye on some gray suit sitting at a table by himself. He looked like he'd been stood up. Black hair, shiny brown shoes, a gold watch he kept checking. Pretty soon I was getting longer looks in my direction. I could feel his eyes on my legs. I saw his wallet on the table. We exchanged a smile.

Then this bleached-blonde pigeon bagged my guy and they left. So it was back to square one. I was on my second iced tea. No other guys were alone. Maybe I was in the wrong bar, I thought. Maybe there was a singles bar somewhere filled with desperation and big bucks. Eight o'clock came and I thought about going back to the motel. Music pumped. Looks were exchanged. Iced tea was sipped. I could feel my disappointment Hulking-over into anger that I'd failed to reel in any big fish.

All I could do was to sit, sit, sit, sit. And I did not like it, not one little bit.

'Can I get you a drink?' a voice offered. A man leaned against the bar.

I looked him up and down, just to appear distant. It was the guy in the leather jacket who'd smiled at me earlier. He was okay-looking. Late twenties, I guessed, though I could have been wrong. If *I* looked twenty-one, he could have been way older.

'I'm solid, thanks,' I said, caressing my iced tea.

'Come on, we can do better than that. Please. You look so lonely sitting there by yourself. It's my duty as a gentleman.' He smiled.

'Okay. I'll have a Coke. Thanks.'

He seemed surprised. 'Sure thing.' He scrolled through a

wad of one dollar bills he got out of his brown leather jacket and placed them on the counter. I slipped down from my stool and made for a table in a dark recess of the bar. Yes, I thought. Just reel him in. Where's he putting the goods?

Inside jacket pocket. Damn, I thought. He arrived with the drinks and settled them down on the table. He was wearing cowboy boots, gold-tipped.

'I hate to ask, but some idiot stood you up tonight, right?' he said.

'Uh, yeah. You could say that. I was just waiting for my knight in shining armor.'

'And along came me,' he said. He had oily skin and curly blond bangs which he flicked out of his eyes. He was good looking in a young country-and-western-singer kinda way. Eyes were watching me from another table. I looked around. The other guys from his party were sitting around a plasma screen in the corner and one by one they all looked away.

'They your friends?' I said, motioning to the TV threesome.

'Yeah.' He leaned in. 'Want me to introduce you?'

'Not really,' I smiled. I felt his hand heavy on my knee.

'Is that okay?' he asked.

I looked down at his hand. 'Yeah.'

'You're really beautiful, you know.'

'I'm not supposed to be here,' I told him. 'I'm not twenty-one yet.'

He shrugged. 'Hey, I'm easy to please.' His hand moved up my thigh a little. I didn't like it.

'Like, nowhere near twenty-one yet,' I said.

He ran his tongue slowly over his lip. 'I had a feeling.'

I got a gross feeling in my belly.

'Ain't seen you around here much. First time in Vegas?'

I nodded, picking up my Coke. 'You?'

'Nah, second home.'

'Really?'

'Pretty much. Come here with a bunch of my boys once or twice a month. Play the tables, have some fun, then roll on home to Austin.'

'Where's that?'

He finally moved his hand and glugged down half of his beer, gasping at the sheer heaven of it. 'Texas. You?'

'Jersey.'

He nodded. I looked at my drink. I sipped. There was vodka in it.

'There's vodka in this. I just said Coke.'

'So you got more than you asked for. Come on, one's not gonna hurt.'

I put my mouth on the edge of the glass and tipped it. I stirred it a little with the special golden Caesars Palace swizzle stick, took out a couple of the ice cubes and pretended to sip it again. I hate alcohol. I hate what it does to people.

'What's your name?'

'Zooey,' I lied. 'With two Os.' I'd read it in a book at school and thought it sounded cool.

'Zooey. That's a beautiful name. Ya want another one?'

'Another name?'

He laughed. 'No, another drink.'

'No, I'm good,' I laughed, my eyebrows raised at the mere suggestion less than ten seconds into an already full glass.

'My name's Steve. So, Zooey, ya here on holiday or …?'

'Yeah. Just having some fun, same as you.'

He leaned in a little closer. He had long nose hairs. I could see the color of his wallet in his inside pocket. I just wanted to grab it and run outta there, but I had the damn killer heels on so it wasn't an option.

'Look, if you want, we could hook up. I could show you around sometime.'

'That'd be good,' I said. It was my turn to lean in toward him. 'You look like a man who knows where he's going.'

He sank the rest of his beer, never once taking his eyes off me. He wasn't drunk enough and I couldn't think how to get the wallet quickly and take my heels off *and* grab my bag all in one swift motion. It just wasn't going to happen. But I needed that money. Money = more Vegas = Dad.

He put the glass down and his eyes seemed to light up. 'You know, it's funny,' he laughed. 'I know we only just met but, don't you think we have a connection? Like we were destined to meet or something?'

'Kinda,' I said. 'So, you staying here at Caesars?'

'Yeah. You?'

'Yeah.'

'I'll walk you back to your room,' he said.

'No. I don't wanna go back just yet. I'd rather stay here. With you.'

'Why don't we go up to my room? It's a suite. It's got a Jacuzzi.' He exhaled, like he was a little nervous, and his breath hit my face. He smelled of leather car seats when your dog's been sick in the back.

He took my hand and stood up. His hand was big and covered mine. Had a strong grip too. He handed my vodka and Coke to me. 'You can take it with you. They won't mind, they know me here.' We walked to the steps and he stopped. 'I'm gonna get another coupla beers. Wait here.'

I did as I was told. It was going too far but I couldn't go anywhere else. Steve didn't strike me as the kind of guy who'd just put up with a girl running out on him. In any case, I couldn't run in those damn killer heels. I put the Coke on the rail at the top of the steps and plunged my hand inside my bag. I rooted around.

Steve looked over and smiled. I smiled back. He'd left me just long enough. I picked up my drink again.

'Sorry about that,' he said, eventually returning with two bottles in one hand. 'Gotta keep hydrated, know what I mean?' He took my hand and led me down the red carpeted steps toward the elevators, just as Caesar himself and a harem of scantily-clad maidens walked by.

'Woah, what's all this?' I asked Steve. He took my hand, squeezed it. I looked up at him but didn't shake it away. I smiled.

'He does this a few times a day,' he said. 'It's a different guy every time. Tourists love it.'

Steve started to get a little huffy as tourist after tourist filed past us to get a closer snapshot of the Roman emperor. We then had a clear runway to the elevators, and there was one already open so we broke into a run.

He got me inside. Two couples were already in there with their cases, but we managed to squeeze in right at the edge and were mirrored on all sides. He pressed me back against the wall and it started to rise. The elevator, I mean. Though I did feel him against my stomach, at first nothing much, but as the elevator juddered and stopped at points where there was no one to be let in, he got harder. He pressed against me more.

He whispered in my ear that I was sexy.

The elevator juddered and some of his beer spilled on the floor. He cussed. A gray businessman threw him a dirty look.

'Problem, pal?' he spat back.

The gray businessman's neck had suddenly stopped working and he focused on watching the floors flash by above.

'You're looking hot,' I whispered to Steve and held my Coke glass to his cheek. 'You want some?'

He moved his face round and I tilted the glass so he could sip. And he glugged half that sucker down. That seemed to make him feel better. Made me feel better too.

We got out of the elevator. Long pink-carpeted corridors stretched off into the distance like a spider's legs, and he led me down one, right to the end. Room 8237.

He took out his key card from the back pocket of his jeans and slipped it in the slot above the door handle. Then he allowed me to go inside first. As I walked past him I got that pukey smell of his breath again. It made my stomach lurch.

If it was a suite, then Steve had been robbed. It was a shit hole and no bigger than our room at the motel. In fact it was smaller. Low roller, I realized. My bullshit shield had failed me.

Fuck.

He locked the door behind us and ushered me through to one of the beds. I looked at him.

'My friend Tommy's in the other one. This one's mine.'

'Oh. You mind if I go freshen up?'

He shook his head. 'I don't want you to go anywhere.' He stepped closer to me and grinned so his bottom jaw stuck out and his eyes were wide. 'I want you to stay here with me.'

'I need to use the bathroom,' I laughed, pushing him away. 'You can wait a minute, surely.' The puke breath was on me again, and now I could smell his BO too.

He placed both hands on my waist, holding me closely and diving in for the kiss. He kissed hard and cold. It was like being pushed into a wall.

I pulled back. 'I want to use the bathroom,' I kept saying, trying to push against his chest, slam my fists against him, but he just kept coming for me, and suddenly I was against the closet and he was undoing his belt and with one hand he held my neck, forcing my head back.

'You fucking stay there! You ain't going anywhere until you do what you came here to do.'

'NO. Get off. Get off me, you sick fuck!' I shouted as loud as I could though my chest was being flattened.

This wasn't supposed to be happening. It shouldn't have got that far.

Then I did something I haven't done since I was a child. I screamed. It was the scream I screamed in the woods when I was six, on the second day of looking for Dad.

It was the scream of lost causes.

CHAPTER TWELVE

Beau

Room 2, Lucky Inn Motel, the Strip

All the way back to our motel I racked my brain, trying to think if she'd told me to meet her anywhere. Nope, nothing. We were at the pool. Then I woke up and it was almost dark and she was gone. I'd been asleep for, like, two hours. Damn the jellybeans!

The clock beside my bed ticked over to ten fifteen. Everything was wrong.

'Where are you?' I said it out loud. I didn't know if I was hoping Paisley would answer back or send me some kind of sign as to where she might be. My tw-instinct, if there is such a thing, was definitely alarmed. I had this unsettling feeling in the middle of my chest that something bad had happened. I was probably wrong. I was usually wrong. She would probably come into the room at any second and slump down on the bed. She'd gone up to the Stratosphere or something, just for the hell of it. Hadn't realized the time. *Stop worrying, Gramps,* she'd say.

But as I watched the numbers on the clock roll over and over, my heart feeling more and more like a steak being pummeled by a meat mallet, I knew I couldn't just sit there. I had to find her.

I caught the Deuce bus just outside the motel but it was slow and seemed to stop every five seconds for more tourists to climb aboard and fumble around looking for loose change. I jumped off as soon as I could and ran the rest of the way toward Caesars. I ran all through the mall, too, eventually finding the casino and the airport-like reception area and the Concierge desk. I felt eyes on me the second I entered the casino. I was like this little alarm bell ringing, wherever I went, alerting the security to the fact that I was way too young to be anywhere near there. Two really thin waitresses asked me if I wanted a drink. They must have known I couldn't drink. All the CCTV cameras must have locked their black eyes on me, my sweat patches, my red neck, my sixteen years of inexperience. Eyes everywhere.

Someone was in front of me talking to the Concierge when I got to the desk, so I had chance to catch my breath. The snooty Smile-Like-You-Mean-It guy who Paisley had been rude to before was gone, so I got a friendly guy instead called Jamal.

'Hey, welcome to Caesars Palace, how can I help you?' he said.

'I've lost my sister,' I said. 'We were by the pool earlier and

I fell asleep, and when I woke up she was gone.'

'Alright, what's your sister's name?'

It was then that I saw her, across the casino. I zoned in on this blonde leaving the bar with this real tall guy with curly blond hair. They disappeared for a second behind a crowd of people in togas.

'Don't worry,' I told the Concierge, heading across the casino floor. What the hell was she doing?

Some guy dressed up in a white toga like Julius Caesar was passing through, with a female entourage to rival that of most rock stars, so I had to wait for them to get out of the way before I could get going again. By the time they'd posed for photos and exited stage left, Paisley and the curly blond guy had gone. One elevator was just closing with an old man in it. Another was broken. I stood outside the other four and watched to see where each one was going. They could be on any floor between seventy-one and eighty. I had to try them all. It would take me forever. I got out of the elevator and shouted along every corridor like a mad man.

'PAISLEY. PAISLEY.' I waited a second. Some inquisitive doors opened but then closed. A couple girls looked out of one door on seventy-five but otherwise nothing.

On eighty, I didn't have to make any commotion. I heard it myself, distant but definite. The worst sound I've ever heard. My sister screaming.

'PAISLEY!' I shouted again, and headed along one of the corridors that branched off the elevators.

I flew. I wouldn't have been surprised to look behind and see a trail of flames. I reached the end door and banged and

- 120 -

slammed against it as if my life—or hers—depended on it.

'PAISLEY!' Eventually it buckled and swung open before me.

'Oh Jesus. Oh my God, Pais.'

She sat on the other side of this double bed. It took a couple seconds before she looked round.

'Didn't know you had it in you.'

I walked toward her. She looked okay. She wasn't crying. I tried to catch my breath. It was then that I noticed the guy on the carpet, pants round his ankles. Unmoving. Mouth open. Dead.

'What's happened? What have you done?' I panted.

She was counting money, distracted as she spoke. 'How'd ya find me?'

I bent over. I couldn't catch my breath. 'I saw you … the bar. He's dead.'

She got up. 'No he's not. I slipped him something. He's sleeping now.'

'I heard you … screaming.'

'Yeah,' she gulped. 'They took longer to work than I thought. Almost had to work for my money. But I'm okay.'

'Are you sure?' I went over and stood in front of her. 'Pais? Look at me, are you alright?'

She was still counting the money. She didn't look up. 'I told you, I'm fine.' She wasn't fine. She was breathing faster and her face was bleeding.

'Tell me what he did,' I said, crouching down in front of her.

'He didn't get a chance to do anything,' she replied.

'What … what did you do to him?'

'Crushed up a couple pills, put 'em in his beer.'

I looked at him. Then at her. 'You drugged him? You DRUGGED him?!'

'Yeah.'

I couldn't believe what I was seeing. She had this shirt on – wide open exposing her black bra – and these black stilettos with heels that looked like medical instruments. And her face was bloody. And her hair was a rat's nest. And her lipstick was smudged. It wasn't her lipstick. Talk about Beauty and the Beast, my sister was both.

'Oh my God. You killed him, Paisley. You're a psycho. You're a complete … psycho!'

She got up, the bunch of money in one hand and a watch in the other. 'I told you, he's not dead. He's asleep. And our kitty's back up to twelve hundred and two bucks and a Rolex.' She tapped the watch and held it to her ear. 'I think it's fake, though.'

'Paisley … we need to call the police.' I looked at her open shirt. It was ripped at the buttonholes. 'If he tried to …'

'I don't think our friend here would appreciate the cops getting involved. What with me being underage and all.' She snickered, like she was laughing it all off. Water off a duck's back. But as she walked over to the desk and pulled out the drawer, I could see her hand. It was shaking. She fished out a piece of Caesars Palace writing paper and a pen.

'I'll leave him a note. To explain.'

I read over her shoulder as she wrote.

To Steve,
If there's anything I can't stand it's a pervert. If there's anything

I can't stand more than a pervert it's a liar. And if there's anything I can't stand more than a pervert and a liar, it's a guy that smells as bad as you do.

Zooey, Aged 16

I couldn't speak. I didn't know what to say or how to say it. She had it all planned out. All sewn up. A little orange bottle lay on the bed. I picked it up.

'Ativan? Where the hell d'you get Ativan?'

She shrugged. 'Virginia's cabinet. I saw it on *ER*. Some kind of anti-anxiety pill, isn't it? I thought it might help.'

'Help who?'

'Me.'

'You get anxious?'

'I get … everything.'

'You … you could've killed him.'

'Just a little bit,' she said and walked straight past me to drop the note on Steve's motionless body. 'How sexy am I now, huh?' she muttered to him. I watched her shaky hand as it lifted to move her knotted hair back off her face.

As we left the room, Paisley pulled the door but, thanks to me, it wouldn't close. Along the corridor, two guys in burgundy uniforms were running toward us.

'What's happening?' one of them called.

'I don't know,' said Paisley. 'I think the people in 8237 are having some kind of party. It's lucky you showed up.'

They hurried past, assuring us they had everything under control.

'Suckers,' mumbled Paisley, and she just carried on walking.

CHAPTER THIRTEEN

Paisley

Deuce Bus stop, outside Caesars Palace,
the Strip

I saw you both on the news. It made me sick to think of you both in that children's home. And when I heard Virginia had taken you in it nearly killed me. That woman is just bad. Real bad. I knew she'd give you stuff, but she's not one of nature's carers. She pulled a gun on me when I came to see you both after finishing my parole. Bet she didn't tell you that. She said neither of you wanted to see me, that you were doing just great and that if I ever came to the house again, she'd call the cops. Tell them I'd been harassing you and acting all violent. That's why I write. I know she probably puts my letters straight in the trash. But I'll keep writing. Maybe one day, one of them will get through.

I was in a bad mood. I had almost been raped to begin with. Hey, that sounds like *A Christmas Carol*: 'Marley was dead to begin with.' And it's important to understand the fact that I was in a bad mood because otherwise you cannot possibly imagine the wonder of what happened after this.

It was a few days after the whole Steve incident. I wasn't speaking to Beau. He'd flushed my Ativan down the can. We were nowhere near finding Dad yet and I was having a real heavy period. And even though we had some money now, I was in a pissy mood. It was a hot, hot day. One of those days when it's arid and dry and there's no air and you've nearly been raped and you can't find your dad and you feel sick from all the candy and the sun seems to hit you harder and harder the more you walk. I could feel the soles of my boots sticking to the sidewalk. I hated that.

We waited outside Caesars for the Deuce. Beau was sitting on the bench eating Jujubes. I stood leaning on the Plexiglass behind him. I couldn't wait to get back to the motel and deal with my underpant situation. Periods are a joke, seriously. I hate being a girl sometimes. They say you lose an eggcup of blood a month. I must be laying ostrich eggs. I was kinda glad to see it at first; I was way late and was worried I might have been sperminated by the train wreck of my life that was Jason. But I had dodged that particular bullet. My periods are always a nightmare though. You'd have thought they'd have come up with a solution to it all by now; all the pain and the moods and the misery. I guess they have. It's called death.

Anyway, this grizzly dude started walking up and down the line with this coupon book. He looked like a hobo. As we stood there, he kept walking past us, again and again, his shabby white Reeboks flopping on the sidewalk like worn-out biscuits. His dirty toes poked through the front of one of them. His left eye was stitched shut like a pirate's and he had this T-shirt on that read, *I stayed, I played, I got laid* and there was this naked woman sprawled out across his chest in silhouette. Made me wanna puke.

As he came closer to us, Beau got up from the bench and joined me standing beside the shelter. He took the slightest step behind me. I knew what he was doing. He was afraid Coupon Guy was suddenly gonna pull an audience-participation thing on him and single him out. Beau had always hated that. All that, *'What's your name, Sonny?'* bullshit. Street entertainers. Magicians. Clowns.

'No smut here, folks. Get your coupons. Family fun. No smut. Pay no money,' said Coupon Guy.

He walked up and down, up and down the line of tourists, back and forth, back and forth, badgering people as they walked by, shoving his books in their faces, saying the same thing over and over. The Deuce was taking forever to roll up.

'No smut here, folks. Get your coupons. Family fun. No smut. Pay no money. No smut here, folks. Get your coupons. Family fun. No smut. Pay no money,' he kept saying, never deviating from the script, exactly the same tone of voice, up and down, taking his tobacco stench as he went and then bringing it right back.

The tourists would sidestep around him or pretend they didn't speak English. If I had a heart I'd have felt sorry for him.

'What is it, a hooker guide?' some guy in sweat pants asked.

'No, Sir, no smut here. Just coupons. Family fun.'

'Why would I want it, then?' the guy shrugged, and two guys with him laughed like morons.

We ignored him for what seemed like an entire millennium, listening to his spiel surreptitiously. 'No smut here, folks. Get your coupons. Family fun. No smut. Pay no money. Hey, buddy!'

For the splittest of seconds I thought he meant my dad, until reality kicked home and I looked behind us to where he had called to see a similarly shabby guy with a beard and a red shirt, watching the news on the Jumbotron outside Caesars.

The bus pulled up and Coupon Guy went over to the other hobo. The bus lowered a little and I stepped up, posting my five-dollar bill into the slot. I took my ticket and waited for Beau. We went to the back of the bus together and sat down. A fat woman fell up the step and some other tourists rushed to help her. I looked out and watched the two hobos, rooting through the trash can together, pulling out wrappers and sniffing them. The Red Shirt guy thumbed through a paper.

'What are you looking at?' said Beau, leaning forward and putting his ticket in his back pocket. 'Ugh, what are they doing?'

'What do you think they're doing—they're starving.'

'God, how desperate do you gotta be to go through trash?'

'Well, you're no stranger to a trash can either, if I remember.'

Beau just looked at me. 'Not by choice. Hey, look.'

The hobos were fighting, shoving each other. Coupon Guy was trying to lay a right hook on Red Shirt guy but the Red Shirt guy was ducking, grabbing Coupon's waist and trying to bring him down.

'My money's on Coupon Guy,' I said. 'He's way bigger.'

Beau frowned. 'That's really sad. They're probably fighting over a moldy pretzel or something.'

'Get outta here, go on!' we heard Coupon Guy shout as Red Shirt moved away. Then he ran to catch him up and kicked his ass again. Red Shirt fell to his knees. Coupon Guy laughed and went back to his line of new tourists at the stop.

The doors clattered shut and the bus started to move away. Red Shirt was walking alongside it for a second. I watched him. He looked up. The bus moved away from him. I saw his face.

Dad's face.

My blood froze.

'Oh my God, Beau.' I shot up from my seat and moved to the back of the bus, watching through every window as it rolled on, hoping to catch another glance. The sun burned my eyes as it burst through every gap in the skyline to stop me getting a closer look. He was too far away.

I came back to Beau. 'It was him. The guy in the red shirt. It was Dad.'

'Are you kidding me?' Then he started frantically searching through the window for him, too.

Tourists had jammed the aisle between the back and front doors of the bus so I had to squeeze my way through, angering some old fart with a camcorder and standing on a kid's foot. The kid cried. Beau was right behind me.

'You gotta believe me, it was him. It was Dad, Beau. I saw him. I saw him.'

'Alright, I believe you. But we're gonna lose him …'

'Go to the back and keep an eye on where he goes. Go on!'

It was him. I knew it was him, I didn't need another look. I'd know my dad anywhere. Dad was like a brown bear, muscly and warm, and he had a smile that told you everything was gonna be alright. And although this guy hadn't smiled and was smaller than I remembered Dad being, I didn't have a doubt in my mind.

I got as far as the driver but she was having none of my sweet appeals to stop the bus. 'Miss, would you please sit down while the bus is in motion?'

'You gotta stop the bus,' I said. 'We need to get off.'

'You can get off at the next stop.'

'Where's that?'

'Up here, by the Bellagio. Now please sit down, Miss.'

Beau joined me at the front. 'He's crossed the road.'

'Keep watching him, Beau!'

'Miss …'

'Oh keep your tube in, I'm sitting,' I shouted, trying to push my way back through the tourists to my seat. They'd formed some kind of human shield like cows do when they're being attacked by a bull, so it was much harder to get through.

'Move out my fucking way!' I shouted. The women clicked and tutted, probably 'cos there were kids around, but they still got the hell out of the way.

The bus driver piped up then, spouting all this bus etiquette garbage and how she could have me arrested for 'abuse.'

The Deuce came to a halt and the doors opened and before any of the cattle could do what they were threatening to do and stop me getting off first, I rammed into them, crawling beneath legs and being as pushy as I could until my feet were on the sidewalk. Beau had stayed with me the whole way and he took my hand and we broke into a run and didn't stop pounding the sidewalks and footbridges and pushing through shuffling tourists until we got to the walkway outside the Bellagio. We two-stepped it to the top of the stairs.

'Where'd he go?'

'This way,' said Beau, panting all the way as we crossed over the bridge. We stopped to stare through the Plexiglass barrier for signs of the red shirt. I looked and I looked and there was no sign.

Then I saw him.

'He's there, he's going past MGM.'

So we raced along and down the escalator as fast as we could, past milling tourists and guys with more coupons books and so-say VIP passes. I caught sight of the red through a sea of people and we kept on pushing through. We caught up with the red; it was the red of a giant M&M greeting people outside the store. We pushed past it and carried on running until we came to MGM Grand. We broke hands.

Dad was gone. Like a ghost.

I kept looking and looking, but he wasn't there. We stood there, spinning round, looking in every single direction for the slightest hint of red shirt, but there was nothing. White shirts. Hawaiian shirts. Spaghetti-strap vests. Baseball caps. Laughing. Joking. Tanned. Happy. Strollers. Suitcases. Camcorders. The big gold lion.

We stood panting.

'Wow,' said Beau, bent over. 'It was really Dad? Are you sure?'

And all I could do was nod. I started walking. I didn't know where I was going. I just had to keep walking.

CHAPTER FOURTEEN

Beau

The Strip

One of the dangers of being a kid is that you always believe that around the next corner is what you're looking for. That if you dig deep enough in the sand, you really are gonna shake hands with someone on the other side of the world. That if you go to that end of the rainbow you're gonna find a little pot full of gold. That if you strain hard enough on Christmas Eve, you can hear the tinkling of jingle bells in the sky. And kids take disappointment real hard.

We had stumbled and crunched through the endless trees, over roots and dark soft earth, walking and walking and walking forever, even though we were both exhausted and cold and out of breath and I was crying. Paisley had dragged me onward, convincing me the whole time that Dad was around the next corner. And the corners were never-ending.

Ten years on, and though we weren't in the woods anymore, but rather on concrete with the full glare of the desert sun beating down on us like the lashes of a whip, it felt exactly the same: running after shadows that could have been Dad and getting absolutely nowhere. I was ready for disappointment anyway; I had been since Paisley saw him from the bus. I knew it couldn't be that easy, not after everything.

We went back to the Deuce stop at Caesars where we'd seen Dad watching the Jumbotron and rooting through the trash. We waited around, thinking he might come back. Paisley would have camped out overnight if she had to. But he'd obviously been spooked by Coupon Guy and there was no sign of him. We walked up and down the Strip for hours, ignoring the dancing fountain displays and flashing lights, paying particular attention to the trash cans and bus stops, looking for red shirts and men with dark brown hair. But we found nothing.

I followed Paisley back toward the big gold lion outside MGM Grand and this time she went inside, along the red-carpeted walkways, past the gift shops and boutiques, until she'd led me to the glass-sided lion habitat. There was a little space between all the photo-taking tourists and she stood at the window ledge and stared in.

I stood beside her. 'So what do we do now? Do you want to go back to the Jumbotron, see if he shows up tonight?'

She didn't answer.

'Talk to me, Paisley. Tell me what to do now.'

She carried on staring in at two cubs playing with a blue ball. A voice-over was narrating their history and what they liked to eat.

I looked in at the cubs. 'I know what you're feeling, 'cos I feel exactly the same.'

She put her head forward onto the glass. 'He's right here. He could be around the next corner.' She looked at me sideways.

All I could do was nod. 'Why don't we try the homeless shelters? Seems logical that's where he'd go?'

She shook her head. 'Dad wouldn't go to a shelter.'

'How do you know? He's homeless, it's possible …'

'He'd rather sleep on the streets. Trust me, I know my dad. He's too proud.'

'You knew him when we were six, Pais.' She threw me a look and I stopped in my tracks. 'I'm starting to think we're not gonna find him. I mean … he's homeless. It's gonna be even harder to get to him now. I mean, you remember what happened last time. We ended up lost and on every TV station in New Jersey.'

The blue ball bounced off the glass right in front of us and Paisley backed off like it had suddenly become hot. Then she looked at me and started laughing. 'Beau, you're a friggin' genius.'

'Oh God, what?'

She stared in at the cubs for the longest time.

'Pais? What is it?'

She looked at me. 'You hungry?'

'Yeah. What is it, Pais, what's your idea?'

'Tell you later. Come on. What do you feel like eating? Pizza, pasta?'

I shook my head. 'I could manage something sweet. A donut, I guess.'

'Donuts. Yes, oh yes, this is gonna be good,' she said, clinging onto my arm and practically dragging me all the way through the front entrance. 'Let's go to Doh-Nutty's.'

'That's not the best donuts. The best donuts …'

'I don't want the best donuts—I want a Doh-Nutty's,' she said.

'Okay,' I said, a little wary of my sister's new-found vigor but hungry all the same and, as always, happy to follow her wherever she went.

So we walked to Doh-Nutty's diner, along the same side of the Strip as the MGM and just around the corner from our motel. There were only four and a half other people in there at the time; a white guy with long dreadlocks sat in a booth nodding his head before a plate of balls, which on a second look I could see were donut holes. A fat woman eating a plate of crepes was sitting beside a stroller. Her baby looked at me, as if to say, *I don't know why I was born either.* A couple in the corner were *Lady-and-the-Tramp*-ing on a churro.

Paisley put her shades down, nudging me.

'Hey, look,' she whispered. 'They're feeling each other up under the table.'

I looked, more fool I. She giggled and studied the lit-up donut menu above the counter.

'Yes please, what can I get you?' said the sweaty, harassed guy behind the counter. As far as I could see he had no reason to be harassed. It wasn't exactly busy.

'Can I get one of every single donut please?' asked Paisley.

'Every single one?' the guy repeated.

'Every single one,' she said, smiling. 'In fact, let's make it two of every kind.' She looked at me beneath her shades and whispered, 'Follow my lead.'

'What?' I said, still a little distracted by the couple in the corner. I came round to discover my sister had a sudden desire to be morbidly obese.

The guy started shoveling donuts into shallow white boxes labeled with the brown-and-green sunshine emblem of Doh-Nutty's.

'Two of every kind for the lady,' he said, looking up at Paisley and giving her the most unctuous of smiles.

Paisley smiled back. 'So how's business?'

'Pretty good,' the man replied. 'You know who comes here for her donuts?' He motioned to the huge billboard across the street, picturing some diva in a sparkly dress.

'I thought she was on low carb?' said Paisley in mock shock.

'Not anymore,' said Doh-Nutty, shoveling in two Double Chocolate Fudge Melts into an almost-full second box and closing the lid.

'Wow,' said Paisley. 'She musta gone back to the trusty two-finger up-chuck. Must be good publicity for you, though.'

The man nodded and smiled, scooping up two Blueberry Whites with sprinkles and two Glazed Maple Creams for the next box.

She nudged my hand. Her eyes glimmered, cheeks flushed with excitement, just like when we were kids.

'Put your shades on,' she told me.

'Why? What are you doing?'

'There you go,' said the man, placing three Doh-Nutty's boxes on the counter. 'Thirty-two donuts plus sales tax equals thirty-six, seventy-five.'

'Cool,' she said, fumbling behind her. 'But I think I can do better than that.' And I watched as her hand dipped inside her bag and pulled out this shiny silver gun. She pointed it right at Doh-Nutty.

Doh-Nutty stared at her in horror, his little ball of chewing gum falling out onto the counter beneath him with a clunk.

'No, please,' he begged, moving backward and fumbling with the key on the cash register. The drawer popped open and he scrabbled around, handing a wad of bills to Paisley.

The Twizzler guy in the corner stood up but made no attempt to come forward.

'It's okay. We don't want the money,' Paisley told the man. 'We'll just take the donuts.'

Doh-Nutty fumbled again with the cash drawer and backed away with his hands up.

Paisley nodded to me to take the boxes and looked up at something behind the counter.

''S that a camera you got up there?' she asked the man. He nodded.

'Can you get sound on that?'

He nodded again, more vigorously.

She looked up and blew the camera a kiss. 'We love you, Dad,' she called out. And as she opened the door for me and pushed me out with the donut boxes, she turned back to

Doh-Nutty and said, 'When they ask you what happened, tell 'em the Wonder Twins did it. You got that?'

'W-wonder T-twins,' he stammered.

Then she smiled at him and walked out as calmly as she had walked in, pushing the gun inside the waistband of her skirt. And I walked beside her, staring, waiting and hoping I was dreaming, trying to keep up and desperately holding onto the three boxes of donuts.

I did this all the way back to the motel. On the way we saw a hobo searching through a trash can. Paisley gave him the top two boxes of donuts with her compliments. Then we walked inside the motel with the last one.

She went straight in, threw the room keys on the desk, and shut herself in the bathroom. I set down the one remaining box of donuts on my nightstand and turned on the light. I heard the flush go. Then she came out, sat on her bed and began looking through the TV guide.

'Is that Goldie Hawn movie on tonight? The one where she falls off the boat and gets amnesia? I love that movie.'

'YOU HAVE A FUCKING GUN ON YOU?' I yelled at her. 'HOW LONG HAVE YOU HAD A FUCKING GUN ON YOU?'

'God, turn your CAPS LOCK off, Beau.' She sighed. 'I knew you'd be like this.'

'How do you expect me to be, Paisley? I mean, am I dreaming? Is this some kind of sugar-induced absurdist nightmare? That's a real-assed gun and you just pulled it on a guy selling donuts!'

'Yeah but not 'cos I wanted to hurt him. I just want to get

- 138 -

us on those news Trons. Like the one outside Caesars. Anyway, it was your idea.'

My mouth was too energetic to find the right shape for my words. I paced the room. 'My ide … wha … ha … what was my idea?'

'You said when we were lost in those woods, we ended up on every TV station in Jersey.'

'And …?'

'We're lost again, Beau. We can't find our dad.' She stood up. 'We need him to see us. To see that we're okay. He doesn't even know we love him. Skank has poisoned his head with all her crap. I want him to know we care.'

'How is pointing a gun at someone going to show him we care? Did you see how scared that guy was? Jesus Christ, Paisley. You're not Al Pacino.'

She put her hands on my shoulders and I shook her away. She grabbed onto me and I tried shaking her off again but she held on.

'Listen to me, Beau, dammit.'

I stopped.

'There's no point breaking your crayons over this, okay? This makes sense. If this makes the news, we'll get ourselves on those screens, on that screen outside Caesars where we know he hangs out. Dad will see us. He was watching the Tron before Coupon Guy started on him. We get famous, we'll be one step closer to finding him.'

'We'll be one step closer to prison, Paisley. Can't you see that?'

'God, when did you become such a prude?'

'I don't know. Maybe the same day you slipped down into the moral abyss?'

She started to protest again but I didn't care what she had to say. There was no excuse. She was making us another crime statistic. And I didn't want to be what everyone expected me to be. I didn't want any part of it.

She sat on the end of the bed and just looked at me.

'Can't we just keep going down to the Tron and see if he shows up?'

'Too hit and miss. And we'll probably always miss. This way, we can really put ourselves out there. We get a snappy little slogan, maybe even uniforms. We rob a few small-time places—donut shops, candy stores, bakeries. That frozen-custard place off the Strip that we walked past the other day. Places people don't expect anyone to pull a gun on them. We're polite, we don't hurt anybody, we take the shit, we leave our message and we go. And then we come back here and wait for it to hit the news.'

I didn't say a word.

She leaned back to pull the gun out of her waistband and put it on the end of the bed.

'Maybe we could graffiti that giant M&M outside the M&M store or something. Kidnap him for a ransom. Ten million M&Ms or Big Red gets it,' she laughed.

I didn't laugh. I just looked at the gun.

'I know how you feel about this, Beau,' she said. 'You don't wanna hurt people. You don't wanna rob people. You don't wanna be one of those clichéd off-the-rails teens. Like me.'

I went to say something but she interrupted.

'But we'll be doing this for one reason: to find Dad. Or at the very least, to let Dad find us. We can get our message to him that we're okay and that we love him.'

'By putting a gun in someone's face and stealing their livelihood,' I told her slowly. 'No, I'm not doing it. No way. There has to be something else we can do. Where the hell'd you get it anyway?'

'Skank's nightstand.'

'It's Virginia's?'

'Yeah, and it's not even loaded. Today is the first day I've even taken it out of the motel. I don't know, I just … wanted it with me today. I thought it would come in useful after Steve the Texan pervert. And it did, didn't it? Besides, I gave away the other two boxes of donuts to that hobo, didn't I? That was a kind thing to do. Steal from the rich and give to the poor.'

I got up and went to the window. 'That Doh-Nutty guy wasn't rich.'

'No.' She got up and stood beside me at the window. 'But when we're famous, he'll get some good publicity out of it and we can pay him back that way. His place'll be jam-packed. He'll be busier than a one-legged man in an ass-kicking contest.'

I shook my head. 'Oh man. This sucks out loud.'

And that was when she started to get angry. 'Put it this way, Beau. You can stay here and keep working your whole Jesus of Suburbia thing if you want, but I'm going. I am doing this. You're either with me or you're not.'

'Not,' I said, turning away from her and slumping down on my bed.

'Fine,' she said. She picked up the gun and tucked it in her skirt, then pulled her shirt out over it, grabbing the room keys from the desk and heading out the door. The door slammed.

I waited a couple seconds. She was definitely gone. I sat up straight and felt my heart thudding, pounding through every section of my body. She had really gone without me. Stay put, I told myself. I leaned against my headboard and just breathed for a while. I picked up the remote and flicked on the TV. There was a Dennis Quaid movie on and I tried losing myself in it but it was pretty bad. I switched it off and felt for stubble on my chin. I took my new disposable razor out my drawer and shaved over it, just in case any stubble came through later.

I got up. I went to the bathroom and checked the mirror. My hair was an insane asylum of knots. I needed to get it cut. I had a little cluster of zits on my chin and bacon grease stains on my T-shirt. I turned the light out and went back to bed.

'Shit,' I said. I got up. 'Shit,' I said again and went to the door. My hand hovered over the handle. 'Shit.'

I walked out into the bright sunlight. And Paisley was standing right there, waiting for me.

'Took your time,' she said.

CHAPTER FIFTEEN

Paisley

Heading north along the Strip, outside Bill's
Gamblin' Hall

It's just like in that song. People really are strangest when
you're a stranger. Everyone does look ugly when you're on your
own.

I couldn't remember who sang it but I knew my dad used to
say it was a classic. And it was so true. I hadn't had one nice
thought since we'd lost Dad in the crowds. I hated everything.
The cowboy fat head who stood right in my path to gaze at the
pirate ships in the water. The dwarf on the walkway to the mall
who called me 'Babe' and asked me if I wanted a bottle of cold
water. The woman in the baseball cap who handed me a flyer

for a strip show. The skinny blonde with her phone on a diamond chain and her heels the height of pencils, who looked like she was headed for a pole-dancing audition. She was real thin. I looked down at my stomach. We had only been in Vegas six days but there was a definite new bulge that hadn't been there when we'd arrived. I pulled my T-shirt out over it, regretting the half-eaten pack of M&Ms in my bag. And the Rainbow Twizzlers in my pocket. And the giant Peppermint Patty.

After checking out the Caesars Palace Jumbotron area for Dad again, we headed for the mall next to the Treasure Island hotel complex. I had decided we needed uniforms.

'You mean a more cohesive statement of fashion sense while we rob people left, right, and center?' Beau had said. The whole way there he laid his guilt trip on me. He was right as usual and I needed to feel better about what we were doing.

'You know I'm not fully on board with this whole robbery thing, Paisley …'

'Yes, Beau,' I sighed, trying to three-bags-full him 'til he shut his pie-hole.

'I mean, it's just such a …'

'… brilliant idea of yours, Paisley?'

'… such a long shot. Think about it for a second. If we get caught, we could do time. Juvey. Or proper jail time, Pais. You know what they do to guys like me in prison.'

'That was in the olden days. They're more like summer camps now. You might get to do canoeing and stuff.'

'I don't care, I don't wanna find out. I don't wanna get caught.'

'We're not gonna get caught.'

'How do you know? Something could go wrong. Someone could get shot.'

I was sweating. 'Beau, for the eighth time, it is not loaded.'

He squinted in the sunlight and screened his eyes with his hand to look at me as we walked. 'How do you know they're not going to hit back? Everyone carries a gun these days. What if they pull a gun on us, what's the big plan then, huh?'

'So the guy who works part-time at Licky's Ice Cream Parlor is gonna pull his Glock out on me just 'cos I don't pay for my frozen custard? Gimme a break, Beau. I told you, they won't be expecting it.'

'You don't know for sure.'

I knew one thing for sure. I had about one nerve left and he was getting on it. But I couldn't help noticing this little tiny sting somewhere inside me. Beau was right and I knew he was right. And him pointing out all the itsy-bitsy things that could go wrong had kinda weirded me out. If I was on my own, I wouldn't be thinking twice. Beau made me think twice.

'We'll cross here,' I told him, stopping at the crosswalk.

'If you say so,' Beau mumbled.

The mall was a little further up the Strip on the other side and by the time we got there, I had managed to steer the conversation over to what outfits we were gonna wear in order to rob people.

'Jeans and T-shirts just make us look like ordinary teenage hoods,' I told Beau. 'I've been thinking about maybe a black-and-white theme, to pick up on the whole Eclipse thing of the gun.'

'Genius,' he mumbled, looking down at his feet as we went up the steps to the huge mall entrance.

I looked at him. 'It is, actually. We wanna get noticed, we gotta wear stuff that stands out. Ordinary stuff just won't work. Bonnie and Clyde had an image.'

'We are NOT Bonnie and Clyde, Paisley. *We're* not carrying guns, *you* are.'

'Whatever …'

'And Bonnie and Clyde killed people. We're not gonna kill people. And anyway, their image wasn't an image, it was just how people dressed in the twenties.'

'Thirties,' I corrected.

'How do you know?'

'It was one of Dad's favorite films. It's one of mine too.'

Beau looked away. I just wanted to shake him and say, Look, we're doing this whether you like it or not so just DEAL WITH IT. But I didn't. Somehow I reined in the old Paisley tendency to shout first, ask questions later. Instead I ignored it and tried to bolster my argument.

'Look at those guys who climbed the Lincoln statue. The dads who wanted to see their kids. They got their message across. They were dressed as superheroes. We gotta have a "thing." An image.'

Beau pushed the door and went in first. I heard him mumbling again but I chose to ignore it before the steam shot out of my ears.

I thought a mall in Vegas would be different to one in LA or Jersey, but it wasn't. I don't know what I was expecting. Maybe more casinos, maybe some circus act on a high wire, zebras on skates, or a roller coaster weaving in and out of the stores. But there was none of that. It was like every other mall you ever saw. Cool from the heat, all white and marbled. Guys swept up your candy wrappers the second they hit the floor. Hip hop pumped out of music stores where happening young guys strolled with blonde bobble-heads with *Juicy* written across the asses of their sweats. Low-key bookstores or over-priced men's fashion houses lulled people in with soft jazz and cream couches. Naked gold mannequins and snakeskin purses in the windows of Oscar de la Renta and Cartier told me I shouldn't even darken their doorsteps, while Cinnabon and McDonalds were ready to welcome me with open arteries.

The entrance was on the third floor. We stopped at the balcony overlooking the second floor event area with its fashion show runway.

'Okay, meet you down there by that runway thing in two hours.'

'We're not shopping together?' he asked, looking mildly hurt.

'No. I'm gonna trust you to get your own stuff.'

'But I don't know …'

'Black-and-white theme, Beau. Use your initiative. Here …' I rifled through my pocket and pulled out the wad of cash left over from chumping Steve, the Texan pervert. I handed Beau roughly half of it. 'Black and white. Stylish. Cool. Go with that. Okay?'

He had this brow thing going on and wandered off, turning back to me, confused, as I shooed him away.

'Two hours,' I called out. He didn't look back.

I needed to not be with him. He was pissing me off to the nth degree with all his guilt-tripping. I wanted to be on my own, work stuff out in my head. I wasn't stupid. I knew what we were doing was risky, not to mention a long shot. Even if Dad *did* see us on the Tron outside Caesars, how the hell was he gonna get to us? I just wanted him to see me, even if I couldn't see him.

I went down to the first floor to a store called Little Madams and they had just what I needed. A white tunic dress which buttoned at the shoulders. I already had my long-sleeved black T-shirt so I slipped it on over that and took my jeans off in favor of black fishnets. My black Doc Marten boots set the whole thing off and I picked up a pair of white-framed shades from a little display case beside the cash register. I paid for it all and still had tons of money left. I mooched around the first floor for a while to kill time. Checked my emails on a laptop in the Sony store. Mostly spam. Tried some lip balms in The Body Shop. And just wandered. It was kinda boring without Beau. Even though he irritated my ass off sometimes, I felt wrong without him. Like in school. It was just wrong when he wasn't there. I went into a bookstore to check out the spines on the YA novels. A blonde girl about my age with black streaks in her hair was checking them out too, with her dad. He was going to treat her to one. I couldn't see anything that took my fancy and I'm not real big on vampires, so I left.

I headed next door to this pet shop, lured by the sound of yapping puppies. There were other animals around too, birds in cages, little mice on wheels, kittens all nestled into their mom in a small sheepskin pod, but I just sat and watched these little pups, about ten little blond guys in a large glass case. There was one lying down in the corner, not yapping at all. His head rested on his outstretched paws, just looking up at me, his brow peaked as if to say, What are you lookin' at? I'd plagued the life out of my dad for a puppy when I was little.

I thought to myself, Go on, buy it. What's stopping you now? No Dad to stop you, no school ties anymore. Buy that little chubby one in the corner. Pull the Eclipse on the sales girl and demand that dog. It'd be something to love.

But it didn't feel right. We're on the road. We're planning robberies. We have to be fast on our feet. It's not fair. He'd be a big responsibility. Who was that talking now? They weren't my thoughts. Must have been Beau's creeping in. Or Dad's. Or they could have been mine. I didn't know anymore.

I got out of there and made my way to the runway area and nearby smoothie kiosk on the second floor. All Shook Up, it was called. I bought a Blueberry Hill Power Pulp and sat down on the marble seat to drink it and wait for Beau. The Eclipse felt awkward in the deep front pocket of my new tunic. It didn't like it when I sat down. It needed to be straight against my body. I put my green jacket on and zipped it up in case it fell out.

Scatt's House was directly opposite the bench so I had no choice but to focus my attention on it. Scatt's was this so-say über-cool clothes store for preppy assholes, and half the stuff looked like it had come from a thrift store. I guessed it was meant to look like that: distressed. I was distressed just hearing the music they were playing. Some rapper shouting. Not my kind of music. I liked the stuff my dad used to listen to.

Timeless rock bands. Classic guitar riffs. Melodic geniuses. I didn't give a shit about hoods and bitches and bling.

There was a topless male model in stonewash jeans on the doorstep, welcoming people inside with squirts of cologne. It was a while before the smell hit me, but then I got it. The dry, clean, aftershavey scent of lemons and dry walling. I inhaled and closed my eyes. I knew that smell. I inhaled again. I felt funny. Like an open gate waiting for water to come rushing through. And right then it all came pouring back through me.

Me and Beau were in the basement of our house in Jersey. We were about five I guess and Mom had shut us down there. We always seemed to be doing stuff that pissed her off. I remember once we'd hid her purse and we both got hit across the backs of our legs when she'd found it in the washer. Another time she told us off for drawing on our newly-painted bedroom door and she had dragged Beau across the room by his arm until he'd cried. I yelled and yelled at her but she kept hitting him. I got so angry I pushed her. Not hard, but enough. She fell back against the door.

It was real dark in our basement and stank of damp and must and old broken furniture. Beau was scared of the dark—had been for, like, forever—so for a while we just sat together on the bottom step and held hands. I remember not wanting to move into the darkness in case I fell down a hole. I told Beau I wasn't scared.

Anyway, Dad came home early. He called out for us.

'We're here. Dad, we're down here,' we yelled out and we heard him jiggling the latch. We ran to the middle of the stairs and he was there at the top.

He ran down to us and squished us both tight.

'Oh guys, I'm sorry,' he kept saying. I can still hear it. He sat down on a step, me on one knee and Beau on the other and looked at our faces. His tears were streaming down, even though he was smiling.

'How long you been down here, kiddoes?'

'I don't know, Dad,' I said, hugging him again.

Beau put a little hand up to his cheek and smoothed away a tear. 'Naughty tear, you go home now,' he said and wiped it on his jacket.

Dad laughed. 'Is that right?'

'That's what you always tell me,' Beau said.

I buried my face into Dad's stubbly neck and clung on. And there it was; the smell of aftershave. The dry, clean smell of safety.

My straw slurped against the bottom of my cup. I tossed my cup into a nearby trash can and went on over to Scatt's House.

The half-naked aftershave model spotted me through the little clique of schoolgirls who had stopped to flirt with him. The smell was stronger. I couldn't get enough of it. 'Would you like to try, Miss?'

I looked at him. 'Uh, it's for men?'

'No, it's unisex.' He handed me a white card and sprayed the cologne on it at a distance. It wasn't exactly the same smell. It wasn't exactly Dad. But it was close. And I loved it.

'There's ten per cent off today …'

'No thanks,' I frowned, walking past him into the store. I

didn't want him thinking I was one of his groupies, though I did want to buy a bottle. Just a little tester that I could smell whenever I wanted.

I sought out an employee and walked right up to this short woman folding pink T-shirts at a table full of folded pink T-shirts. The shouty music was deafening and the place reeked of the not-really-Dad cologne the model was spraying.

'Excuse me, what's the name of that cologne …?'

She didn't even look at me, just carried on chewing her gum and folding her T-shirts. 'We don't have anything black here.'

'I'm sorry?' I said.

She still didn't look at my face and carried on chewing. 'And you can go tell your little goth friends outside that if any more of you come in here looking for their wrist-slitting uniforms, I'll call security.'

'Oh …' I said, totally cave-faced.

'Mm hmm,' she said dryly, looking over my threads before going back to folding her T-shirts. *Chew chew*.

Okay, so I was wearing black pantyhose and boots, but my dress was white and my jacket was green. And my hair was blonde. How fucked-up is that? And anyway how rude was she? If I *had* been a goth I'd have bitch-slapped her good and plenty.

I decided to leave, turning around and mumbling about her being in the wrong job, when I stopped. I couldn't let it slide. I turned back. 'What's with the 'tude?'

She actually looked me in the eyes then, still chewing. 'All day I've had kids coming in here asking for black this and black that. I'm tired of it.' *Chew chew*.

'I'm wearing white. And I don't wanna slit my wrists. I just want some of the goddamn cologne that Brad Pitiful has out front, if you don't fucking mind.'

Her face dropped like a bag of wrenches. I followed her eyes. My green jacket had shifted. My gun was sticking out the pocket at the front of my tunic.

I smiled. 'This is what I gotta do to get some respect around here, is it?'

She stared at me. She gulped something down. Her gum.

'So where's the cologne?'

She didn't take her eyes from it and stepped backward, scrabbling around for a small box on a display table near the cash register. The T-shirt she had been folding dropped to the floor. She handed a box to me. 'Take it.'

I took it. 'Thanks. Try to be a little more fucking helpful next time, huh?'

'Please don't …'

'And ask your manager about getting some black stuff in. Seriously. If that many people are asking for it, maybe you got a little gap in your market.' I motioned to the cologne. 'Thanks bunches.'

So I strode on out, giving the model a dirty glance as I did, and went on up to the third floor, feeling mighty pleased with myself, bolstered by the Eclipse once again. As I reached the top of the escalator, I saw Beau coming out of Dude Wearhouse.

He looked unbelievable. Like some kind of model, striding out of there with his jacket slung over his shoulder and one hand in his pocket. Confident. Deadly sexy. Ugh. He was my brother! But he looked absolutely not my brother. To kick things off, he'd had his hair cut so I could actually see his face. It was slicked back and flicked out a little behind his ears. He looked super flashy. Stylish. White shirt, black waistcoat, black pants. His skin glowed. His baseball boots shone. He'd gotten new Chuck Taylors. We're talking *Vogue*. We're talking rock star.

'Oh … my … God,' I said, smiling. 'What did you *do*?!'

He smiled. 'What do you think? Is this what you meant? I tried to be mostly black but my shirt's white. I got some new white laces, though.' He looked behind him in a store window to check his hair.

'Beau, it's so … not you.' I couldn't think what to say. He put me to shame a little, what with my cobbled-together-in-under-five-minutes ensemble from Little Madam's. And I already had black pantyhose so all I'd really bought was my white tunic and shades. He'd had the works and then some.

'I got the full prom king treatment in the salon on the top floor.' He gestured toward Dude Wearhouse and chuckled like a little kid. 'And the guys in there fixed me up with a suit and tie. I kinda spent a lot, though.'

'That's okay. I kinda spent a little.' I pulled him aside to the balcony so I could keep an eye on what was happening down below at Scatt's.

'You look cute, Pais. Real cool.'

I patted his hair at the front. It was rock solid. I wrinkled my nose up.

Beau sighed and put his bags down. 'Go on.'

He smiled. I loved how well he knew me. I rolled up his shirt sleeves and loosened his tie a little. Then I tried to mess up his hair a little at the front.

'Hey!'

'It's okay. It needs to be less rigid, more just got out of bed. There, *now* you're über-cool.'

'What's über-cool?'

'Freezing,' I said, which he seemed happy with. He turned to check his reflection again in the window.

'Hey, what do you think of this cologne?' I asked him, opening the box I got from Scatt's and spraying a little into the air before him.

Beau sniffed the air. 'It's okay.'

'Remind you of anything? Of anyone?'

He shook his head. 'No. It's good though. Can I?'

I handed it to him, a little bummed that it didn't remind him. A security guard ahead was speaking into his CB radio and looking around.

'You been busy,' I said, slipping my green jacket off and folding it into one of my bags.

'Yeah,' he smiled, picking up his bags. 'I got these cheap canvas totes from Hot Topic. They got rock band names on 'em but it doesn't matter …'

'You don't like rock bands. What do you want with those?' I rooted blindly in my bag for a scrunchie and tied up my hair.

He stared at me, like some alien had landed on my face. 'For the swag. To put what we steal in.'

'Oh yeah,' I laughed. 'I didn't think of that, Beau, well done.' I put on Beau's suit jacket over my white dress.

'Nah, that doesn't look right over your dress,' he said, 'take it off.'

A security guard ran past me at that moment. He had his radio held up to his mouth and I heard this scratchy but distinct voice say '… long blonde hair, green jacket …' He headed for the moving staircase.

I guessed he was on his way to Scatt's House. I started making for the exit and Beau followed my lead.

'So you're finally on board then, are you?' I said. 'No more questions and worries and giving me shit over doing this?' I said, glancing behind me as we walked.

'I'm not on board. It's still hare-brained. I just figure that if we're going to do this, we should be prepared.'

'Good. See, your old boy-scout days are paying off at last.' I could see the automatic doors of the entrance far ahead up the white marble walkway, the sunlight from outside, blinding, like it was the gateway to heaven.

'The lady said I looked sexy.'

'What?' I said.

'In Dude Wearhouse. She said I looked sexy.'

I looked at him and snickered. He blushed.

I picked up my pace, glancing behind me. 'Where are your shades?'

'Right here,' he said, putting all his bags in one grip and grabbing his shades out of his front pocket with the other. Totally black. Totally cool. 'Why are we going so fast, Pais?'

'Put them on,' I told him, pushing down my own white-framed shades off the top of my head.

'Why?' he said, a little out of breath now. 'Are we going to go for it? Now?'

Another security guard ran straight past us, followed by a

second. I watched from the balcony as the first one went into Scatt's House below us. The exit was in sight and the light from outside was dazzling.

'Yeah. But not here. We'll try the frozen-custard place off the Strip.'

'I thought you wanted to do M&Ms? Or that candy store on …'

'Beau, we gotta dip out. A.S.A.F.P. I did something.'

Beau's face darkened like a little cloud had appeared above his head.

'Paisley? What did you do?'

And then I grabbed his arm and we started running.

CHAPTER SIXTEEN

Beau

North Strip, toward Circus Circus and
Stratosphere

I wasn't listening. I was too preoccupied with running as though my life depended on it. Sweat streamed off me and my new white shirt was soaked on the back and under the armpits. My side ached. I thought I was gonna cough up blood.

'I saw it on YouTube,' Paisley panted as we ran. 'The fathers who hung … this banner at the Lincoln Memorial.' We were clear of the mall and heading toward the very far end of the Strip, our boots pumping on the sidewalk, dodging tourists, looking behind us, running faster.

'What?' I heaved, a biting pain in my side. I had to stop and bend over. Little droplets fell from my forehead onto the sizzling hot sidewalk.

Paisley stopped too but stayed upright, her hands on her hips. 'They've gone. We're okay. But … do you see what I'm saying? "We are the Wonder Twins, tell Buddy we love him" is too long for a slogan. I'll forget half of it.'

'So … we need to shorten … our slogan. 'S that … what you're saying?'

There was a rank of stores behind us and a bus stop with an old dude in a coat huddled up in the corner. A tacky souvenir shop, a tattoo parlor and a wig-maker's.

'We could make a banner,' she suggested. *Pant pant.* 'Something written down. Spray paint?'

'We can't spray paint people. I draw the line at vandalism.'

'Oh, you draw the line?' she mocked, wiping her forehead.

'Yes. We're not causing any more … damage than we have to.'

She muttered under her breath, and then did a double take at one of the shops. 'There's a Kinko.'

'Huh?' I grimaced.

'A copy place.'

'You wanna print flyers or something?'

'Why not?'

She started walking toward it, and I pulled her arm back. She tugged it away, frowning at me. I let go. 'People will just think it's a publicity stunt.'

'Well, it is, isn't it?' she said, and carried on walking.

As it turned out, though, we didn't get flyers. Paisley got a better idea. We got stickers. Hello My Name Is … stickers, about the size of a credit card. White with black writing, saying, 'Wonder Twins.' Two hundred of them.

'We'll just stick one of these on the counter each time,' she said, peeling one off its paper and attempting to stick it to my forehead. With all the moisture it just dropped off. 'So all we have to say is …'

'… tell Buddy we love him.' I nodded. I got it. 'Yeah. We could even sign them for people if we get famous.' It was either a genius idea or the longest shot in history. We'd rob these food outlets, unsuspecting little places selling stuff no armed robbers would ever wanna rob. Yet all of these places would have CCTV, potentially warning off kids and hobos trying to pull off sly little five-finger discounts. Paisley would do her thing, we'd run off without paying, leave the sticker and the message about Dad, and then go into hiding and wait for the heist to hit the news. The frozen custard place was just around the corner from the copy store.

'So, are we going for it then?' I said.

'Yeah.' She pushed her shades up onto her head, pulling her tote bag up to her shoulder from where it had slipped down.

Inside General Custards it was hustly and bustly and there was an explosion of color from the walls, floors and tables. It smelled of burned sugar and body odor and the song playing was scratchy with a hint of maracas. I wondered if the serving mama would hear us telling her to 'Stick 'em up' over all the noise.

An endless line of people stood waiting to order. I joined it behind Paisley, who didn't seem in the least perplexed by the people or the noise. She waited her turn, hands clasped before her, studying the overhead menus. They had every flavor sundae in the world: Butter Pecan, Strawberry, Marshmallow,

Peach, Cherry, Chocolate Brownie. There was the choice of hot fudge, chocolate sprinkles, whipped cream, nuts, and marshmallow blobbies, whatever you wanted on the top. Two little boys at one of the tables were having foot-high shakes.

There were some girls sitting around the counter by the window, scooping out frozen custard from little blue cups and huge waffle cones. I thought one of them was checking me out but I wasn't sure. I thought maybe she was waiting for someone. She had red hair. I saw her glance over at me.

I asked Paisley, 'You see those girls back there by the window? No, at the counter. Don't look. Are any of them looking my way?'

She peered over my shoulder. 'No,' she said nonchalantly, going back to looking at the menus. 'Why? You got a chubby for any of 'em?'

'No,' I said, feeling my cheeks glow. 'One of them looked over when we walked in.'

'Probably waiting for someone.'

Zzrak! The electric fly killer claimed another victim. The staff shouted at each other in Spanish.

'That one on the end, with the red hair. She looked at me. Twice.' I looked slowly behind again. We caught each other's gaze and she turned away.

Paisley saw it too. 'You're right. She is checking you out. Why don't you go and put the moves on her?'

'You think I should?'

'Sure. Now you've had your makeover, your junk's bringing all the girls to the yard.'

We were next in line to be served behind a woman who

must have had fifty kids out waiting in the car. She spent like sixty bucks. I had a wedgie, but I didn't dare try and pluck it out with the redhead watching. I looked back at her. We locked eyes again. She smiled. I smiled. Wow! I couldn't believe it. I'd always imagined having a girlfriend and doing stuff that couples do together. Not gross stuff. Stupid stuff really, things couples take for granted or don't even think about. Holding hands. Sharing a milkshake. Buying birthday presents. I never had that. But I could see it all happening with this girl. I could see our future like a rainbow-colored bubble on the air. I'd be such a good boyfriend, I thought. I prepared myself to go over to her, checking my hair, straightening my clothes.

Paisley spoke to me through gritted teeth. 'Stop fidgeting. You gotta be cool now. We need to make a good impression for the news.'

'She's cute. I should go over,' I said. 'I'm gonna go over and just say hi.'

Paisley elbowed me in the stomach. I *oomphed* and bent forward to relieve the pain. 'You're not going anywhere,' she said. 'We got work to do.'

'Why'd you do that, huh?' I groaned, guarding myself in case she did it again. I looked back. The redhead was still there, smiling into her custard. She'd seen me *oomph*. She was laughing at me. 'I can't go over now. She thinks I'm stupid.'

Paisley turned and brought her face up close to mine. We were exactly the same height. She said it slowly and quietly. 'We're about to commit armed robbery and all you can think about is picking up chicks. What's wrong with this picture, Beau?'

Zzrak! Another one bit the dust.

Our grandmother would say exactly the same thing to me all the time. *What's wrong with this picture, Beau?*

'That really hurt, Paisley. Totally embarrassing …'

'Can you please just shut your pie-hole and keep focused?' said Paisley. 'We can see about getting you laid afterward. You've waited sixteen years, what's another hour?'

I gave her my filthiest look. 'Paisley.' She paid no attention.

Waiters rushed out from kitchen doors with double triple quadruple chocolate custard sundaes and Belgian waffles dabbed with melting balls of frozen custard. The guys all kinda looked the same and the way the woman was ordering them about in Spanish from the counter gave me the impression they were her sons.

'It's gettin' real busy,' Paisley noted. I didn't say anything.

The waiters ran around the tables, filling coffee cups, clearing dishes, flinging themselves in and out of a swinging door, taking orders, while others banged and shouted in Spanish in the kitchen beyond. One dude hurried through wheeling a large refrigerated box, ushering the line of customers out of his way.

'Jeez,' Paisley whispered, leaning back toward me. 'Now they gotta do a heart transplant as well.'

I didn't laugh. She always did that, pissed me off then tried to act like nothing had happened and make me laugh. She could say some pretty hurtful stuff and I never deserved it. Like just then. She knew how much I hated even mentioning that I was a virgin. I wore my inexperience like an albatross around my neck. I hated even saying the word 'virgin.'

'You ready?' she whispered back to me.

I didn't answer.

'Beau?'

'Yes,' I spat back. My chest had begun to throb. The woman in front paid and moved away with her eight gallons of custard. I knew what was gonna happen next. I looked behind for the redhead. She had gone.

'Next please,' barked the short, sweaty server lady.

My sister stepped up. 'Yeah, can I get four gallon buckets of custard; one chocolate brownie, one pistachio, one French vanilla, and one mint.'

'You want blobbies? Chocolate chips? Jimmies? Nuts?'

'No, can I get some of those rainbow sprinkles on all of them, please?'

The woman was on it before Paisley had finished speaking, sliding back metal doors on freezer cabinets, clattering plastic buckets, hollering into the back for help. A short man with two large facial moles and pit stains appeared and started flicking switches on machines and shoving the containers underneath the taps. The four buckets were placed on the counter. The ice crystals in the custard sparkled like daylight stars before the woman flung some rainbow sprinkles on and snapped the lids down shut.

'Forty-seven ninety-five,' she barked.

Paisley reached into one of her front pockets, muttering that she could never find her wallet when she needed it. The woman shifted around on her feet, her palm flat out for the money.

Paisley pulled out the Eclipse. 'Tah-dah!'

The woman froze.

'Beau, take the buckets.'

I'd frozen too. I couldn't get used to seeing her with that gun. It was pointed directly at the woman's chest.

'Nobody move!' Paisley ordered, sweeping the Eclipse around the whole place, back and forth like she was scattering sugar. 'Nobody say anything or do anything.'

A girl screamed at the window counter. A baby hollered. An old man gasped. One waiter sank to his knees. Some kids our age in a booth were recording it on cellphones. Another waiter approached us, and it looked for a second like he was gonna be the big hero and wrestle my sister to the ground. Paisley zoned in and he stopped in his tracks.

'TAKE THE BUCKETS,' Paisley yelled. I grabbed hold of the plastic handles and fumbled around for the canvas totes I'd bought. The buckets just fitted inside them, two a piece, but they were heavy. Real heavy.

'It's done,' I said, and backed out of there, pulling the door open and standing with my back to it to wait for Paisley.

She was doing her piece to camera and had a sticker peeled off ready. She ordered the woman to put her hand on the counter and stuck the sticker on top. We backed away. Paisley stopped and blew a kiss at the kids with the cellphones. They smiled in stunned awe.

'ANGELO!' The woman screamed.

'Okay, go, GO!' Paisley shouted, pushing me out and stuffing the sheet of stickers, minus one, inside her tunic pocket. Outside and along the street we ran. I looked back. The short man with the moles was running after us, shouting, calling us names in Spanish and cursing. I heard *'Policia'* and I picked up my pace, encumbered somewhat by all the bags.

Paisley stalled to take one of the totes from me, shoving the gun inside, and we carried on running.

'Jeez, they're heavy.'

'What did you expect?' I shouted, looking back for signs of Angelo. He was distant but he was still in hot pursuit. 'What the hell do we want with four gallons of frozen custard? It's all gonna melt before we eat it.'

'It's not about the custard, is it?' she yelled back at me, over-taking. The lid had come off one of the custard tubs in my tote and it was leaking through the fabric, streaming custard behind me in vanilla ribbons. We were headed back down the Strip toward our motel, crossing roads without warning, paying no heed to the cars who had to brake hard and honk at us, nor the tourists we had to shove past, wetting their legs with our leaking bags of custard. My chest heaved, my feet hammered the steaming concrete, my head ran with sweat, my mouth poured with *sorry*s and *excuse me*s.

Boomph!

I didn't see it until I was on the ground. Well, *we* were on the ground.

'Oh my God, Beau!' my sister laughed breathlessly as she U-turned and grabbed my arm to help me up. The giant red M&M lay there on the sidewalk, its legs floundering. 'Get up,' she said, still laughing as she pulled on my arm. My legs were in shock; I couldn't stand up. People had gathered around. A blonde woman in a yellow M&M shirt came running out of the store to see what was happening. She bent down and put her hand on me, asking if I was okay.

'He's fine,' Paisley chuckled as I got to my feet. 'Come on.'

'I'm sorry,' I yelled back, still grasping my bags of melted custard.

We had to get off the Strip. We were too conspicuous so Paisley found us a nice dirty backstreet to run down which she swore would lead to the back of our motel if we followed it right to the end. We dragged our sorry asses through the alleys the flashy Vegas hotels don't want the tourists to see. Concrete breeze blocks walled our escape, while broken glass, cardboard boxes and the odd mumbling-drunk hobo lined our route.

Paisley started walking. We reached the alley running alongside the back of our motel and I stopped to bend over and relieve yet another stitch in my side. I wanted to throw up. I gagged a little but there was nothing. So I just spat.

'That was a little close for comfort, sheesh!' she puffed, coming to a halt. 'Reminded me of that bit in Indiana Jones when he's got to grab his hat before the stone block comes down on him. If that Angelo had got his hands on you, you'd be toast, buddy.'

She threw her totes down by some trash cans and stepped up onto a pile of empty cardboard boxes to climb the wire fence.

I dropped my bags to the floor. 'Paisley, that whole thing was shit.'

She turned around, one leg on the top of the fence. 'That whole thing was … fu-larious! That M&M did not see you coming.'

'You're not listening to me. This ends now.'

'What does?'

'This whole effed-up situation. You pulling guns on families. Kids. Old people.'

'Not guns, Beau. *A* gun,' she panted, mounting the fence and jumping down to the other side. I scowled at her through the holes. 'What's up with you? You keep doing this brow thing …'

'I'm pissed, Paisley. If you can't see that …'

'I told you what we were doing. I gave you an out, you didn't take it. You're in this up to your neck now.'

'Not this. I didn't sign up for pointing guns at kids, Paisley.'

'I didn't point it at the kids.'

'No, you pointed it at their parents.'

'But did you see those kids with their cellphones? We'll be on YouTube this time tomorrow!'

'I don't care, alright? I don't fucking care.'

I looked away from her. I'd heard a siren in the distance. I looked back. Paisley had barely raised her eyebrows. She turned and started walking across the back lot to the motel. Then she stopped. She walked back to the fence. I hadn't moved.

'What, are you embarrassed because you tripped over an M&M?'

'No I'm not.'

'Then it's about that girl, isn't it? The redhead. You're pissed because you wanted to score and I wouldn't let you.'

'I don't wanna talk about it.'

'I think we've got to.'

'Paisley …'

'Beau, she was a cooz. Let's leave it at that.'

'Wha …?' I couldn't see straight I was so mad. 'I just wanted …' I kicked the stack of boxes again and again until my foot went straight through the side of one.

Her eyebrows were right up. 'All better now?'

I pouted. 'Leave me alone.'

She hesitated, then came closer to the fence. 'No.'

I didn't know what to say. I was just grabbing at words as they came to me.

'I just … it's so damn … all you can think about is Dad. Dad. Dad. Finding Dad. Gotta get to Dad. Even if it means we gotta make people afraid. Steal their stuff. I hate it. I hate this.'

'There's no alternative.'

'Yeah, you made that pretty clear.'

Paisley sighed, scuffing the broken glass and crumbs of concrete at her feet. 'Don't you wanna find him?'

I didn't answer. I thought about the redhead. 'I didn't sign up for this …'

She scratched her head and laughed. 'Why did you come with me, Beau? You thought about that? What was the alternative? Staying in LA as Grandma's little house elf? Getting beat on by kids in high school? Shutting yourself in your room reading weird French books and writing poetry? Hiding away?'

'You kinda burned my bridges though, didn't you?'

'You could've gone off on your own. I didn't force you. You willingly came along with me.'

'Yeah, more fool me.'

'Beau …'

'I just wanna be a normal kid. I want … a girlfriend. I wanna go to a nice school. Study. It's all I've ever wanted. Just … simplicity.'

'Yeah, well you're shit outta luck, 'cos you're my twin and I hate simplicity.'

I backed away from the fence and folded my arms.

Paisley moved toward the fence her side. 'If you'd have gone over to that redhead, she'd have ignored you, laughed at you to her friends and you'd have walked away feeling like the biggest loser in the world. I know girls like that. She was a butter face anyway.'

'A what?'

'You know. Okay body, but her face ...'

'For Chrissakes, Paisley.'

She came closer to the fence, until her forehead rested against the wires. 'Maybe General Custards'll make the news and we won't have to do any more stings. We can get on that screen and Dad'll see us and somehow we'll get to him.'

'How? How are we gonna get to him? Alright, so he might see us. What then, huh? What do we do then?'

'He'll know we love him ...'

'SO?' I shouted. I didn't mean to. It just came out. 'He won't know where we are and we'll be on the run. The longer we keep doing this, the more people who'll be after us. We'll have to leave. Go on the road. And we'll never find him.'

'I have to let him know that we still care,' she said, her finger going round and round inside one of the wire holes in the fence. 'Do you understand?'

I thought about Dad's letter. The one I kept in my back pocket.

Beau, I still think of you as this real quiet little boy. You're probably totally different now. I'd give everything just to see your face. Just to know how school's going. I remember you were real good at

English and I wonder if you still keep up your baseball. You were a great little pitcher even as a kid. I think you took after me. Your brown eyes and dark hair. It's the Italian in us Argents, or 'Argentos' as we were known once upon a time. Paisley takes after your mom's side—blue eyes, blonde. We had the best of both worlds with you two ...

'Alright, so it's a shitty plan,' Paisley said. 'But it's the only one we got. And when we get on that big old screen, then it'll be over. We can go out somewhere and celebrate. Whatever you want. Make some friends.'

I couldn't help smiling. The idea of Paisley making friends was just funny. I tried not looking at her but it didn't help.

'What's so fu-larious?' she said, all offended, pulling back from the fence. The little wishbone-shaped crease appeared between her eyes.

'Nothing,' I said, stacking the boxes again to climb over the fence. It took me a while. I wasn't as nimble as my sister and I was struggling. She offered to help me down but I didn't let her.

She stood there, one hand resting in the front pocket of her dress. 'Still best sister?' she said. We always argued the same way. Like a mini volcano going off and then nothing, nothing but ashes. She never apologized, just always said that. Still best sister?

'I guess,' I said to her, keeping a little distance.

CHAPTER SEVENTEEN

Paisley

Mandalay Bay shopping mall, south of
the Strip

Our next week in Vegas was hard and fast. It had to be. If all went to plan, our black-and-white uniforms would soon have us sticking out like two zebras trying to get into a parrots-only party, so the idea was to do as many stings as possible then ditch our threads. We bought another week at the Lucky Inn and made a plan.

And then we just did it.

We screwed over the Chronic Chocolate Company, Jellies from Heaven, a couple little cupcake places, Cookie Lookin', a churro stand and another ice-cream parlor, all on different blocks jutting off the main Strip. We'd do one a day, and when we were done we'd head back to our motel the long way round, through the back alleys, and lay low until the next morning. Every day we'd check the news. But every day, nothing. We steered clear of all the obvious places to hit, like M&Ms and Krispy Kreme, figuring they'd have super-duper alarm systems and automatic shutters, and only did one store on the whole Strip—Mandie's Candies in the Mandalay Bay mall.

The joint looked like Candyland on acid and was playing all these songs with "sugar" and "sweet" in the title. Fluorescent pink throughout, it had this annoying little squirrel motif everywhere with speech bubbles coming out of its mouth saying stuff like, *Try 'em, you'll like 'em!* and *Don't forget to brush yer teeth!* The store was near the back entrance to the complex and the nearest security guard was stationed at the far end of the casino, so by the time whoever was on the staff had alerted anyone we'd be long gone. It was an easy raid.

Claire the candy girl was pink, sweet-natured and helpful, and the store was empty, probably because it was eight thirty in the morning.

She got all upset when she saw the Eclipse so I tried to make her feel at ease, I really did. 'My, that fudge smells yummy. Can I get a bag of that too? Fresh, though. Don't try goofin' me with yesterday's.'

She helped us shovel little white bags full of candy noodles, chocolate-covered peanuts, raisins and raspberries, Jujubes, Lemonheads, Laffy Taffy, Tootsie Rolls, Mike and Ikes, Rainbow Twizzlers, Dum Dum Pops, and soft chunks of rum fudge. We got packets of fairy dust in lemon, strawberry and lime, small buckets of fizzy snakes, cola bottles, luscious lips, gobstoppers, gum and gummy bears that looked like little rubber jewels. We got rainbow twizzle sticks. Licorice bootlaces in black, green and yellow. Small tubs of flavored hot chocolate, so-say the *Best in the West*, and she even threw in a couple T-shirts saying *Mandie's Candies* for good measure. Pink for me, blue for Beau. Guess what, Beau didn't want one, so I stuffed it inside his waistband.

'It's free, Beau, just take it,' I told him.

'It's not free though, is it?'

As Claire was putting it all in bags, a tear fell from her eye and splash-landed on the counter.

Beau made for the door.

I leaned in. 'I'm not gonna hurt you,' I told the girl. 'You're doing great. Would you like a sticker?'

She looked at me, then nodded. I told her to put her hand out and pasted it down on top. 'There,' I said. 'Tell Buddy we love him.' She gave me the customary look of confusion and I followed Beau out of there with the bags.

On our way out of the back entrance to the hotel, we bumped right into this shock-headed rock dude in shades. I dropped one of the candy bags.

'Sorry,' he said, scratching his head behind his ear. I thought I recognized him. I think he was famous. He had on a sleeveless vest, and there was a really neat tattoo of a burning rose on his shoulder. It reminded me of the rose tattoo Mom had on her ankle.

He picked up the candy bag I'd dropped and handed it to me. I didn't feel like being nice back.

'Get an eye dog!' I snapped at him, pushing past. I didn't

even hear Beau apologizing on my behalf as he usually did. I don't think he said one word.

I felt bad then and I didn't know why. I'd been in a fairly good mood as we were robbing the crap out of that candy store. But now I felt all at sea again and that ain't easy when you're in the middle of the desert.

It was getting late in the day, the final day of our heists. Outside the Ace of Cakes, about a mile from the back of the Mandalay resort down Blue Diamond Road, I had another flashback, like the one I got about Dad when I smelled the cologne. This time it was about Mom. The shop front was full of the most unreal cake specimens I'd ever seen. A three-tiered carrot cake with tiny little carrots all round the edge over the frosting. Huge chocolate cream cakes. Sparkling fruit tartlets. Someone had worked real hard on making every single one just perfect for the window. At the back of the store was the wedding-cake section. A 'Love Me Tender' special with an Elvis statuette on top, standing before a little plastic bride and groom with a prayer book. Another cake, designed like two big red dice, had *Take a chance on me* written on the top in swirly writing. Others were made to look like huge poker chips or horseshoes. One like a cowboy hat, another like the MGM gold lion.

The cake I zoomed in on was at the bottom of the window in the corner. It was on special, I guess because it wasn't selling, a one-tiered sponge cake with pink frosting and covered in tiny marzipan strawberries.

It was our sixth birthday, one of the few days I remember our mom being our mom, not just some psycho drunk woman.

Mrs Wong's kids came over and so did some other randoms from school. Dad wasn't there so Mom was in charge. She managed to do us rainbow sandwiches like we'd asked and she even baked a cake. We helped her to frost it and put on the letters that spelled our names and a big '6' candle that went right in the middle.

Me and Beau were out in the backyard with our friends, wearing our Princess Leia and Luke Skywalker costumes, and we looked real cute. There's a photograph of us dressed like this somewhere but I guess all that kinda stuff was left at the house. Mom had tried doing the Leia buns in my hair but she couldn't do it so I just had pigtails. We had some real cool presents from our friends. Beau got a microscope and I got this Barbie hair-accessory kit with this little hairdryer and stuff, and a Moo Box which made everyone laugh when I kept turning it over, the way kids do, taking a good joke and stoning it to death. I ran inside to show Mom.

She was in front of the open drapes in the living room, head back, downing the dregs of a glass. She poured herself another. The banner above the doorframe had come down at one end.

'Y'all opened your presents?'

I nodded.

She went over to the mantel and put down the glass. 'What'd you get?'

'Barbie hair stuff. And this …' I tipped the box upside down and it made the moo noise. Mom didn't laugh. She just nodded and picked up the glass.

'And Mikey got Beau a detective kit with an invisible ink pen …'

'Go cut the cake now,' she said, looking at me over the top of her glass.

'Dad says we mustn't touch the knife drawer.'

'Dad's … not … here … is … he?' She said it very slowly.

I hesitated. I shouldn't have 'cos she started yelling.

'JUST GO AND CUT YOUR FUCKING CAKE.'

I ran into the kitchen. The back door was open. Everyone was gathered around Beau's microscope under the tree. I went to the knife drawer and took out the largest one I could find. My hands were shaking so much I had to use both to hold it. I cut everyone a raggedy little sliver and set them down on seven paper plates.

I cried when our friends went home. I get the same feeling every birthday.

'So are we doing this one as well today or what?' said Beau from the doorway, where he was putting on his shades.

'No,' I said. 'I don't wanna do any more today.' And I started walking back down Blue Diamond Road. The sun was just starting to go down but it was still hot. Damn hot and damn dirty. Flyers and candy wrappers clung to the soles of my feet as I walked. A couple yards down was a thrift store and we took the bags of candy and chocolate in there and dumped them down on the counter. The place was big and jumbled, like a Macy's sale, but gray and stinking of moldy vegetables. I held up my sleeve to my nose and breathed in the Nearly-Dad scent I'd sprayed there.

We approached the desk. 'Can you take these to some homeless shelter please?'

'Sure,' said the little hobbit guy, standing on tippy-toes to peer inside the bags. 'Ooh, candy. All this? Thank you.'

The odds were in his favor. He'd be dipping into that candy the second we left the store, I thought.

Beau piped up. 'Is the homeless shelter nearby?'

'Yeah, there's one down the street. It's between Paradise and Pebble. Would you like it all to go there?'

'Uh, yeah,' he said. And I could see the cogs whirring behind his eyes. 'You know what, we'll take it ourselves if that's okay?'

'No,' I said.

'Oh, well if you're sure …' said the Hobbit.

'Yeah. Thanks anyway.' On the way out, Beau was suddenly Beau again. 'This feels good, Pais. This actually feels like a lead. There's a shelter less than a mile away from where we saw Dad. He could easily be there.' After days of pissing and moaning over the robberies, he was almost giddy.

'He's not there, Beau, I'm telling you. He wouldn't.' I rummaged around in the Mandie's Candies bag for a Dum Dum Pop and pulled the paper off. Lemon.

Beau put his arm around me and squeezed, as though to inject me with some of his glee. I'd come over all emo since seeing Mom's cake in the window. I didn't miss Mom, it wasn't that. But that night, our birthday night, Dad had come home after work and he took us out for pancakes and we played kick-ball in the street. And it made everything okay again. That's why I'd forgotten Mom's outburst; Dad made me forget it. He was like magic. The thought of finding him in some homeless shelter with all these rejects was disgusting. But the thought of *not* finding him there made everything feel so much worse.

It was a long walk to the shelter and I knew we were getting near it because there were less and less tourists and more and more homeless people. Men bundled in blankets lying in doorways. A guy with no legs lying on the sidewalk by an upturned wheelchair. Some crackhead having a fight with an invisible man in an alley, screaming at the top of his voice. It was a kid, about our age.

Typically grim and grimy, the entrance to the shelter was like the box office in an old movie theater. A woman in a Plexiglass booth was reading *People* magazine, all dolled up like she was Cinderella in some shitty-assed pumpkin carriage. She looked up. She had large eyes, and even larger eyelids to cover them, caked in glossy purple eye shadow.

'Women's check-in is at four forty-five; men's at six o'clock,' she drawled. I took it she thought we were checking in.

'No, we're donating some candy,' Beau said, holding up one of the bags to show her. He was sucking on a Dum Dum Pop too. He'd gone for strawberry. 'And we're looking for somebody. Our dad. He might be here.'

'You don't want beds? If you just want a meal, dinner's served at seven …'

I pulled out my Dum Dum Pop. 'No we don't want beds, or dinner. We just wanna make a donation and see if our dad's here.'

'You can't just go in, Miss. Women's check-in is at …'

I scowled at her and nudged my brother over so I could speak through the hole in the Plexiglass. 'Four forty-five, yeah, you said. I don't *want* to stay here. I *have* a bed for the night.' I breathed out, trying to get rid of the poisonous anger that was building up in my lungs. I tried again. I even tried smiling as I dumped the candy on the desk. 'Do you have a list of inmates or whatever you call 'em? Could you just look up a name? Please?'

Beau nudged me back and leaned in to speak.

'His name's Buddy Argent. He might be under Michael Argent, though. If we could find him, you wouldn't need to put him up. We'd take him off your hands.'

He smiled real genuine at old Purple Eyelids, which actually stirred her into action. She started tapping on her keyboard and hit the space bar, looking briefly again at Beau. I watched him. There was a small but definite bat of eyelashes. He was playing her like a piano. I'd created a monster. But it was working.

'Yeah, here you go, Buddy Argent. Bed thirty-seven.' Beau looked at me. I looked at Beau.

'Oh. My. God.' We both stood there, white sticks in our mouths, mirror images of each other. *Suck on that.*

Purple Eyelids swiveled her chair round and produced a long chain out of her pocket that was tied to her belt. There were keys on the end of it and she found the right one to unlock her little booth. She didn't even say thanks for the candy, just shoved it inside and locked the booth up again.

'Follow me.'

I didn't dare get too excited. I'd been there before, preparing myself the whole way from LA to Spurina. I kept it at bay, like a puppy who just wants to lick your face.

We went through these double doors into what looked like a high school gymnasium, littered with metal-framed beds. On the bars at the end of each bed dangled collections of cherry and vanilla Magic Trees. They didn't make the place smell any better. It just smelled like cherry-flavored ass crack. Grizzled men in baggy sweats on stained mattresses looked up at us briefly before going back to sleeping, scratching, playing cards, talking with each other. I saw torn football jackets, T-shirts, patchwork blankets. One old guy in a Yankee cap was puking into a blue bag. I looked for the red shirt.

The beds weren't numbered, so I didn't know how she knew where bed thirty-seven was, but soon she brought us to it. On the far side, next to a door marked 'Women's/Family Rooms,' she came to a stop. A man was lying curled up with his back to us, like a big baby, wrapped in a muddy gray raincoat.

'Hey, number thirty-seven, wake up,' said Purple Eyelids, kicking the metal leg of the bed.

The man turned over and saw her. Then he saw us. It wasn't Dad. I threw my Dum Dum stick on the floor.

'I'll give you a coupla minutes,' she said, smiling at Beau and leaving.

The man had a green baseball cap on and turned it round so it was back to front on his head. 'Who're you?' he garbled, still half asleep.

'We're Buddy Argent's kids,' said Beau. 'And you ain't Buddy Argent.'

I was still slaloming down Mount Disappointment. I knew who the guy was, though. It was Coupon Guy from the day we saw Dad at the Deuce stop. I remembered the gruff voice and the stitched-up eye.

Coupon Guy sat up on his bed. He was fat for a hobo. He had a real-assed belly on him. I kicked at the brown paper bag by his bed. There was a stack of those coupon books behind it.

He leaned up on one elbow. 'Lookin' for Buddy, are ya, Princess?'

'Yeah, what have you done with him?' I said, all annoyed and foot-stampy like he'd hidden my teddy bear and I wanted it back.

'I ain't done nuthin' with him, Princess. I was just borrowin' his name.'

'Why couldn't you use your own name?' asked Beau.

''Cos I done that once before in here and they threw my ass out.'

'Why?'

He tapped his nose, as if to say, *That's for me to know*. 'What do you want anyway?'

'What do you think we want, we want our dad!' I yelled in his face. Beau stepped in and held me back. My hand went to the Eclipse tucked safely in my tunic. Beau's hand went on top of mine to stop me.

'Then I can't help you. I ain't him,' he grinned. Across the far side of the room, there was a clanging of metal. 'Now if you don't mind, I'm gonna wash up for dinner.' He started to untie the luggage straps which were holding up his pants. 'Unless there was something else …?'

'Do you know where he is?' said Beau. 'It's real important …'

'I might,' he said, getting up. He was about two feet taller than us and had a belly like a nine-monther.

'Leave it, Beau. I don't want this mooch's help,' I said, making to leave.

My brother grabbed my arm, force-whispering, 'Paisley, he knows Dad. We can find out where he is, get a message to him. We need this guy. He's our best bet.'

I shook him away.

Beau looked back to Coupon Guy and attempted a smile. 'If you know where he is or how we could reach him, we'd be real grateful.'

'How grateful?' He stroked his chin and pulled at the spiky hairs.

Beau shrugged. 'I don't know. What do you want?'

Coupon Guy looked at me. Then he looked back at Beau and scratched his chin. 'Oh I don't know. Maybe some dead presidents?'

Beau nodded. 'We have money. We could buy you dinner, you could tell us what you know.'

Coupon thought for a second. Then tied up his pants again and did the buttons on his coat. He smelled so strong of so much stuff. Cigarettes, gasoline, cabbage, whiskey, piss. If I'd had a lit match I'd have thrown it at him and done everyone else in the place a favor.

'Money, dinner, and I'll tell you where you can find him.'

Beau nodded like a little puppy. He picked up my Dum Dum stick off the floor and put it with his, tossing it into a nearby bucket which served as a trash can. 'Cool. What's your name?'

'Well, my name's Trenton. Trenton Anthony Ford. And you are?'

'Beau Argent. And this is my sister, Paisley,' he said.

Trenton's good eye zoomed in on me. I could feel my nose

twitch up in a sneer. 'Well, Paisley and Beau,' he said, picking up his brown paper bag, 'buy me dinner, I'll tell you what I know.'

We went to this yellow diner a little further up hobo street and Beau got the Early Nerd special: a warm pastrami sandwich with Swiss cheese and a chocolate shake. Trenton ordered a double short stack with bacon, eggs, sausage patties, syrup and whipped butter. I had to sit dead opposite his saggy old bung-hole so I just ordered a coffee.

'What's Dad doing now?' Beau asked. I kept my mouth shut for once as he asked Trenton all the questions. They were getting on like my grandmother's house on fire. But my top lip kept doing this little Elvis thing whenever Trenton's eye caught mine. I sat with my arms folded, leaning against the back of the booth, my stomach churning at his eating habits.

He had egg hanging from his chin. 'We hang out. Shoot the shit.' Every time he said an S word, he sprayed pancake crumbs across the table.

Beau nodded in understanding. He had eaten half his sandwich and pushed the plate across to me as a hint that I should eat something. I pushed it back. He hunched over his shake and started popping the bubbles on the top. 'How'd you end up on the streets, Trenton?'

His brown paper bag was on the floor under the table, out of the way. I wanted to know what was in it.

'Little woman kicked me out. I fooled around. You know how it is.'

'Did Dad talk about us?'

'Oh yeah. All the time. Talked about you two and your

mom. Said you were most 'portant things in the world to him. I saw him a couple days ago.'

'Yeah,' I said, slowly pulling the bag toward me with both feet. 'We saw him from the bus. You were giving him shit and he made off. We couldn't catch up with him.'

'Do you know where he went?' said Beau.

Trenton shrugged. 'He hangs around. Doesn't come in the shelter. He doesn't think he deserves to.'

That was so something Dad would say. He'd have much preferred to live out in the open on benches than admit he was destitute and go to a shelter. I bent forward, feeling around for the bag.

Trenton carried on eating his pancakes. I hadn't touched Beau's sandwich or my coffee.

'More coffee?' asked a waitress, appearing with a jug full of it. I looked at my cup and then at her. She just waited.

'No, I got floaties. I'm good, thanks,' I said. She had a lot to learn if she thought I was gonna leave a tip.

I continued with my undercover bag-opening attempts. Trenton was more focused on his plate.

I looked down. The bag was open. Something white. Something silver. Candy wrappers. A beer bottle. A lighter. Silver coins. Roll of police caution tape. Daredevil action figure still in the packaging. Something silver.

He was still talking to Beau. '... shit outta luck,' I heard him say. 'No one's gonna hire an ex-con with no fixed address, are they?'

I reached down into the bag. Tentatively at first, and then I had my fingers on it. I pulled it up, like a little crane pulling up a wreck from the ocean floor.

It was my mom's necklace.

I would know it in a mountain of jewelry. I liked playing with it when she was unconscious. I remembered not being able to open the clasp. I held it tight in my fist.

I pushed the bag back slowly across the floor.

'… my bet is he's still hanging round Caesars trying to get work.'

I flashed back to the other day. Coupon Guy and Dad arguing at the bus stop. He'd robbed him. He'd robbed my dad. That's why Dad wasn't coming back to the Tron. Trenton had told him to stay away from his patch.

I leaned forward, my eyes so sore it felt like they were being scored by a knife. 'Did he talk about our mom?'

'Yeah,' he said. 'Just how much he missed her and still wanted her back.'

'He seen her recently?' I said.

Beau looked at me. Trenton shook his head, slurping up a dangling, chewed lump of sausage. 'He wanted to get back in touch with her, though. Thought they could make a go of things. For you two …'

I dipped my head and thought. I came back up. 'Did he say why he left us?'

Trenton put another heaped fork into his face, probably so he could think up another lie. Then he just said, 'Sometimes dads just leave …'

I smiled, though I felt tears finally falling from my eyes. I couldn't hold them in anymore. Everyone has a limit. This was mine. This was definitely mine.

'Kiss me, Trenton,' I said.

'Huh?'

'Kiss me. I like to be kissed when I'm being fucked.'

Trenton looked at me. My bullshit shield was tingling all over. I shot up out of the booth and lunged at him.

'YOU FUCKIN' LIAR,' I shouted right in his ear, plunging his head down into his butter-soaked pancakes. 'You evil … fucking … leech,' and with every syllable I dunked him again. And again. 'How d'you like me now, Princess?' I shouted, and each time I pulled his head up there was more crap stuck to it.

It took every muscle Beau had to pull me off of him, then I marched out of there, the heat of the day bombarding my face from the air-con coolness of the diner. I left Beau trying to stem the *maître'd's* concerns and probably leaving twice what our bill came to. I kept walking, right to the end of the block, taking insanely deep breaths the whole way. The tears kept coming and coming and coming.

I soon heard quick footsteps running up behind me.

'PAISLEY!'

'Fucker,' I shouted. 'I should have choked him. BASTARD!' I shouted back up the street. 'God, why are people such assholes, huh? Why, Beau? Why are we being dicked at every single turn?'

'Alright, calm down. It's okay …' He held my wrists down like Dad used to.

I stopped. 'He doesn't know Dad, any more than he knows Mom. Didn't even know he was in jail.' I held up my fist. 'And he obviously didn't know the truth about this.'

Beau looked at me, then gently prized open each one of

my fingers and took the necklace from my hand. The chain tickled my palm as it went.

'Where did you get this?'

'From his bag. It's the necklace from Dad's letter. It's Mom's necklace.'

His eyes were going all soft and he started leaking tears too.

'I always thought it opened. I can't open it. Stupid fingers.' I wiped my cheek.

'Uh … I think you gotta slide it,' he sniffed, fumbling and rubbing it until unexpectedly it split open into two, like scissors' blades. Two little sections. A little child's face in each one: Beau one side; me, the other. Both grinning to show the little gaps in our top teeth.

'That was Dad's fault,' Beau smiled, his tears trickling down over his lips as he spoke. 'Too much candy.'

A memory flashed into my mind. Of me, tugging and twisting at that tooth and getting all covered in blood and spit. And of Dad, holding my head and reaching in to pinch it straight out with his finger and thumb.

And of the dollar Mom put under my pillow.

I leaned over to Beau and put my head against his and we looked down at it in his hands. And we both just cried and cried.

CHAPTER EIGHTEEN

Beau

Room 2, Lucky Inn Motel, the Strip

We went back to our motel. Neither of us wanted to do anything else. Paisley threw up. I didn't know if it was all the candy we'd been living on or the shock of finding Mom's necklace. Probably both. I was feeling a little sick myself. Our room looking like the refuse pile from Wonka's factory wasn't helping either.

Paisley hadn't once let go of Mom's necklace. The chain was coiled around her hand, the pendant gripped tightly in her palm. She came out of the bathroom and we lay on my bed with a bottle of this cologne Paisley swore smelled like Dad. We sat our stuffed toy owls, Two Wit and Two Woo, between us, and we talked into the night about everything. Stuff we didn't usually like talking about. The times O'Donnell and his gang had trash-talked or kicked the shit out of me at school. This Jason guy at Paisley's school in Jersey, whom she said meant nothing to her but who I could tell had broken her heart. Well, maybe not her whole heart, but he'd definitely bitten a chunk out of it.

I guess unless you knew Paisley really well, it was hard to tell when she was hurt. She liked to bury stuff kinda deep and pretend it didn't matter. But I knew. It could just be a look, a shrug, a fake smile. But I could see it. She talked about her counseling sessions. And I told her what had *really* been bothering me about doing the robberies – it was starting to feel like we were little again. Like we were in kindergarten or something. It was just like in that song from the dance machine.

And I wonder
When I sing along with you
If everything could ever feel this real forever
If anything could ever be this good again …

I was beginning to enjoy myself.

I couldn't hold the gun without shaking and I couldn't demand money from store clerks. But just watching my sister, yelling at her to run, us fleeing each scene, pushing past tourists and vaulting over wire fences to run back to the motel and eat candy on our beds. Even falling over that damned M&M. I felt part of something exciting again. I felt like I was a kid again.

'You better hope me and this O'Donnell guy at your school

never cross paths. Because if we do, I'll probably kill him,' she said.

'Yeah. And I'll probably let you.'

We talked about being lost in the woods when we were six.

'I don't remember much about it,' I said. 'Do you?'

Paisley was staring up at the ceiling, chewing on some of the blueberry gum from Mandie's Candies, the chain of the necklace still wrapped around her fist. 'Little bits. Waking up and just seeing leaves. All these leaves. Trying to find open sunlight. And this real tall tree that I couldn't see the top of. I remember going to pee behind it, and when I got back you were crying 'cos you thought I'd gone somewhere without you.'

I laughed. 'Yeah. Always the wuss.'

'No. You were a kid. We were both scared.'

'I don't remember you being scared.'

She looked at me and stopped chewing her gum. 'Yeah. You know me. Wouldn't give a fuck if I had a bag full of 'em.'

I looked at her. She had the oddest twinkle in her eyes.

She looked back up at the ceiling. 'I remember finding the Wonder Gummies in my coat pocket. We ate them that second morning. And I remember just walking and walking and my legs aching 'cos we never got anywhere. And just being so tired. But I knew we had to find Dad. And that if we found him, we'd be heroes. We'd find Dad and he'd save Mom and everybody would love us.'

'You really thought we'd be heroes?'

She nodded. 'The third night I gave up. You were asleep all the time so I was by myself. I cuddled up to you in this little burrow I'd made out of twigs and stuff and I just drifted away.

We musta kept each other warm.'

'Just like Hansel and Gretel,' I said. 'Still are I s'pose. Except we're leaving trails of stickers now, not breadcrumbs.'

'I guess.'

'I don't remember being found at all.'

'You were pretty out of it,' she said, levering herself up and hawking her gum toward the little trash can across the room. Amazingly it went in. She took a fresh one from the nightstand and began devouring it. 'I remember opening my eyes and seeing this giant above me with the longest legs that stretched up and up into the trees. I thought it was Dad at first. But he said, "My name's Officer Worley. You two are gonna be alright."'

'What happened then?'

'These two women cops got us orange juice that tasted like warm medicine, but it was the best drink I ever had in my life. Then we were put in the ambulance. They were saying all this stuff like, "Oh my God, I can't believe we found you," and "You two are all over the news. Everyone's so pleased you kids are okay." I just remember wanting Dad. And him not being there.'

She took the lid off the cologne and sprayed a little into the air. She sniffed and put the lid back on.

'If he hadn't been in jail he would have been at the golf club. You were right to go there, Pais.'

Paisley held out Two Wit to kiss Two Woo.

'You know what I finally realized?' I said.

'What?'

'You remember when Dad took us into the city? And we went to the Roosevelt and we'd play with Eddie and go up the stairs and eat candy and stuff …'

'Yeah.'

'They were casing the joint. Him and Eddie. And those two other guys.'

Paisley sat up and hugged her knees to her chin. I thought she was gonna call me a douche for even considering such a thought. She bit her bottom lip. 'I try not to think about it. I always tried to believe he took us there 'cos he wanted to show us the places he worked. He did it for us though, Beau. To get money for us.'

'Always sticking up for him,' I smiled.

She smiled. 'Like he was sticking up for us,' she said, then blew out her cheeks and spat up her gum in the direction of the trash can again. This time it missed.

'Great,' I said. 'I'll be picking that one outta my socks all day tomorrow.'

She chuckled. 'So did Hansel and Gretel make it back to their dad?'

'Um, yeah, in some versions they just find their way outta the woods and make it home. Others, they have to cross a river on a white duck.'

'A white duck, huh?'

'Yeah. A white duck carries them across the water on its back.'

'How come you know the different versions?' Paisley said, lying back down.

'I read 'em all. I went through a little phase of being kinda obsessed with it. I thought it was us. Because it is us, isn't it? We are those kids in that story …'

'Tell me it,' she said, closing her eyes. 'Especially the bit when Gretel pushes the witch in the oven. I wanna think happy thoughts.'

And as I recalled the tale of Hansel and Gretel, the stresses went out of her limbs and the wishbone crease in her forehead disappeared and she became heavy beside me. I couldn't switch my brain off as easily. I stared at the walls for a while before carefully reaching out to the nightstand for the remote. I pressed Power.

Someone was being sexy and dramatic on The CW. On the History Channel it was the biography of some saint. Discovery was in the ocean. Disney was something colorful and unfunny set in a diner. On HBO some shock-headed rock band was screeching live from Mandalay Bay. The seven o'clock bulletins were just starting on ABC, CNBC, Headline, Prime, CNN, The Fox Report and Eyewitness. Breaking news was the President's meeting with the Australian PM. I clicked back to Fox. Two old guys debating; one of them loved it, the other thought it 'deplorable and dangerous.'

I switched to *Fairly Odd Parents*. Paisley stirred and levered herself up.

'What time is it?' she garbled, rubbing her eye.

'Just gone seven. Wanna go get somethin' to eat?'

She nodded, a little blonde firework party dancing on the back of her head. 'I need a shower first.'

The bathroom door closed. I sat up and reached for the half-bottle of blue Gatorade that had been on my nightstand for a few days. I winced at the warm syrup as it trickled into my mouth. I twisted the lid back on and threw the bottle over to the trash can under the desk. It missed, but knocked over a stack of stale pretzels. I lay back again, feeling my eyes go heavy. I heard the water go on. I turned over and shut my eyes, my ass pressing down on the remote. *Odd Parents* turned into the news. It got louder too, and before I could find the remote to turn it down or off, I heard this …

… *Police still don't know who the duo might be or how old they are. They say they could be anything from sixteen to twenty-four. The pair are shown here on a surveillance tape robbing a Las Vegas candy store* …

That's when I looked up.

… *known only by their code name the Wonder Twins* …

'HOLY SHIT.'

… *Internet sites already set up in their honor, all trying to work out their curious message, 'Tell Buddy we love him.' Anyone with any information is being urged to contact the Las Vegas Police Department.*

Paisley came running out of the bathroom, all sudsy and wrapped in a bath towel, stinking of vanilla. 'What the hell …?'

I pointed at the screen like a loon, jumping up and down on my knees, barely able to get the words out. 'It's us. It's us, we're on TV. We made ABC!'

'You gotta be kiddin' me!' she yelled. 'Oh my God!'

The next news story was about premature babies.

'Try another channel,' she said. I hopped through the six news channels. Custody battles. Traffic reports. The latest CGI technology. Iraq. And then …

… *though it is still unknown why this M&M representative was knocked to the ground in such an unprovoked attack* …

'Oh my God, Beau! That's the M&M you floored! He's being interviewed on *Eyewitness News* for Chrissakes. We did that, we made that M&M famous!'

... Welcome back to CNN. Police in Las Vegas are investigating a series of robberies on bakeries and candy stores ...

'WOAH!' squealed Paisley, jumping on the bed. I turned up the volume.

... The duo, known as the Wonder Twins by the strange calling card they present at every crime scene, have been caught on security camera in retail outlets along the Las Vegas Strip. Holding this shop assistant to ransom at Chronic Chocolate Company, the female of the duo is heard shouting the words, 'Tell Buddy we love him,' before applying a Wonder Twins sticker to the assistant's hand. The duo leaves every scene with chocolate bars, cakes, or candies before disappearing. It is thought they are still in Las Vegas and aged between sixteen and twenty-four. The public is warned not to approach either member if seen, but to contact Las Vegas police immediately ...

'I can't believe it,' I said. 'I just can't believe it!'

No other channel was carrying our story, or if they were, we had missed it. The two biggest national news channels were, though. NATIONAL news!

'Okay. Okay,' I said pacing the floor, trying to be decisive but having absolutely no idea what to do. I stopped and bit my nail. 'What do we do, Pais?'

She was staring blindly at the TV screen, in a little daze. 'I need to get some clothes on and rinse my hair.' She snapped out of it. 'We gotta get down to the Jumbotron. See if he's there. See if he's seen it!'

I could feel my face fall. Of course, Dad. He was the reason we were doing this. Not just to get on the TV, to find him. Didn't I want to find him? Yeah, of course I did. I think. I liked it being just us for a while, together again, no friends or grandmothers or schools getting in the way. I didn't know what I wanted. It felt good to be on the news, though. Really good. I looked cool in my shades, in my uniform. I looked good.

We couldn't wear our uniforms to go down to the Tron. Now we'd made the news, we had to go incognito in case any cops were around. Paisley suggested we wore our Mandie's Candies T-shirts and jeans instead. I said this was kinda like advertising our crimes, but she wanted us to look the same and I didn't argue anymore.

A lot of people were milling around under the Jumbotron; waiting for the bus, coming back from the volcano or the pirate battle or heading to the Bellagio for the eight o'clock dancing fountains. Buying bottled water or monorail tickets.

We looked and we looked and we waited, but Dad didn't show up.

The news was still on and we sat on the bench for a while watching it. It wasn't the same footage as before. This time, they named us.

… A quite extraordinary story now. We've been updating you all this week on the exploits of the duo dubbed the Wonder Twins, caught on security camera holding up various candy stores and bakeries in the Las Vegas area over the last couple of weeks and now we can name them. It turns out that these two candy bandits are none other than twins Beau and Paisley Argent, whom some viewers may recognize as the Wonder Twins who first hit the headlines ten years ago …

'Candy bandits, yeah, I like that,' my sister grinned.

'They know who we are now,' I said. 'They'll know all about us.'

They were talking about Virginia.

… The twins' grandmother, former actress Virginia Creed, identified them from a news item shown yesterday. She was also able to tell us that the 'Buddy' to whom they refer during their robberies is their father Buddy Argent, who has been in prison since the twins were six years old. In a further twist to the story, Mrs Creed claims the twins stole one thousand dollars from her before setting fire to her house and stealing her car …

'She gave that money to us!' Beau shouted.

'God, when's she gonna fuckin' flatline?' said Paisley. Then she chuckled. 'She must be so jealous. We're more famous now than she ever was. She's gonna pin everything on us so the cops ratchet up the charges. Any unsolved murders in Vegas recently?'

Virginia had appeared on screen. The news crew had taken her back to the charred remains of her house. She was trawling through the wreckage.

… I've brought them up. I've given them a good home and love and care …

'Liar,' said Paisley.

… and this is the thanks I get. She started to cry. *I'm living in a motel with my partner, Matthew.* Matt appeared stage left. He held her hand and rubbed it.

'"My partner, Matthew"?' Paisley again. 'Sorry, I thought they just had afternoon delights in her sauna. I didn't realize they were *partners*.'

... They've stolen my money, ruined my life. I don't know why. I think they've gone completely off the rails. So many teenagers do nowadays. She looked into the camera. *It's not surprising. I don't think punishment is the answer, but they need to know what they've done is wrong. They can't do these things to people. They can't do this to me.*

I couldn't stop looking at the screen. It froze on Virginia's face for a couple seconds, a glitch in the broadcast. The look in her eyes sent a quiver straight down my back. It made me more afraid of her than I'd ever been.

The news guys were back in the studio talking about the Super Bowl.

Paisley was still looking around for Dad. 'What about him?' she nudged me, pointing to a huddled mass in the shelter of the Deuce stop. The bus pulled up and the mass got to their feet, and we saw it was a black guy wrapped in blankets.

We both turned round and continued to watch the bulletins. Tourists on their way to and from shows along the Strip would pass every so often, laughing about *Spamalot*, carrying posters or Cirque du Soleil programs. Drunk and disorderly. Bemoaning large gambling losses. Then a small gaggle of teenagers appeared, about our age, and stood under the Tron. The bulletin came on again and they cheered.

'We love you guys!' they shouted at the screen. They booed at Virginia.

Paisley looked at me. I sank in my seat a little. She pretended to look at something else. Both of us were still listening.

'We should get T-shirts printed,' one of them said as they walked past.

'Yeah, a ton of people have asked for them on the site.'

I looked at Paisley and smiled. 'Wow. Did you hear that?'

'Yeah,' she said. 'Did they say site?'

'We must have a website. Already?'

'How can we check it?' She grabbed my arm and pulled me to my feet. 'They got computers at the Fashion Show mall. In a store. I checked my emails on one of them the other day when I was waiting for you.'

'The mall?' I said. 'Where you pointed a gun at a woman in a clothes store and scared the crap outta her? Won't that be like returning to the scene of a crime?'

She shrugged. 'Wanna check the Internet or not?'

Hey everyone, it's Nancy Nightmare here, official President of the Argent Army website. This is the place to come for the absolute latest info on what the twins are up to, and THE place to come for your official Argent Army T-shirts. Due to overwhelming demand, we even have fantastic new Team Paisley and Team Beau shirts, available in either pink or blue, and wristbands with a variety of slogans, including 'Buddy Argent, We Love You' and 'How much custard will this get us?' So hurry on over there now. Stock is selling fast!

'Unbelievable,' I laughed. We cruised in and out of websites set up in our honor, read through countless message board threads, and after a while became so brainwashed we weren't sure who we were anymore.

'What?' said Paisley, coming back over to the computer where I was standing. I was quicker with computers and she was better at fending off sales attacks from over-diligent Sony staff. She'd already tried out a new digital camera, MP3 player and surround-sound TV, but she kept popping back over to check what I'd learned.

'Does that say, *ever since the fire*?' said Paisley, loitering. 'We've had fans since then?'

'Yeah, apparently local LA news reports picked it up. Then there was a Facebook group, A told B, B told C; you know how it is. Once they found out it was,' my voice dropped to a whisper, '*us* doing the robberies, the whole thing just snowballed. The kids love us!'

'What about *Perez*? Did we make *Perez* yet?' she asked, nudging me over. I'd minimized the two celebrity gossip pages I had opened. I maximized one of them again to show her. We were all over it.

'Cool!' she shrieked.

A Sony store clerk came over. Paisley turned and asked him which one was their biggest TV.

What dreams have you had about the Argents? What presents would you buy them? Where are they: The Latest Sightings! The 'We Hate Buddy Argent' thread. Help Celebrate National Beau and Paisley Day. What would you do to show your love for them? Baisley: fan fiction.

'Ugh. That's disgusting.'

'What?' she said, coming back to me.

Black or blond: Which hair color best suits Beau? CCTV pictures thread. Is Beau Argent gay? Is Paisley Argent gay? Paisley and Beau: early years news footage. Who is Buddy Argent? They're looking for their dad! What places would you like to see them rob? Which celebrity's home would Paisley and Beau rob? What animal is Beau most like?

'Ooh, I gotta see this,' she said, taking over the mouse and clicking the link.

NANCY NIGHTMARE: I think he'd be a little koala bear 'cos he's so cute and he's got little sticky-out ears. LOL.

'Shit. Do I?' I said.

WONDER GIRL: No it has to be a puppy, 'cos of his brown eyes. I swear his eyes are so beautiful I could just drown in them! It's like he completes me.

'Give me a break,' said Paisley, and went back to the clerk and the 'TV she couldn't leave the store without.'

I clicked on the eBay link at the bottom of the page.

Now available: Own the cutlery used by the Argent twins at Denny's yesterday evening. Starting bid: $1,700.

'Seventeen hundred bucks! Jesus Christ!'

I clicked on the discussion board. 'Argent Angst.'

LITTLE MISS BOSSY: I just had the worst day ever. My mom's been crying a lot lately since my dad left, and seeing Beau and Paisley doing their stuff makes me so happy. Paisley's so the girl I wanna be. And Beau is just so amazing. I just wanna hug him …

NANCY NIGHTMARE: Aw, I feel bad for you, hon. But I know what you mean. Beau and Paisley are awesome. I wish we could help them get their message across.

CLUELESS: It's really hard for me. Since my dad died, I feel like there's no one who understands what I'm going through. I see people way older than me who still have their dads and I'm so jealous. Sometimes I wish other people's dads would die or just leave, and I feel guilty for thinking that but I just want someone to feel the way I do. When I saw on the news that they're doing all this stuff to find their dad, I thought it was so cool. Beau and Paisley know exactly how I feel. They'd do anything to find their dad and so would I.

TWINZ ADDICT: I know what you mean. I really do. I'd do the same thing if I thought my dad gave a rat's ass about me. LOL. Sometimes, the only way people will listen is if you fucking make them listen. I wanna go with them!

BUNNY BOILER: Srsly you guys, I don't think I can live much longer without Beau Argent being my husband. He is the most beautiful person in the whole world. There was a little yellow blob with hearts coming off the top, followed by a line of smooching red lips.

Paisley returned. 'I didn't buy the TV. Not big enough. Find anything else?'

'Oh my God. People love us, Pais. I'm serious. We are in demand. Some of the discussions are weird, though.'

'What?'

'They're talking about me and you, like as a couple.'

'We are a couple.'

'No, like a … sex couple.'

'What?!'

'Yeah, I know.'

Paisley grimaced like she was trying to swallow her fist.

'… and some of these girls are talking about doing stuff to me and they're like thirteen?'

'So? I know girls like eleven and twelve who've done it. It's no biggie.'

'Oh, I'll put that on the website shall I? *Have sex, kids. It's no biggie.*'

'Stop being so judgmental. Get that smug twitch out your eyebrows.'

I looked back at the screen. 'These guys really love us.'

Paisley peered at it. 'They're mostly girls,' she said. And it's mostly you they're loving. As far as they're concerned, I might as well be a piece of shit. They all think you're adorkable. I can just see the double-pager in J-14. You wait 'til they find out you read books.'

'It's more than that, though,' I told her. 'It's like we're helping them. Look at some of the stuff they're saying. This one girl's dad just lost custody of her, and she's looking at us and we're helping her.'

'How?'

'Because she's gonna stand up and fight for her dad. She says she's gonna run away and go find him.'

'Woah. That's pretty weird,' said Paisley. 'I never helped anyone before.'

'Yeah. The message boards are going insane.'

'Let's leave them a message,' she said.

'Yeah? What do you wanna say?'

I set her up and she nudged me out of the way and started typing.

Dear Fans,

Keep Wondering …

Luv P & B

'There,' she said. 'What do you think?'

'Sweet, Pais. Pretty sweet.'

'Why, thank you.'

'But we gotta do more.'

'What?'

'We gotta do another one. Robbery. To keep our profile up.'

'Well, there's turning worms and changing tunes and then there's you, Beau.'

'Just once more. My way. Then we'll lay low.'

'If you want. I still got the Eclipse on me ...'

'No. No Eclipse. No uniforms. My way, I said. Not so aggressive, not so rude. We got a little fame now. We can trade on that.'

She held out her hands in surrender. 'Fine. Do it your way. Where, then?'

I signed off. We walked out together. The mall guide was right outside. We stood looking at the map. 'Cornucopia,' I said. 'Popcorn shack. Top floor.'

CHAPTER NINETEEN

Paisley

Cornucopia, Fashion Show mall, north end of
the Strip

'Hey, can I help you?'

My big macho brother stepped up. 'Yeah, can I get one salted, two sour cream and chive, one caramel, two chocolate and one cheese please.'

'Cans or cartons?'

'Cans please.'

'Tiny, Small, Medium, Large, Extra Large or Super-duper?'

'Uh, tiny please.'

I threw Beau a look as if to say, *Why bother?*, but he got his money ready.

'What are you doing?' I whispered. 'We're not gonna pay.'

'I'm just throwing him off the scent.'

'I'll say. What d'you get cheese for? I hate cheese popcorn.'

'I don't plan on eating it.'

The Corn Dude got seven little cans ready, which looked like see-through paint cans, and went over to the huge glass machine behind him. It buzzed and hummed and there was this little fountain in the middle of it spewing out fresh popcorn. At the bottom were the five trays for the five different flavors they sold. Somewhere deep inside that machine, those popcorn kernels were given their flavors then sent to the right tray. The Corn Dude kept looking back at us as he opened the chocolate tray and scooped out enough for two tins.

He came back to the counter. His badge said his name was *The Corn Dude—Danny*.

'Hey, you guys were on the news.'

'Oh you recognize us, do you?' said Beau, turning to look at me.

'Yeah. Shit, you guys are way cool!'

'Yeah?!'

'Yeah. Wow. Can I get an autograph or something—or, no, wait—one of those stickers? Please? Wow, this is awesome.' He continued shoveling out our order but chuckling, barely taking his eyes off us.

'Sure,' said Beau, reaching into his back pocket for some stickers.

I stopped his hand. 'Beau, you can't do that. We only give stickers to people who deserve it. People who we've robbed.'

'Yeah, but this guy seems nice. He might give us a discount.'

Corn Dude Danny wiped his palms down his white apron and held his hand out ready. Beau peeled a sticker from the paper and pressed it down.

'Cool. Thanks man. Hey, Paisley, could I get a kiss from you?'

'A kiss? Why do you want a kiss?' I looked at Beau. 'No, you can kiss him.'

Corn Dude Danny laughed. The machine behind sent out another rush of popcorn to the empty caramel tray.

'Just kiss him. Call it public relations,' said Beau.

I looked at him, my hands on my hips. 'So we can't rob people anymore but you're quite happy to pimp me out to any mook that comes along, are you Beau?'

'No, it's just a little give and take …'

'I can't let ya have all this stuff for free, though,' said Corn Dude Danny, stacking up our tins. 'Sorry. Kinda company policy.' He chuckled again. I felt a little sorry for him. He had, like, no teeth.

'But it's good publicity, isn't it? Us being here?' said Beau.

'I guess,' said Corn Dude Danny.

'Kids are going batshit crazy for us. You said yourself we were on the news,' I added.

'Yeah, but I got my job to think about.'

I turned to my brother. 'Whatcha gonna do now, Beau?' I said. 'Danny don't wanna play with us.'

Corn Dude Danny rang up what we owed on the cash register. 'So that'll be sixty-eight ninety-five.'

Beau huffed and got out his wallet. 'Well, that's not gonna get our message out there, is it?' he said.

'No,' I said, 'but this is,' and I pulled the Eclipse once again from my waistband and held it out in front of me, pointed at the glass popcorn machine, my finger poised on the trigger.

Corn Dude Danny stopped laughing. Beau dropped his wallet. My finger pulled back.

PEEOW! PEEOW! CRASH. WOOMPH! The glass exploded and a fountain of popcorn came flying out, ricocheting off every wall. Corn Dude Danny ducked behind the counter. It was still raining popcorn as I grabbed the cans and ran out front.

'I knew you wouldn't let me handle it,' Beau shouted, running along beside me.

'What did you expect?' I laughed.

We ran out of there into the near-empty mall on the sound of ringing bells and the smell of burning popcorn. The once again brilliantly tardy security staff were nowhere to be found, so we checked out the nearest exit and made our way back along the Strip into the dense tourist cluster of Treasure Island. Another pirate show was in progress and we lost ourselves in the crowd.

'Tron!' I shouted out to Beau. He caught up with me at the fountain outside the entrance to the Forum shops, where we sat on a bench to catch our breaths.

I looked across at him before he even had the chance to say anything. 'Yeah, I did know it was loaded.'

He leaned forward and shook his head, still out of breath.

'Aren't you going to start yelling at me? Tell me I could have taken someone's eye out? That a little bit of glass could have severed an artery or something?'

He leaned back, still breathing hard, prizing open one of the chocolate corn cans and picking out a couple bits of corn. He shoved them in his mouth and shrugged.

'I'm sorry I put you through all this, Beau,' I said. He offered me the tin and I took a handful. 'I know you wanna be one of those kids who doesn't run with the crowd, and you wanna go to Paris and read all your French books and stuff.'

The lights on the big screen illuminated his face. 'It's okay.'

'No, it's not. I know it's worked, this whole weird, psychedelic, scary, gun-toting adventure of mine. But I'm sorry you had to be a part of it, okay? It's my thing, not yours, I know that.'

'Pais, you do know we're gonna have to leave Vegas pretty soon? Cops aren't gonna have to search for long. Especially now you've pulled the trigger.'

'I guess.'

'We need to go pack our stuff.'

I nodded. 'What about Dad?'

Beau put his arm around me and squeezed. 'We're okay as we are, aren't we?'

I looked at him. I knew what he wanted me to say, so I nodded.

The news was still on. We were on. I looked back to see grainy footage of me flipping the bird to the camera in Chronic Chocolate Company.

… *Tonight we take a closer look at the twins whose story is once again captivating America. I'm right here in Las Vegas where the Argent twins, once America's sweethearts, are thought to have embarked on something of a crime spree. I'm Amanda Peace and that's all coming up on Peace of the Action.*

'Ugh, can't stand that cooz.' I sat down on the bench and prized open a can of caramel corn. There she was again. Every half-hour bulletin her smirky face would appear: thick fringe, perma-tanned and talking about us through her nose like she could smell the shit we were up to our necks in. At the ends of her sentences she'd dip her head and look intently into the camera as if to say, *This is serious everyone. This is sooooooo serious.* Like she even *cared* about those stores we'd robbed. Those 'decent hardworking families' I'd pointed the gun at. Or us. Very least of all, us.

After commercials for the Diaper Genie and Oreo cookies, she appeared again.

… Las Vegas law enforcement officers are keen to apprehend the sixteen-year-old brother and sister duo who have been dubbed the new Bonnie and Clyde. And though they are wanted for a string of crimes including arson, car theft and robbery, many young people see the twins' exploits as heroic. The Argents have become modern-day celebrities, gracing the covers of the current issues of Teen Times *and* Face It. *Like Bonnie and Clyde before them, the duo perpetrate their crimes in an era of severe economic difficulty. And they've become nationwide celebrities because of it. Their raid at a frozen custard outlet in Las Vegas has already notched up over one million hits on YouTube. Internet sites have been set up in their honor, web forums are inundated hourly with messages of support, and, believe it or not, items alleged to have been used by the twins in various restaurants have even been found up for grabs on eBay …*

Our mug shots came up again: the grainy black-and-white

one of me flipping the bird at the CCTV at Mandie's Candies, and the one of Beau, full color, at General Custards.

Amanda Peace spoke to some teenagers hanging around the base of the Stratosphere.

'They're just so cool,' said one girl with red cheeks. 'They haven't hurt anyone. I don't think they'd be doing it if they didn't have to.'

'It's not like Mickey and Mallory,' said a black-haired boy. 'Beau and Paisley don't kill. They're not sadistic. They're just cool.'

'And Beau is really sexy,' said an older woman with a lip ring, laughing.

I could feel Beau looking at me out the corner of my eye as he stretched out on the bench like a cat stretches after sleep. He was smiling.

The state governor came on TV. He had a total hair up his ass.

... *Nevada State Police hope to capture the Argents within the next twenty-four hours. The net is closing in on them. Everybody knows what they look like thanks to the websites and magazine articles, so they'll be pretty easy to spot now. People will be sleeping easy in their beds by tomorrow, of that I have no doubt.*

'Asshole.'

'Everyone knows where we are, Pais ...'

'Yeah, well. Maybe we *should* get caught. Maybe that's the quickest way to find Dad.'

'Or the quickest way to jail.' Beau looked at me. He looked down at Mom's pendant around my neck. 'It looks good on you, Pais.'

'Thanks,' I said, offering him the caramel popcorn.

Then there she was in billions of pixels, Granny Dearest. The old Vaginasaurus herself, against the backdrop of the ruined, smoking remains of her house.

... I've lost everything. I just don't know why they would do this. They've set fire to my house, they've stolen my car, jewelry, valuables. I brought them up well, gave them everything I could. Jane was privately schooled and ... they had a good life after the trauma of losing their mother. I don't know what I'm going to do now ...

'Squeeze a little harder, Skank, you might actually produce a tear.'

'She must be real pissed with us,' said Beau.

'With me,' I said, digging around for popcorn in Beau's can.

'What do you mean? I was there too. I'm an accomplice.'

'Yeah, but you're Golden Boy. She'll hang me out to dry. And once the cops find out about my expulsions and ...'

'I'm not Golden Boy.'

'Yeah, y'are. She's always loved you. You're the one who never makes any waves. You don't even tell her when you get beat up at school, do you?'

'That's not true.'

'Oh, really? You've told her about O'Donnell and his crew and what they do to you? The head-flushing and the spitting and the locker graffiti?'

'No, of course not.'

'That's why she kept Dad away. She'd sell me down the river in a heartbeat, but she'd never let you go.' I closed my can and opened a sour cream one. 'She ever tried anything, you know, sexual?'

He looked at me from under his hair. 'Paisley …'

'I'm just asking. It happens. Something-Ophelia. I heard about it. Like necrophilia but when old women get horny for young guys. She's already bagged our infant gardener. She ever get you alone and …?'

'You are unbelievable! You're twisted. Have you ever thought that maybe she just prefers me because you're the difficult one? You're the one who doesn't take any of her shit, whereas I'm the doormat.'

'Well you know what they say, a boy's best friend is his grandmother.'

'Shut up.'

'Aw, Beau. If I'm outta line, just tell me to fu—'

'Fuck off,' he spat.

'Alright.' I smiled. I always appreciated him more when he told me to fuck off. I did need to be told. I'd have told myself to fuck off if I thought I'd listen.

'Come on,' he said, leaving his tins on the bench. 'Let's go back.'

I did the same and got up. I followed him through the flood of people who were headed for the on-the-hour dance of the fountains outside the Bellagio. They looked just like they did at the end of that George Clooney movie. All these huge bursts of water from all over the pool were shooting straight up into the black sky on the beats of the music. It was amazing. Hundreds of people had gathered all round the pool to watch and all the best spaces at the front were taken. I wanted to get closer.

I went to see if I could push in.

I peered over, jumping up to see if I could see somewhere we could stand and turned around to tell Beau where to head to.

But he had disappeared.

CHAPTER TWENTY

Beau

Bellagio Fountains, the Strip

She came toward me like a tiger stalking through long grass. Except the long grass was a crowd of tourists. And the tiger was my grandmother.

I turned around. 'PAISLEY!' I shouted. I didn't know if she heard or saw me. Matt gripped one of my arms, Virginia the other, and together they dragged me through the rest of the tourist mêlée. I wriggled and writhed to be free of them but the more I squirmed, the harder they held on. I didn't stop, though. It wasn't like before, outside the house with Matt squeezing my neck. There, I didn't dare breathe for fear of what he might do to me. But this time I kept on, pulling and pushing and making it as hard for them to take me as I could.

Neither of them said a word, all the way to the motel. They didn't ask me where we were staying, they just knew. They must have been trailing us. In the parking lot, Matt manhandled me while searching for a room key. I squirmed in my grandmother's grasp, shouting for help, hoping someone might hear and come over.

'Gimme the key or I'll bust it open. Your choice,' said Matt. I just smiled at him. He busted it open.

Once inside, Virginia pushed me face first onto my unmade bed as Matt set about binding my hands together with a length of rope. The same rope he used for marking off planting areas in our grandmother's garden.

She bent down so her face was level with mine. 'Where are my antiques?'

'In the closet,' I mumbled, burying my face in the bed sheets.

She went over to the closet and pulled one of the handles, immediately spying the beach bag. She pulled it out and searched inside. 'Good. It's all here.'

'You don't need to tie me up,' I said, as Matt wound the rope round and tied it tightly, checking my hands wouldn't slide. Then he did the same with my feet and left me on the bed. I lay there, my wrists and ankles throbbing with the rope pressure. 'You've both got what you came for. There's only me here.'

Virginia walked back over to the bed, slowly swinging the bag. 'This is just the down payment, Beau. YOU'RE what we came here for …'

'Me?'

'Uh huh. We're going to the lake house, Matthew and I. And you. We're going to live there. Just the three of us.'

'What, you're gonna hold me to ransom?' I said, my mouth once again getting my ass into something I seriously couldn't handle. But I didn't understand it. 'No one's gonna pay that for me. You know we don't have that kinda money.' I nodded towards the piles of candy and boxes of donuts around the room. 'We can pay you in jellybeans. We got plenty of them.'

She grabbed a fistful of my hair and yanked my head back. Upside down her features looked all distorted, like a melted clay pot. She raised her eyebrows and chuckled, like Jack Nicholson in *The Shining*. 'Your mouth's running away with you, Beau. You were always so eager to please me. What's happened since you've been away?' She came down closer to my face so I could feel her breath on my skin. 'If I have to lock you up for the two whole years you'll stay …'

'Two *years*?'

'Well, eighteen months at least.'

My follicles screamed in agony. I thought my eyes would pop out of my head. She gave me a look, right up close, like she didn't know if she was gonna kiss me or hit me. 'Then you'll get our fund.'

'Yes,' she continued, 'once I've got that, you're as free as you want to be. We've got a long time together, boy. I suggest you play nicely. I may even throw in a little cash bonus for good behavior.'

She would have let go if I'd said something nice, something palliative. But I didn't have it in me to be nice to her anymore.

That old Beau had gone. Well, I hoped he had gone, anyway. 'Paisley will kill you for this.'

Her mouth screwed up in a knot. 'I don't want to hear that name again.'

'She will. She'll know where you're going and she'll find you and she'll kill you. You don't know what she's capable of.'

Matt scoffed and took the bag from Virginia, heading outside to the parking lot.

Virginia gripped my hair harder. My eyes bulged. 'You don't know what *I'm* capable of. And I've had a fair idea of what your sister can do. I watched my home burn to the ground, remember?!'

She finally let go and shoved me back down onto the bed.

My scalp throbbed. 'Is that what this is, a revenge thing?'

She reached behind me and picked something up. Two Wit. She didn't take her eyes off me, but clutched my toy owl with both hands and started pulling it, until the stitching came away at the neck and it was two separate pieces of useless white stuffing. She took a handful of it and crammed it in my mouth. Then she took Two Woo from Paisley's bed and, still looking at me, did the same again, except she threw all of the stuffing behind her into the trash can.

'Where's my gun?'

I didn't answer.

'Where's my gun, Beau?' She came over to the bed and stared down at me. I lay on my back looking up at her, still with a mouthful of stuffing. I laughed in her face. She slapped me hard and some of the stuffing came out. I laughed again. She hit me again, twice as hard and this time with nail digs for good measure. I laughed again, though my eyes were running with tears.

She pulled the rest of the stuffing out of my mouth and yanked me upright on the edge of the bed, gripping the sides of my face in her claw. 'Where ... is ... it?'

'You know where it is,' I coughed.

Matt came back inside and closed the door. 'You ready?'

She nodded. 'Take him.'

Bundling me over his shoulder, Matt took me out to his pick-up. There was a large sheet of blue tarp over the back, folded over to one side. I didn't know what Virginia was getting up to but she hadn't yet come out of our room.

Matt threw me down on the bed of the truck. I lay next to a pile of old tools and a lawn mower on its side. He took a roll of duct tape out of the muffler pocket of his hoodie.

My heart was hammering so hard I didn't think my breath would make it out of my chest. I just said it before I could edit myself or think about what Matt would do to me once I'd said it.

'You won't see a penny of that money. Think about it. If she's doing this to her own grandchildren, what's a two-bit gardener mean to her, huh?'

He tore off a length of duct tape and plastered it over my mouth. Then he looked at me, as if weighing something up. I gulped. The last thing I remembered was the fist coming toward my face.

CHAPTER TWENTY-ONE

Paisley

Lucky Inn Motel, the Strip

I made it back to the motel, all pissed with Beau for going on ahead without me. The door to our room was hanging off its hinges. And something was burning.

I ran inside. In the middle of the orange carpet a fire was burning. And the fuel was Dad's letters.

'Oh shit!'

I ran over to the little burning mound to try and stamp it out, but the flames were too big. And it was still catching. The carpet was catching, the skirt thing on Beau's bed was catching. I saw the mess all over the room: my clothes all torn up and scattered around the floor; the candy stash strewn across the carpet; my backpack empty, dumped beside my bed. I scrabbled around and found the one letter of Dad's that I kept apart in the front pocket. I opened it. It was okay. I folded it up and put it inside my bra. The closet was wide open. I ran to it and saw the bag of antiques was gone.

'Fuck!'

All our stuff was gone, except for a stack of Wonder Twins stickers on the nightstand. I grabbed them.

The fire was all along Beau's side of the room now, right up to the drapes, which caught within seconds. There was no way I could get out the way I came, not without burning up myself. So I had to go through the bathroom. I stepped up onto the sink unit and sized up the window for my head, shoving the stickers down into my boot. I could just squeeze out. The catch caught on my belly as I writhed and wriggled and squirmed like a caterpillar to get outside, landing with a *flump* on the ground. Inside, something exploded.

The window banged shut behind me but I didn't look back. I got to my feet and just started running, filled with a rage so painful I could have torn off limbs. I didn't know where I was going, I just ran.

All hope plummeted like a bird shot down. All my stuff was burned. Dad's letters were burned. Beau had vanished. I just knew the Skank had taken him. She'd done it and she'd do more if she didn't get what she wanted. No matter how hard I ran or how deep I breathed to control it, I couldn't stop my own tears. I stopped in a sheltered doorway, some defunct record store just off the Strip, trying to stifle the huffs caught in my throat. I breathed hard and heavy, *in, in, in* then *out, out, in, out*. I stood back against the wall, feeling the cold tiles against my calves and hands. I was sweating; my hair had become stuck across my face as I ran, but I didn't move it away. I didn't know what to do. I couldn't hold it in any longer. I sobbed.

I sat in the doorway until two hobos came stumbling along, shouting that I was in their spot. They were still shouting at me when I began running back along the Strip. What was it about that fucking block that kept me coming back to it? Dad, that was what. I'd seen him there, I knew I had. I watched people walking along, hand in hand, on holiday, smiling, laughing, taking photos, sipping through curly straws. Families. Little girls with dads. I watched groups of guys strutting past with calling cards for hookers. More hunched-up hobos shuffling along, holding their hands out for spare change. I watched drag queens shimmying past on their way to a show, acting like the whole world owed them a favor. None of the faces I saw was Dad's and that made me hate them all. I hated the world. It was all so dirty and loud and complicated. Everything was f-ugly. Everything was wrong.

I didn't stop walking for hours. I moved about unseen in the crowds. I didn't know what to do, I had no money, nowhere to go, I hadn't found Dad—and, worst of all, I now realized—I'd lost Beau too.

I was totally lost.

My chest felt like it was being crushed, like a piano had fallen on it or something. The pain squeezed and squeezed and there was nothing I could do about it. I thought about hamsters. Hamsters get on their wheels when they're stressed out, didn't they? I needed to get up, walk around, run if I had to, run it all out of me.

I ran down the Strip, weaving in and out of tourist clusters until I found Walgreens. I bummed up and down the aisles with no intention of buying anything. Thumbed through magazines without even reading them. Picked up packets of shit I couldn't even identify through the water in my eyes. As I came to the end aisle, I scoped the shelves displaying the Scotch. There were so many kinds but only one that meant anything to me. One particular bottle came into focus. Black-and-white label. I grabbed a bottle and walked to the entrance. Then I ran like a bitch. I could still hear the alarm screaming as I reached the Tron outside Caesars. I sat down on the bench, watching for police or security guards—nothing. Nobody. Nobody gave a shit about me and I gave a shit about nobody. I twisted off the lid of the bottle and brought it up to my nose. It smelt disgusting. Like the living room the day we found Mom. Like my grandmother's breath when she was shouting. My stomach turned over at the thought of drinking it.

I sat there with the open bottle between my knees and watched the Tron. We were on again. Two old dudes were debating the effect we were having on teen America.

… It's a sorry state of affairs if these are the kinds of role models we are producing for our younger generation …

'They don't want to be role models, Glenn. They're doing this because they've lost their way, that's all. They're lost souls. Society has failed them …'

If in doubt, blame society. I put the bottle to my lips and swigged. I held it in my mouth. I spat. I tried it again. I held it in my mouth for longer. I tried swallowing again but my damn throat wouldn't let me. I spat it out and heaved into the trash can. On my third swig, I swallowed. I shivered. It was disgusting. But I needed it. I needed it to forget where I was. Who I was. I understood Mom. For once, I understood my grandmother. I felt the swig going down my throat, into my stomach, like a little rush of Band-Aids traveling to all the places in my body where it hurt. My heart. My stomach. The pain deep inside my body which no doctor could ever get to. The more I drank, the less it hurt me. Beau being gone. My dad not showing any interest in watching us on the big screen, or being kept away from it.

Whatever.

Whatever.

Whatever.

What-fucking-ever.

I laid my head on the arm of the bench and watched our news reports into the night. Pretty soon I closed my eyes.

And when I opened them, the Jumbotron was still twinkling above me. They were looping the old dudes. They were on again. Bad role models. Lost souls. The crowds hadn't thinned out either. Moms and dads and kids and friends and grandparents and boyfriends and couples and hobos and brothers and sisters and guys in red shirts. Guys in red shirts. No, not guys, *a guy* in a red shirt. A guy standing there, watching the screen. Watching the Tron. Watching *us*.

He had his back to me, hands in his jean pockets.

I thought I was dreaming. I thought he'd disappear like a ghost. Like the day we saw him from the bus. But he didn't.

I sat up. He was still there. I stood up. I came up to his shoulders. He was still there. I was wobbly on my legs but I walked up to him. He still didn't turn around, just carried on watching the Tron. They were still screening the manhunt for those dastardly Wonder Twins.

I reached out and put my hand on his back. I still thought he would disappear even as my hand touched his shoulder blade. He twitched.

He turned around and looked at me, frowning at first like he was gonna tell me to fuck off. And then he really looked at me. And he frowned even more. And I started to cry.

'Dad? Are you my dad?'

'Paisley? No! Baby, 's that you?' He was smaller than I remembered, not just 'cos I'd gotten taller. He'd lost a lot of weight, too. His face was hairy. He'd grown a thick beard and mustache but underneath it all it was my dad, alright. His face lit up like there was a candle under his skin when he said my name. Just like when I used to run into his arms when he came home after work.

He was shaking. 'Oh my God. Paisley ...' He went to hug me, but stopped and put his hand over his mouth, like I'd told him not to.

'I can't handle this,' he said and started to cry. He had white bits stuck to his clothes and he smelled like he'd fallen down in a public toilet. But it was my dad and I didn't care, so I touched one of his hands and he grabbed onto it. I leaned over and hugged him. And he hugged me right back. His cheek was cold and quivery against my face. And he held me like we were going to jump off a building. Normal hugs don't last long. A quick hug, a pat on the back and then you come undone. Not this one. He was there, like all my sunrises at once. My dad.

'Please tell me this isn't a dream.'

'It's not a dream, honey,' he said, pulling back to look at me. 'God, I can't believe you're here!' He kissed my hair and breathed it in, his tears forming a little damp patch on the top of my head. He held my face in his hands.

'I knew it,' I told him. 'I knew if we got on that screen you'd see us. I knew we'd get to you somehow,' I said, holding onto him again so tight. I didn't ever want to let go. I didn't even care how dirty he was. I buried my face into his filthy red shirt and breathed him in like he was lavender. The last time I'd hugged him, I'd only come up to his waist. Now my head was on his shoulder. We stood for the longest time. I had my dad and he loved me. And that was all that mattered …

I pulled back. 'Dad …'

'We've got so much to talk about, Paisley,' he said, wiping his eyes on his shirt sleeve. 'God, look at you. You're so beautiful. My little girl. I've been watching the news. I saw you.' He rubbed his eyes. His fingers were blackened with dirt. He saw the bottle of Scotch in my hands and took it from me. 'What are you doing with this? You don't need this.' He aimed it at the trash can he'd been searching through days before.

'Dad, everything's gone wrong. We've done some pretty bad things. Well, I have.'

'Yeah, I saw …'

'No, before the robberies. Beau and the fire and I … shit, sorry, I don't know where to start … I got expelled … like, five times.'

'Well that's—'

'And I punched a girl.'

'Okay.'

'And I burned down Virginia's house.'

'Woah.'

'And I drugged a guy and robbed him.'

He pulled back a little and held his hands up. 'All in good time. But I saw you guys on the news. You did that for me, didn't you?'

'Beau said it was a stupid plan.' Beau, oh my God, where was he?

'It *was* a stupid plan,' said Dad. 'But it worked. We're here, together. That makes it a perfect plan.' He hugged me again but I just stood there like some stupid pillar. Everything was so fast in my head, it had made my body completely still. Dad was still talking and stroking my face.

'My baby gone all Bonnie Parker just for her old dad?' he laughed. 'I can't wait to see Beau. Is he alright? Paisley? Paisley?'

I snapped out of it when he said my name twice, like he used to when he caught me doing something I shouldn't, like crayoning on the wall or blocking the toilet with Legos. 'I … I lost him in the crowds. We were headed back to our motel, but … oh God, the fire, Dad, our room was on fire. Our stuff … it's Virginia, she's got to him.'

'Woah, what do you mean, got to him? Where is he?'

'She took him, her and her gardener toy boy thing … they've got him, I know it. They probably been trailing us for days. They trashed our motel room, set the letters on fire …'

'Set *fire* … were either of you hurt?'

'No. She just burned the letters you sent.'

He looked at me. 'You got them? You kept them?'

I nodded. 'She kept them from us. We got the last one you sent from Spurina. That's why we came. The guy at Green Mango Road, Eddie, he told us to come to the Strip so …'

'Where did they go?'

'I don't know. Dad, I don't know!'

'It's alright, it's alright …'

'No, it's not, Dad. I have to know! What's she going to do to him? I'll kill her, if she hurts him I'll fucking …'

'Paisley, watch your mouth.'

'I'm sorry, but Dad …' A thought hit me like a wrecking ball. I could hear Beau's voice in my head.

The lake house. In Utah. I saw a picture of it in her desk drawer. Lake Peligno. She bought it a while back. It's pretty remote … for holidays, I guess. A retreat.

I almost spat it back out at Dad. 'The lake house, she must have gone there!'

He held my hands, just like he used to when I had one of my tantrums.

'Alright, calm down, talk slowly.'

'I can't! We have to go there now. We have to get Beau!'

'You think that's where they've gone?'

'I can't think of anywhere else. Beau said it's remote. She might kill him, Dad. She might wanna come after me and kill me. Just so she can claim all the money …'

'*What?* What money?'

And just then he looked down. Mom's necklace. I didn't

think he could cry anymore. He kind of cry-laughed.

'You got it back for me. You got it back,' he spluttered.

We hugged again.

'Oh Dad, I've got so much to tell you.'

CHAPTER TWENTY-TWO

Beau

Somewhere heading north along Interstate 15

I woke up, my brain feeling like it had been kicked around on cobblestones. All I could see was blue. My body was being bumped and jerked around, and as I fully opened my eyes to see the scratchy blue sheet lying over me, I remembered where I was. My heart started pounding. I was in the truck. I was tied up. My mouth was stuck fast behind a strip of tape. It was daylight outside the blue sheet. I could feel the sun. The truck clattered on, metal clinked, loose tools rattled. Lying beside me was the lawn mower, and as I turned onto my side I stared straight into the blades. Bits of lawn cuttings were stuck to them. I could hear some country and western song coming from the cab. Hear voices over the top of it.

Virginia's voice. 'You're very quiet.'

Matt's voice. 'What?'

The music went off.

'I said you're very quiet. Something the matter?'

'I was just thinking over something you said.'

'What?'

'About keeping him chained to a water pipe for two years.'

'It's not two years. It's barely eighteen months.'

'You'd really lock him up?'

'He's always had a strict curfew ...'

'Yeah, but that didn't involve tying his hands together.'

'We'll have to see how he behaves. If he promises to comply, we won't have to tie him up, will we?'

Matt's voice. 'What if he gets out again? He'll go straight to the cops.'

'No, he won't. The police are already after them for everything else. Arson. Car theft. Armed robbery. I don't think they're going to pay much mind to a tiny case of kidnapping between family members amidst all that, do you?'

'What if he won't play ball? Goes on hunger strike or something?'

'It won't get that far. I told you, Beau's a pussycat, he won't cause us any trouble.'

'Yeah but—'

'Matthew, darling, I'm getting a little tired of all these arbitrary questions. Don't you trust me?'

'Yeah ...'

'That almost sounded convincing. I'm starting to think

your heart isn't in this.'

'I just gotta think about the pitfalls, Ginny. I don't wanna go back to jail. I wanna go straight now.'

'Yes, and won't it be nice when all this is over to go straight with millions of dollars in the bank? Your own business?'

Silence. The radio went loud again. Then down again.

Matt's voice. 'What if she comes back to get him?'

'She won't. Darling, she's been away at boarding school for months. She doesn't even know we bought the house. She won't have a clue where we are. And he won't put a foot wrong.'

'But if she does find him …'

'Matthew, if I ever see that girl's face again, I'll make sure I never have to see that girl's face again.'

'What does that mean?'

No answer. I didn't need to hear anymore. If it came down to it, our grandmother would kill us both, of that I had no doubt. She had nothing to lose and everything to gain.

I had to get off the truck. I twisted my head round to see a wooden board propped up against the cab. They couldn't see me. I wrenched my hands but they wouldn't budge. The rope was coiled around them six times. I wrenched my feet, but the rope was too tight and I was too weak. I couldn't even open my mouth with the tape there. I lay back and closed my eyes and felt the tears coming. There was a clattering from the other side of the truck. The blade from Matt's hedge trimmer, a large jagged blade, was jutting out the side of his toolbox. I writhed over to it and held my hands up to the blade and started to rub along it, trying to get some friction going.

Rubrubrubrubrubrubrubrubrubrubrubrubrubrubrubrubrubr ubrubrubrubrub …

Every breath I took into my nose was laced with the stench of hot rotten grass and gasoline. Sweat beads trickled down my forehead and into my eyes, but I didn't stop rubbing that rope until a fray appeared.

I lay back down to catch my breath for a second, rubbing my forehead against the wooden board I lay on to wipe away the sweat. Then I started again. *Rubrubrubrubrubrubrubrub rubrubrubrubrubrubrubrubrubrubrubrubrub* …

A strand from one coil of the rope came free, making it easier to cut through the rest of the pieces. *Swip swip swip* went the rope as it loosened and fell off my wrists. The relief was amazing. I had my hands back. I arched them back and forth and stretched my fingers out. Lying back, I brought my legs behind me and set about undoing my ankles until my legs were unburdened by rope, too, then stopped and caught my breath again, my chest rising and jumping with the heaving from my lungs. My shirt was soaked through with sweat and I pulled the neck up over my face to wipe it. Must have been a hundred and five degrees under that tarp. Another hour and I reckon I'd have cooked under that scratchy sheet.

'I love this song!' I heard Matt shout.

The music got loud again inside the cab.

It was the song from the dance machine. I was sure of it.

I snaked under the tarp and crawled my way along to the other end of the truck, poking my head up at the other end. The sunlight was blinding outside. I craned my neck over and looked back at the cab. I couldn't see Virginia or Matt, so hopefully they couldn't see me. I looked over the back of the truck to see the desert road stretching out behind us. It was like the road we'd taken from LA to Vegas, but it definitely wasn't the same one. The mountains were closer and the concrete was darker and there were no cars around. The truck was moving pretty fast but there wasn't another car for miles.

I closed my eyes. 'Come on. Come on,' I muttered. I could feel the tears coming again. It was all my *carpe diem* moments rolled into one. Every time I had to take the plunge into a cold swimming pool. Every time I'd had to walk into class after summer vacation and look into O'Donnell's eyes. Every time Paisley pulled the gun out. It was being back on Stratosphere, about to go on Big Shot.

And I wonder ...

I heaved up my upper body to rest on the end of the truck. It wobbled. Any moment, the chain could have snapped and I could have fallen out onto the road. The tears came. I jabbed myself in my stomach with my fist. 'Come on!' I muttered louder. I punched myself again.

If anything could ever feel this real forever ...

I had to get on that road. I had to stop going where I was going. I had to be free of our grandmother.

Gotta promise not to stop when I say when.

I had to jump off the truck.

CHAPTER TWENTY-THREE

Paisley

Caesars Palace Jumbotron, the Strip

'Oh my God! Paisley? Is it really you, Paisley? Guys, it's Paisley!'

'I'm sorry?' I said as this fat, straggly black-haired woman darted toward me, her sandals slapping on the sidewalk as she ran. She had a lip ring and emblazoned across her chest was the black-and-white screen cap of mine and Beau's faces from the CCTV at Doh-Nutty's. A girl, about the same age as me and wearing a black AC/DC T-shirt just like mine was eating a burrito but dropped it and ran over. Then another, a skinny blond boy in a marching band jacket with big gold buttons.

'Oh my God, this is a total honor,' said AC/DC. 'You and

- 236 -

your brother, you're like … our heroes. You're legends!'

'We've been following your story and we've set up this website for the Argent Army, which is like this group of kids who just adore you,' said Lip Ring. She had gray strands in her hair and a huge boil next to one of her nostrils. 'We got like seven thousand members to the site. The hits go up every day.'

'Seven thousand members?' I said.

'Yeah, and there's other sites too. There's Totally Argent.net and Wonder Twins Inc too. You two are teen idols. Everybody loves you. Well, kids love you. We've come here from Ohio. I'm Vicky, Vic for short, this is my daughter Eliza and this is Eliza's boyfriend Robbie. I remember you guys the first time round, when you went missing. We sent teddy bears to the hospital in Jersey. Oh my God, is this your dad?'

'Uh, yeah,' I said.

'Where's Beau?' said Marching Band.

'He's …' I didn't know what to say. I couldn't think of a lie either, so I just came out with it. 'Our grandmother's kidnapped him.'

All three of them laughed hysterically, then stopped when they saw my face. I thought Marching Band was gonna start bawling.

'We thought you were joking,' said AC/DC. 'Oh my God, we're so sorry. When?'

''Bout three hours ago,' I said, reaching for my dad's hand.

Lip Ring snorted through her nose like a dragon. 'We knew it. We said when we saw her on the news, that woman won't let this lie. She'll be after them. Didn't I say that, Eliza?'

'Yeah,' said AC/DC. She opened her bag and got out a

rolled-up copy of *Teen Times*. 'Could you sign this, please?'

She handed it to me with a small Sharpie. Me and my brother's grainy black-and-white faces were on the front and the headline read, *Bonnie and Clyde for the New Millennium*. I scrawled my signature across my own face. Marching Band offered me a small thick journal, plastered with pictures of me and Beau cut neatly from newspapers. I looked through it and found my own page to sign. He had written a short poem entitled 'Paisley's Ode.' I can't remember much about it but he likened me to a starfish and I liked that. I scribbled underneath, *So not worth it. Lots of love Paisley xo.*

He smiled like a dolphin and eagerly showed the other two. 'Look what I got. Look what she wrote. Oh wow. Oh wow.'

When I'd finished my signing and photo calls, the three of them stood there looking at me. I didn't know what they were expecting.

'What? You want me to open a vein or something?' I said. They all laughed again. Then Lip Ring looked at Dad, who had just been standing there the whole time by my side.

'Is this really your dad? Is this Buddy?' she asked. I nodded. She pulled him toward her and hugged him like they were good old friends. 'I've been following these kids since they were little and they were on *Oprah,* and when we heard what they were doing now we had to come here and show our support. They've done all this for you. Oh my God! It's an honor to meet you, sir.'

'A real honor,' said AC/DC. 'Your kids are amazing, always have been. My sister lives in Jersey and she went out with one of the search parties when they went missing. Never thought they'd find them. But they did! And here you are.'

Marching Band turned to my dad. 'Can I shake your hand?'

Three hours ago, he was rooting through trash cans and washing in public fountains. Now he was getting called 'sir' and having his hand shaken? And *I* was amazing? I didn't know what was happening. I thought it might be some prank. I turned and walked away, pulling Dad along with me.

'Wait! Where are you going?' called Lip Ring, and the three of them caught up with us. I kept walking. So did they.

'I'm sorry, but I'm not this big hero, alright? All me and Beau did was hold up some candy stores, and we only did that to get on the news. So we could tell our dad we love him. So we could find him. Alright? I've found my dad now. That's all I wanted. You can get on with your lives now. Stop stalking me.'

I carried on walking. Pretty soon, I'd noticed they'd stopped following. So had Dad. I turned around. They were all stood on the spot a couple yards away, staring at me, their three little faces falling to the floor.

'Dad?' I said.

'Paisley, apologize. These people have come a long way to see you.'

'What? I didn't ask them to, Dad …'

'Paisley …'

'Okay, I'm sorry. But, I didn't ask for any of this, okay?'

'But you got it,' said Dad, walking toward me. 'So what are you gonna do with it?'

I shrugged.

'We've got a car,' said Lip Ring. 'If we can drive you guys

anywhere, it'd be a total honor. Do you know where your grandmother might have taken Beau?'

'No. Well, I got a hunch but it's risky …'

'We know the risks,' said AC/DC. 'If your grandmother wants to kill us, it'd be a total honor.'

'Yeah,' said Marching Band. 'We don't mind getting shot. I'll get shot for you.' He bowed his head like he was totally embarrassed.

'You're so cool,' said Lip Ring. 'Everybody loves you guys. Well, everybody under fifty at least.'

I shook my head. 'But I don't get it. Why so stalky? Just 'cos we got a gun and there's some montage of us on YouTube with a Bon Jovi soundtrack?'

'It's The Who actually,' said AC/DC.

'"Baba O'Reilly"?' said Dad.

'Yeah,' smiled AC/DC.

'Cool,' he said. Look at my dad, I thought, down with the kids.

'We just want to help you, like you helped us,' said Marching Band. 'We want to show you our gratitude. Please. We could help you find Beau.'

'How have we helped you? Me and Beau are thieves, guys. We're not rock stars, we're not heart surgeons. We steal from people to get money to get to places we need to be. That's all. We're not exactly role models.'

'We don't want role models,' said Lip Ring. 'We're sick of role models. You're the coolest thing to hit the States since Bonnie and Clyde. It gives us all hope.'

'Yeah. And I know what it's like to lose your dad. I'd do

anything to get mine back.' AC/DC shot Lip Ring a knowing glance and the woman reached for her hand and gave it a squeeze.

'And the state governor hates you,' added Marching Band. 'He says you're an example of everything that's wrong with America.'

'Praise indeed,' said Dad.

'I think you need us,' said Lip Ring. 'We could really help you out.'

I looked at Dad. He raised his eyebrows, like he always used to when he was waiting for me to make up my mind which cereal I wanted for breakfast. It was always the chocolate one.

'Okay, guys,' I said. I remembered what Beau had told me about one of the Hansel and Gretel stories. How they got out of the woods on a white duck. This was our white duck. 'We're in your hands, I guess.'

As the three of them leaped up and down in utter joy, they didn't look much like white ducks. More like baby black rabbits.

So we went to find Lip Ring's car. It was beyond cool. A black Trans Am with scratches and dents and zebra-print seat covers. When we were on the road, Marching Band told me they were turning it into the Wonder Mobile, black-and-white themed throughout, and they were gonna follow us in it everywhere, wherever we went. Keeping their distance of course. They didn't want us to get caught. They just wanted to be near us. Batshit, I tell you. Totally batshit.

Somewhere on the I-15 to Salt Lake City, Lip Ring said she needed gas, so we stopped at a little rest stop called Moriarty's Diner. Dad was starving, so me and him went inside to get him some pie to take with us. The TV was on in the corner.

CNN BREAKING NEWS: WONDER TWINS BANDIT FOUND IN ARIZONA DESERT.

—*Welcome back, the headlines again on Monday, September twenty-ninth. I'm Kim Slaughter and we can go live now to the Dixie Regional Medical Center in Utah, where Jake Williamson is waiting. What's the latest, Jake?*

—*Thanks, Kim. Yes, I'm standing outside the hospital where Beau Argent, one of the Argent Twins, who have been causing mayhem in the city of Las Vegas over the last couple of weeks by holding candy stores to ransom, has been admitted. Early reports say he has suffered a head trauma after having jumped or been pushed out of a moving vehicle. He was found on the roadside off the I-15 near Cedar Pocket Road around five thirty this morning by a fisherman heading to the reservoir there, and was brought here to the Dixie Regional Medical Center in St George.*

—*For those people watching who may be out of the loop when it comes to the Argent twins, Jake, can you tell us a little more about them?*

—*Well, Kim, in recent weeks these kids have become kind of Bonnie and Clyde figures for a whole new generation, and as you can see behind me there are literally hundreds of young people who have gathered to show their support for Beau Argent and to light candles, wave banners and wait for news of his condition. They're also waiting to see if his sister, Paisley, shows up. She has, perhaps, been the more vocal of the pair and in every robbery it has been Paisley calling the shots, so to speak. Last night it is believed the twins pulled off their last robbery at Cornucopia in Las Vegas, before firing shots at a popcorn machine and causing thousands of dollars' worth of damage. There are a lot of very worried fans of the Argent twins, but you can bet store clerks all over Vegas won't be saying any prayers for these two right now, Kim …*

—Thanks, Jake. More details on that story as we get them. In other news …

'They don't know if he's alive, Dad. He could be dead. It's all my fault. I did this to him. He was better off without me …'

Dad stopped and stood in front of me. 'You just did what you thought was best,' he said. 'It was her. It was your so-called grandmother who did this to him, not you. I mean, we don't know for sure she pushed him out …'

'She did, I know she did. She left him for dead. If he hadn't been found and taken to hospital …'

'Yeah, but he was, wasn't he? And they're making him better. You gotta hold onto that, Paisley. And we're gonna go get him. Okay? Are you with me?'

I nodded.

'It's okay to be scared sometimes, Paisley.'

'No it's not. I need to be angry.'

'Why?'

'Because then I can kill her. If I see her again, I'll kill her. I need to be angry.'

He held my hands. Somewhere, a plug was being pulled out and the fire was running out of me. Dad looked into my eyes. 'You still got the gun you did the robberies with?'

I nodded.

'Let me have it.'

I tucked my hand into the back of my skirt and grabbed the Eclipse. I handed it to Dad.

He shook his head. 'This can only lead to no good, baby. Okay? I don't want you getting into no more trouble.' He tucked it into his own belt. I hadn't realized it until then but he was still wearing his wedding ring.

'Come on,' he said, and we ran to the car and told the White Ducks about the news report.

'How many fans are out front at the hospital?' said Marching Band, biting his bottom lip.

'It looked like a lot, maybe a hundred,' said Dad.

'Were they all wearing black and white?'

'Most of 'em yeah, why?'

'That'll be Totally Argent,' said Lip Ring. 'One of our sister sites. If it was Wonder Twins Inc they'd be wearing candy colors and the Argent Army wear what they like. They're not dictated to by anyone, not even you guys.'

'God,' I said.

Lip Ring started the engine as I squeezed into the back with Marching Band and AC/DC, and my dad fiddled with the radio from the passenger seat.

'There were police there, too. And doctors and press. How

the hell are we gonna get past all of them and find Beau?' said Dad.

'You need a diversion,' said AC/DC, 'and we can give you a diversion.'

CHAPTER TWENTY-FOUR

Beau

Dixie Regional Medical Center, St George, Utah

Not for the first time in the last few weeks, I woke up wondering where the hell I was. I felt like I was juiced, like my head was being put through a pencil sharpener and my whole body was turning in circles. As my eyes focused, I saw white bed sheets. A TV on a shelf in the corner. Sunshine blazing in through a window between walls the color of a rainy day. It wasn't the motel room. There was no other bed. It was just me and a TV and white bed sheets. A little red light was on the bottom of the screen. I had a nightstand to one side of me with the remote on. I reached for it, but found I couldn't move. My left arm was in a sling, plastered up. I tried to wrench my body slowly over so my other arm could grab it, but everything hurt. I couldn't move. The door opened. A nurse came in.

'Where am I?'

'Oh, you're awake. You're in St George, in the hospital, sweetie.'

'Where the hell's St George? I was in Las Vegas.'

'Well you're not in Vegas anymore, you're in Utah. Boy, you musta banged up your head pretty good.'

'Utah?'

'Yeah. How you feeling?'

'I'm in Utah? I can't be. Where's Paisley? What's happened?'

'You got a badly broken left arm, multiple bruising and a nasty head wound. From what I hear you been damned lucky. We're keeping you in overnight and then I'm afraid you got some explaining to do.'

'Are the cops here?' I asked her.

'Here, there and everywhere. You got one outside the door just in case you pull anything, and a dozen trying to keep the crowds at bay out front.'

She sighed, and went round my bed to the window to open it a crack. 'Can I get you anything, a drink?'

'I'm not allowed. I'm sixteen.'

The nurse chuckled, pointing to the water jug by my bed.

'No, I wanna see the TV. Are we still on TV?'

'Yep,' she said, reaching for the remote and stirring the TV into life. They were broadcasting live from outside the hospital, where there was some kind of riot going on.

'What's happening?'

'I don't know. Looks like your fans are going crazy out there.

Fighting over who loves you the most.'

There were all these kids on screen outside the front entrance, waving makeshift cardboard placards spelling out *We Love You Beau and Paisley* in glued-on candy. Some of them had linked arms and were chanting. Others were throwing donuts at cameramen, others being restrained by cops. Most of them wearing black and white outfits.

All for us.

All 'cos we robbed some people.

All 'cos of Dad.

'Is my sister here? Is Paisley here?'

The nurse shook her head. 'No. Though I wouldn't be surprised if she turned up. She'll wanna give *them* a wide berth if she's got any sense ... but coming from the same family as you, I'm thinking maybe she ain't got a lick of sense neither. Jumping out of cars ...'

'I jumped out?'

'You don't remember? Some fisherman passing through Cedar Pocket found you lying by the side of the road. Like a bloody carcass awaitin' the crows.'

'Shit. Why don't I remember?'

'When you kids ever gonna learn that horseplay always leads to no good?'

I smiled again. 'I did it. I jumped out.'

'Y'all need anything else, just give that cord a little pull, okay? When you're feeling up to it, someone'll be in to show you how to use those,' she said and nodded to a pair of crutches leaned up against the corner by the door.

'Okay,' I said, as she wobbled out of my room.

I really jumped. It was all coming back to me. I'd heard Virginia talking about us and how she'd do whatever it took to get to the money. Locking me up for another two years. Killing Paisley if she had to. And I jumped. And between jumping and landing here in whatever middle-of-nowhere hospital I was in, I remembered nothing.

The TV flickered on in the corner. Girls were taking their tops off and parading around half-naked, cops trying to cover them up with their jackets. Girls were painting *We Love You Buddy* in melted chocolate on the hospital windows.

How come they loved Buddy? I didn't even know if I did, and I was his son.

Was I thinking straight? Didn't I love him? Didn't I want to see him? Not as much as Paisley, I knew that. Not enough to get us both killed. Not enough for all this.

Not enough.

Amanda Peace was being accosted by a kid in a military-style coat and a big girl wearing an AC/DC shirt, just like Paisley's.

And then I heard a little voice in the room.

'Beau?'

And Paisley was standing there in a candy striper's uniform.

'Oh my God!' I said and she shushed me and came over, throwing her upper body on top of me in a hug. I groaned.

'Oh shit. I'm sorry,' she said drawing back.

'It's okay,' I said. 'I'm just a little bruised. How did you find me?'

She nodded at the TV. 'The news. God, I'm so glad to see you, Beau. I'm sorry, I don't care if it hurts,' and she hugged me again.

I laughed in my pain. 'By the way, what are you wearing?'

'Don't ask,' she said. 'We haven't got long. The cop outside your room went to get coffee from the top floor. Coffee machine on this floor's broken. Somehow. You hooked up to monitors or anything? One of those bags you piss into?'

'Uh, no,' I said.

'Good, 'cos we gotta get you outta here.'

'Who's we?'

'Oh, I met some people. Made some friends.'

'YOU made some friends?' I laughed. 'You gotta be kidding me.'

She eased me up to a seating position on the bed and then gently swiveled me round. 'Can you walk?' she asked me.

'I think so,' I said, standing up. I stepped forward. My whole body was screaming with pain, throbbing in too many places, but I could walk.

'Come on, we gotta get out of here before that cop comes back. Where are your clothes?' She found my Converses and my jeans and Mandies Candies T-shirt folded neatly on an armchair in the corner and dropped them on the bed. 'I got a car waiting at a back entrance but we got like a five-minute diversion before they start getting suspicious.'

'Where did you get a car from?'

'The fans out front,' she said. 'They're giving it to us. Like a gift. They said they'd be honored.'

'They're rioting for us? You did that?'

'Of course. So we can get you outta here.' I was shuffling a little from all the pain and she was urging me to hurry up. 'We're not gonna get very far like this. I'll go get a wheelchair.

I saw some old lady using one a couple doors down. I'll go and scam her.'

As she opened the door, a man stood there in a red shirt with a white doctor's coat over the top. A scruffy man with a thick brown beard.

I felt my heart sink.

'What's the problem, Pais?' the man said. 'Is he awake?'

'Yeah,' she said. 'But it's slow going. I'm gonna grab him a wheelchair.'

'I'll carry him if I have to,' the man said, coming in to the room. He stopped when he saw me, as though waiting for me to say something.

She'd found him. I knew she would.

'Dad,' I said, without thinking. He was a little grayer and he'd lost some serious pounds, but it was still him.

He walked over, smiling, though there were tears in his eyes. 'Hey, son. You need some help there?'

'No, I'm okay,' I said, throwing off the bed covers with my good hand before he could get to me. I didn't want him to hug me. Paisley must have hugged him half to death. My whole body was screaming in varying degrees of pain, but no way was I gonna show him that I couldn't manage. I didn't want anything from him. I didn't need anything from him.

I stood up carefully and purposefully, holding onto the nightstand until I was sure I wouldn't stumble.

'Y'alright, Beau?' asked Paisley.

'Yeah, I can manage,' I told her.

CHAPTER TWENTY-FIVE

Paisley

Dixie Regional Medical Center, St George, Utah

So here's where you want us all driving into the sunset, Dad throwing candy back at us like he used to, and me and Beau bundled up in blankets on the backseat. That's what I wanted too. But life's not that kind.

'Which car is it?' said Beau. Dad's hand had been clasped around his good shoulder all the way down the fire escape.

'Over here,' I said, running ahead across the parking lot to open the back door of the Wonder Mobile. The sunlight was streaming across the concrete. Beau got inside.

'Won't they want it back?' he asked me, squinting up in the sunlight.

'Nope,' I said, holding the top of the open door. 'And they're gonna keep the cops away from this side of the building for us so as we can get away. Pretty sweet, aren't they, our fans?'

'Yeah, pretty sweet,' he winced, obviously in agony as he leaned back against the other door. Dad took his jacket off and bundled it up for Beau to rest his head on. Beau lay down and closed his eyes.

We could hear the fans chanting from around the front of the hospital, so we knew the cops would be busy for a while, but we still had to hurry. The only thing I could see for miles around was dust. Dust and desert and rocks and beyond the rocks, mountains. Where the hell would we go now? Dad would know what to do. He always knew.

Dad shut the door, and when we turned around, there was the Skankmother and her gardening minion, standing beside Matt's pick-up. She had a gun. It was pointing right at me. The gun looked exactly like the Eclipse.

'Shit.'

'Didn't know I had another one, did you? They came as a pair. Two for one. If only you'd bothered to look harder, Jane, you might have found it.'

'Maybe if you'd bothered to look beyond Beau, you might have seen me coming,' I said.

She laughed and swept the gun across to Dad, her long red nails clutching the handle. Then I got kinda nervous. She hated me, but she truly detested my dad. Suddenly my heart was a madman slamming his head against a stone wall. I felt myself move over to Dad. I wasn't going to lose him again.

'Where's the other gun?' she said.

Dad looked at me and took the Eclipse out of his pocket.

Virginia held hers with both hands. 'No funny business. Empty it and put it on the ground. I'm warning you, Michael.'

Dad did as he was told and emptied the chamber. *Plink plink plink,* the shells fell to the ground. He didn't take his eyes off her. Then, both hands raised, he walked a couple steps forward and placed the Eclipse down by his feet and kicked it over to her.

'Now you, Virginia,' he said, standing against Beau's door. 'We can settle this without violence. We don't want trouble. We'll just go, okay?'

'Michael, you're quite the unexpected irritation. They didn't mention you on the news.'

I'd never heard anyone call my dad by his real name before. He was always Buddy to everyone who knew him. But not the Skank. She called everyone by their proper names. I hated that.

Dad didn't take his eyes from her gun. 'Yeah, well, I fly under the radar these days.'

'My lawyer tells me that in the sad event of your deaths, I am legally entitled to your estate as your next of kin.'

'What you gonna do, kill all of us?' he asked her, still staring down the barrel. 'That's what you want, isn't it? To get us out of the way so you can lay claim to their money.'

She shrugged. 'I've got my future to think about.'

I scoffed, starting forward, ready to wring her scrawny chicken neck. 'Stop pointing that gun at my dad!'

Dad held me back. 'What if we signed it all over to you? Legally,' he said.

I looked at him. 'Dad?'

'It's okay. Let her have it, if that's what it takes to leave us alone. What do you say, Virginia?'

She shook her head. The gun moved over to me and it didn't waver. 'No. We have to do things the hard way, I'm afraid. I was quite willing to take your children as down payment until the time came. And I was more than happy to settle just for Beau, but then he listened to his pathetic excuse for a sister …'

'Aw, if it weren't for us pesky kids,' I said.

It was my turn to look down the barrel. 'Shut up. Shut your dirty mouth, you pathetic little whore.'

'Don't call my daughter that,' said Dad, his hands still raised.

I didn't think I could love my dad any more than I did at that moment.

Virginia was still spluttering her fumes at me. 'Your brother could have died and it's all your fault. Anything bad that has ever happened to you two has been your fault. Beau was happy with me. You are the root cause of everything, do you under-stand me?'

'You mumble a little bit, but I get the general idea,' I replied.

'Vile girl!' she spat, the Eclipse wavering in her rock-hard grasp. It was strong on me now. I wasn't worried. It kinda worried me that I wasn't worried.

'Don't you dare talk to her like that,' said Dad.

Yay Dad.

'She's said far worse to *me*,' said the Skank, holding the gun out further in front of her, making the bullet's flight an inch shorter. I watched her trigger finger. Dad moved across me. 'So there really is no other option. I have to get rid of all three of you right now. Which one of your twins do you want to see executed first? The boy or the girl?' She moved it so it was locked on the rear window of the car, where Beau was, then back to me. Then back to Beau. Then back to me.

'Eeny, Meeny, Paisley, Beau. It's like *Sophie's Choice,* isn't it?'

'There are hundreds of fans out front,' said Dad. 'And cops. They hear three gunshots going off, they'll be round here faster than you can scream. They'll find you. You'll be seen. How the hell d'you expect to get away with it?'

'Who's going to miss you three?' said Skank. 'A vagrant and two thieves?'

'I take it you haven't been watching the news then,' he said.

She cocked the gun.

'You hate that, don't you, Virginia?' Dad smiled. 'You hate the fact they've gotten more famous in a couple weeks than you ever were in your entire career.'

She squinted a little, aiming the gun right at Dad's head.

And with that, Matt turned and made for his truck.

She looked around at him. 'Matthew …?'

'I can't handle this, Ginny. I'm sorry. I have to go.'

'You stay there. You damn well stay there!' She pointed the gun at him.

His hands flew up, his face gurning in sheer terror. 'What, you gonna shoot *me* now?'

'You're in this up to your neck anyway, sweetheart. Even if you go and I do get caught, I'll name you. Don't think I won't.'

'You bitch!'

'Bitch with brains. I want that money. And you are going to help me.'

She turned back to Dad and cocked the gun again. 'First things first. Let's deal with the irritation.'

There was no time. No time for anything else. My legs started moving and I went with them. I can't remember what I screamed. I ran toward her and I got hold of the gun. I shook it. I pulled it away from her. I had it. Dad was there. A shot rang out. Dust flew up.

And Dad went down.

It was just like the movies. Everything went all slow. My legs wouldn't move.

'DAD!'

I dropped the gun. Dad was slumped against the back wheel of the car, blood pouring out of him. I went to him. He was crying in pain.

'Oh my God, Dad. I didn't mean … Dad, I'm sorry … shit … SHIT … you need a doctor. Beau?! BEAU! Go get a doctor!'

The sun disappeared behind me as the shadow of Virginia loomed larger than ever. Laughing.

'You shot him! You shot your precious daddy! How awful. That's so awful, I don't think I'll ever stop laughing.'

Her words burned me slowly but she was right. I had done it. I had pulled the trigger, whether I had been aiming at him or not. It was me. She had the Eclipse again. It was poised to take my head off. I stood up. I stood up and looked at the face I'd only ever back-talked, bitch-slapped, or shouted at. And I begged.

'Please.' Suddenly I didn't care anymore about our pathetic little war. I just wanted my dad to be okay. For Beau to be okay. I didn't give a shit about anything else.

'What?' she said.

I held my hands out. They were shaking. Tears poured down my face like rain. 'I'll go with you. You can tie me up, whatever, I don't care.'

'Paisley, no, stop it. Get in the car,' Dad mumbled. I thought blood was gonna come out of his mouth but it didn't.

Beau was getting out of the car.

I turned to Dad, my hands still out front waiting to be tied. 'It's okay. You go on inside the hospital with Beau and they'll fix you up.'

My chest thumped like a thousand marching soldiers. There was a horrible silence. I shifted across the rocky ground toward Virginia on my bare knees.

She was still laughing. 'You think I'd trust YOU, after all you've done? I wouldn't trust you as far as I could throw your miserable body, Jane Argent.'

'Tie me up, then!' I shouted. 'I'm giving you myself on a plate. Gag me if you want. I don't care. Just let them go. Dad needs a doctor.'

She looked over at Matt. He still had his hands in the air. 'Matthew?'

'I'll get the rope,' he said and walked backward to the cab of the truck.

She glared back at me. 'If you try anything, anything at all, you know what will happen, don't you?'

I nodded. 'You'll let them go then, yeah? Let them go.'

The gun was still fixed on me. 'Who shot your father?'

I looked at her. I hung my head. 'I did.'

'I didn't quite catch ...'

'I DID. I SHOT HIM!' I shouted and thrust my hands out further.

She smiled. 'They can go.'

Beau was helping Dad to his feet. Dad had his hand pressed against his shoulder and blood was seeping out between his fingers.

'No, Paisley.'

'There's no other way, Dad.' I got to my feet.

Beau appeared by my side, his good hand clasping my arm. 'Paisley?'

'She'll kill Dad if I don't, Beau. You know she will. I can handle it. It's my turn. I always said I needed locking up anyway.'

'No, no way,' he said. 'No way, Paisley. I can't leave you with her.'

'You'll be better off,' I sniffed through my tears. 'Look what I did.' We both looked at Dad. 'I have to go. You go get a doctor.' My voice dropped to a whisper. 'Tell 'em it was me. They'll come looking for me.'

An engine started, a screech of brakes, a door slammed. Matt was getting out of there, ducking behind the steering wheel.

KA-BLAM! BLAM! BLAM! Skank fired at the truck, cracking the windshield, smashing a light, running after him, but Matt drove on, drove away. Left her.

'You bastard! You lying bastard!' she screamed after him.

Everything changed in a heartbeat.

'Quick!' said Beau. 'Help me get him in.' He flung open the back door and I helped him put Dad into the back seat of the car and propped him up. 'Get in with him.' I climbed in beside Dad and scraped away my tears with the back of my hand. I looked at him. His head was back and he was sweating. I looked at his chest. I felt over it. His shirt was soaked in blood. My hand got to his shoulder and he winced in complete agony. I snapped my hand away.

'I'm sorry, I'm sorry!'

Beau shut both of us in and limped around to the front of the car. Once inside, he slammed the driver's door and jammed down his button. I jammed down the other buttons in the back.

'Has he got an exit wound?' Beau asked, turning to me but keeping an eye on the Skank through the window while cowering down.

'What?'

'An exit wound, does he have an exit wound?' he asked again. I couldn't fuse the two words together in my brain and before I understood what he meant, he clambered awkwardly through the seats to check it himself, propping Dad forward with his good arm and looking at his back. Dad howled.

'Yeah, it came out,' said Beau. 'That's good.' He climbed back through, *ouch*ing and *aargh*ing as he caught his bad arm on the seat.

'How is that good?' I asked him.

'The bullet came out. Means we can patch him up ourselves.'

'But he needs a doctor, Beau. Look at him.'

'Get back here!' Virginia was screeching to Matt's pick-up as it reversed at full speed out of the parking lot.

'She's coming back!' Beau yelled. 'Keep applying pressure to his shoulder, Pais. Use one of your socks or something, turn it inside out.'

'Okay,' I said, taking off my boot. The stack of Wonder Twins stickers dropped into the foot well. I'd forgotten all about them.

BLAM! BLAM! BLAM!

I leap on Dad and pushed him down. He cried out in pain. Beau was huddled down in front, his head between the seats. He was okay. Dad was okay.

BANG. A bullet plinked off the metalwork. Glass tinkled at the window. Shattered pieces fell on my bare legs. I didn't dare move them. They became stuck together with sweat.

'How many more she got left?' Dad whispered.

'I don't know,' I said, my head hard against his.

The driver's door slammed.

Me and Dad both jolted. I looked up. Beau was making his way slowly, slightly limping, around to the front of the car where our grandmother was standing, pointing the gun at us. We watched as he walked right up to her, took her gun with his good hand and threw it to one side. He then grabbed her by the throat with the same hand. Beau had one arm in a sling but he grabbed our grandmother by the throat. I couldn't believe what I was seeing.

He talked the talk too. 'What you got now, Grandma, huh? What you got for me now?!' He looked her hard in the eye. She was shaking, pawing away at him but he held on. Gasping for air, she pleaded. She *begged*. Beau had her begging. He had her on her knees. He was a fucking superhero!

The Skank stumbled and twisted in his grasp, wide-eyed and helpless. He seemed taller. She seemed older.

'Beau, there's no need for this, please,' she writhed, pawing at his grip with her false nails. 'Oh God, let … please, you're hurting me!'

'You come near my family again, I won't need a gun. I will kill you with one hand.'

And he shoved her down onto the dusty floor of the parking lot and limped back round to the driver's door. He stopped. He opened it and got in.

He started the engine and wound down the window.

Virginia crawled in front of the car.

'If you don't move, I'm gonna fucking run you over!'

Our grandmother scurried away, like a frightened mouse looking for a hole in the sand. My brother, my little geeky wuss of a twin brother, shifted us into drive with his good hand, holding his broken one against his chest. We drove out of the parking lot and back onto the road.

Nothing else happened for several minutes, nothing but the sounds of my breathing, Dad's breathing. The lull of the engine. Glass tinkling at the window. Beau said nothing and he didn't look back at us. I couldn't pick out the right words either, so I just stayed quiet and held my bleeding dad in my arms. Aside from holding my sodden red sock against his shoulder, I didn't have a clue what to do.

'You knew she didn't have any bullets left, didn't you?' I said eventually.

My brother looked back at me. He smiled. I smiled. We started laughing, but it was a weird laughing. Beau couldn't stop himself. He laughed until he had wet eyes, I could see them in the rear-view. Nothing was funny. I guess it was just relief. But it didn't last long.

'We need to get Dad to the hospital,' I said. 'I can't stop it bleeding.'

'We've just come from the hospital.'

'Another hospital, then.'

'No we don't, I'm okay,' Dad piped up, trying to act the martyr but all the while I could see in his eyes he was scared. And in so much pain. 'Blood would be darker if we had anything to worry about.'

Beau looked at him in the rear-view. 'You been shot before, Dad?'

'No, just watched a lotta movies.'

'Sure?'

'Yeah. We'll go to a rest stop or something. Buy some dressings, sterile solution. Fix me up.'

'No,' I said, 'you have to see a doctor, it might get infect—'

Beau looked back at me, his good hand on the wheel. 'You can't just go into a hospital with a gunshot wound and get treatment, Paisley. The cops'll be onto us in a heartbeat. We gotta keep on driving.'

'Keep on driving where?' I said, folding the sock over and pressing it down again on Dad's arm. I looked at Beau in the mirror.

He shrugged. 'I didn't plan on being alive for this part so your guess is as good as mine.'

'Don't say that, Beau.' I couldn't believe what he was saying. Me and him had totally switched places.

'It's true. I could have taken my chances with Matt and Virginia but I chose to jump off that truck. I never thought I'd make it.'

'But you did make it. And so did Dad. And so did I. We can go anywhere we want now. We're a family.'

'No we can't,' said Dad.

'Why not?'

'Because we're outlaws now, Paisley,' said Beau. 'And outlaws gotta watch themselves. We make ourselves known too much, they'll send you and me to Juvenile Hall, they'll send Dad back to jail and that will be that for another ten years. At least. Face it, Paisley. We gotta keep running.'

I nodded. He was right and I hated it.

I looked at Dad next to me. His eyes were scrunched up like he was trying to think real hard, trying to concentrate on something other than the pain. The pain I'd caused him.

'I'm sorry, Dad,' I said. 'I just wanted to find you. Beau was right, I shouldn't have taken her gun in the first place. I shouldn't have done a lot of things, then maybe this wouldn't be happening to you. It's all my fault. I'm sorry.'

He opened his eyes and looked up at me. He smiled and the pain disappeared from his face. 'It's alright, Paisley. I'm gonna be alright. I got my Wonder Twins back.'

He raised his good hand to my face and stroked my hair. I would never, ever touch a gun again. It was then I caught sight of the stickers in the foot well. I reached down, grabbed them and threw them out the broken window. They fluttered behind us onto the empty road.

I looked in the mirror at Beau again. He caught my eye. If he could sense my anxiety, he didn't show it. His face was unmoved.

'So what do we do now, Beau?' I asked him.

'Try and get some sleep, okay?' he said as we juddered along through the rocky desert. 'We got a long drive.'

Acknowledgments

Barry Cunningham and everyone at Chicken House.

My Mum for always believing in me even when I don't. My big sister Penny Skuse for showing me *Platoon* when I was eight and for teaching me to always swim against the tide. Nan. Auntie Maggie and Uncle Roy. My big brother Jamie, Angie, Alex, Josie, Joshua. Matthew and Emily Snead, for all the years I spent at your mansion while mine was being decorated. Karen and Danny for letting me burn their house down.

Wendy Griffin at Yew Trees Nursery for keeping my job open throughout my studies.

Julia Green and all the Creative Writing staff at Bath Spa University. Dawn, Diana, Titania, Lila, Eden, Roy and my fellow witches Fliss Crentsil and Ali Killeen.

Gill and John McLay, Barry Timms, Owain Gillard and Jo Baker, for their advice.

My Chemical Romance, Linkin Park, Blind Melon, Killers, All Angels, Limp Bizkit, Slipknot, Feeder, Kings of Leon, Paramore and Foo Fighters for always unlocking the block when I needed it.

Gerard Way, Jeffrey Dean Morgan, Bonnie and Clyde, Brothers Grimm, Grant Morrison, Jack Nicholson, Anthony Perkins, Al Pacino, Quentin Tarantino. Whether you know it or not, you've all helped in some way to make my dustland fairytale come true. Thank you.